PITY THE MOVIE LOVER

By

Martha Kemm Landes

Elemar Publishing

Though very loosely based on a period in the author's life, this is a work of fiction.
Identities and situations have been greatly embellished.

www.marthalandes.com

Pitymystery@gmail.com

Print ISBN: 978-1-956912-00-5
e-Book ISBN: 978-1-956912-01-2
Audiobook ISBN: 978-1-956912-02-9

Cover design by Tahomina Mitu

First Edition

Dedication

Dedicated to friends and family who helped me navigate my busy, exciting, and sometimes crazy single years - especially my two sweet daughters, Emily and Elizabeth. Special thanks to my sister, Kathy, who was available by phone day and night to give feedback about the plot. And to my ever-supportive husband, Dan, a heartfelt thank-you for being my in-house copy editor.

Pity the Movie Lover

Martha Kemm Landes

Movie Watching Tip #1
You can usually tell in the first five minutes
if the movie will be good.

She bent forward to pull the two-year-old from his car seat, her hair blowing across her face with each passing car. Frantic to move her sleeping son away from the busy highway, she strained as she carried him across the muddy ditch.

Why had she swerved to miss the little dog? And why did she leave her phone at home? Now she couldn't call for help. Could this day get any worse?

Just as they cleared the bog, the groggy boy lifted his head from her shoulder and said with wide eyes, "Fwuck!" His pudgy finger pointed to a red truck barreling toward them. Horrified, she heaved the toddler as far away from the road as she could, then scrambled through the muck to join him. The boy didn't cry when he landed, but sat up, blue eyes staring at the wreckage. Once reunited, they heard the terrifying screech of metal on metal. The mother yanked the boy closer just as a loose tire whizzed past her foot.

Eerie hisses and groans filled the air as both vehicles rocked to a halt and she cringed at what little was left of her Corolla. She croaked, "Fwuck is right.

Tears filled her eyes as she worried about the driver of the truck, but moments later, there was a creak and a man emerged from the smoke, with his hand on his head. When he spotted the two, he called out, "Are you alright?"

"We're okay, just shaken. And you?"

He loped toward them. "I'll live. There was a damned dog in the road and I swerved to miss it. I couldn't even see the car in this fog until I hit it. I assume it's yours?"

"It is. And the same little dog landed us in the ditch."

He looked back at the debris. "I'm glad you got out before I came along."

The dark-haired man limped up the muddy bank and helped her stand up. The beam of the headlights hitting his face revealed his turquoise eyes and fresh scrapes on his right cheek.

He held up his hand to the child, ready for a fist bump. "Hey there, big guy."

The mud-covered boy ignored the gesture and pointed to the wreckage. "Fwuck!"

She shrugged. "He's not very good with his T R's yet."

The man smiled and said, "At least he'll do well with my name – it's Frank."

She blushed and said, "I'm Angela."

"Mom, this is a stupid movie. Let me guess…the beautiful blonde falls in love with Aaron Winston and they live happily ever after. He always gets the girl. And I'm just sayin', I don't like him with dark hair."

I paused the DVR and turned to my 16-year-old daughter, Lauren, "Give it time, Ren. You can't judge a movie by its first five minutes." Although based on my vast movie-watching experience, I knew you could.

"Well, I'm going to go call Jennifer and see what she's doing." Ren stood, stretched her arms over her head, revealing her toned, bare midriff, then turned to leave.

I announced, "OK, but you're missing a great movie. You know Aaron Winston was nominated for Best Actor for this role!" I watched as she shrugged and walked to her bedroom, leaving me with my youngest daughter in the living room.

With a waggle of my head, I said, "Well, sometimes she just doesn't get in the spirit of our movies, right, Ree?" Hearing no response, I turned to see my silent 13-year-old, officially named

Marie, lying on the couch so engrossed in a book, she hadn't even noticed I paused the movie.

So much for family movie day. I pushed play and focused again on watching the movie on my new 55" flat-screen TV. The two beautiful people indeed got together amid heartaches and several mishaps. Oh, and of course, the dog both drivers swerved to miss, became their family pet. The story was a little lame, but I love Aaron Winston in anything and the little boy was adorable, especially when he called Frank "Fwank".

I sighed and said, "Personally, I liked it even more today than the last three times I saw it. What did you think, Ree?"

When she didn't respond this time, I turned around again only to find her sound asleep, book open on her chest and her long blonde hair dra   the side of the couch. The only one still watching TV w   as my trusty sheepdog, Harriet. She licked my hand as he   of the movie. I patted her head and shook mine as I sto   alked quietly to peek in Ren's room. My eldest was cc   t on her bed, surrounded by posters of swimmers, ac   her favorite singers.

I shrugge   can't beat 'em, join 'em. I mean, a nap on a Sunday afte   nded like a pretty darned good idea. Just as I got comfy under my quilt, my phone rang. I groaned as I answered, "Hello?"

"Sooo, did you read the paper this morning?" It was my best friend, Lin, sounding very excited.

I shrugged. "No. I guess it's still on the porch. Why?"

She spoke so quickly, I could hardly understand her, especially with her northern accent. "It's in the Local section. They're gonna film a movie in Tulsa. And you'll never guess who's in it. Not in a million years, you won't."

My eyes widened, "Is it someone I like?"

"Oh, you betcha," she said.

I guessed, "Chris Hemsworth? Will Ferrell?" I got faster as I went. "Adam Driver, Dwayne Johnson, Aaron Winston?"

"Yes!" she screamed.

I sat up and threw off the covers. "Well, which one, Lin? When do they start filming? Do they need extras? Oh My Gosh, this is so exciting!"

"I can't believe you didn't see it in the paper. It's Aaron Winston! He's coming this week and yes, they need locals for extras. The casting call is today at 3:00."

As soon as I heard the name Aaron Winston, I bolted to the front door and grabbed the paper from the porch. Back in the living room, I slid the rubber band off the rolled paper so fast that it shot across the room, hitting Ree on the leg.

"Ow!" she yelled, sitting up with a start and grabbing her thigh.

I grimaced. "I'm sorry, Ree. It was a rubber band. Are you OK? Aaron Winston is filming a movie here and I need to know the details!" Thankfully, that's all the explanation she needed, since she's seen me spaz out for much less.

"That really hurt." She rubbed her leg with one hand and her sleepy eyes with the other.

Carrying the paper with me, I ran to the kitchen, grabbed a piece of ice, wrapped it in a damp washcloth and handed it to Ree, all the while dismantling the huge Sunday paper.

A tiny voice said, "Hello? Hello?" Oops. I guess I'd put Lin in my pocket to open the door. I held the iPhone back to my ear. "Oh, sorry, Lin. I had to get the paper. I'll call you back in a minute. And thanks for cluing me in."

After finding the local section, I read about the upcoming movie. Aaron Winston was really going to be the star. Ooh, Alison Baxter was the female lead, and Joel Mason the director. I imagined being an extra and meeting all the stars. Too bad it wasn't during Spring Break when I'd have all kinds of time. But since I hadn't used any of my three personal days, a few days would be doable. "Ree, they start filming this Tuesday!"

I devoured the article, getting more and more pumped as I read. Lin was right, try-outs were at three o'clock today. I looked at the clock. It was already two; barely enough time to get ready.

Ren entered the living room yawning, probably to see what the hubbub was about. She squinted. "What happened in here? February is kind of early for tornadoes."

I looked at the scene through her eyes. Maybe I had been a little exuberant in disassembling the paper. Colorful ads and sections were strewn everywhere throughout the large room.

Ree rolled her eyes and droned, "Mom found out Aaron Winston is making a movie in town and got so excited she nearly killed me! See?" She lifted the washcloth from her leg to prove how badly I'd injured her. I was relieved to see nothing but a light pink spot from the ice cube on her pale thigh. She made a face. "Well, it really hurt anyway."

Ren smiled. "Oh boy, Mom, your favorite, Aaron Winston. So, let me guess, you're going to find a way to meet him?"

She always had been a good guesser. "Yes. Exactly. I'm going to be an extra and watch all the action. It's my chance to meet a real, live star!" I tore out the article and folded it for safekeeping.

Ren shook her head as she picked up pieces of the paper from the floor. "Well, I doubt he's going to become your bestie – or wanna date you." She looked at me with eyebrows raised.

"Ooh, I hadn't even thought of that. He is single, isn't he?" I closed my eyes:

There I was, laughing as I rode with Aaron in a sporty red convertible. I pointed out Tulsa's landmarks, starting with my favorite, the Golden Driller statue, and continued south. Aaron's wild blonde hair blew in the wind as he steered along Riverside Drive. He flirted with his cute Southern drawl as we played on the equipment at Gathering Place. After touring Brookside and Cherry Street we went downtown and stood in the Center of the Universe. Aaron bent over and whispered, "This has been the best day ever, Pity", and his voice echoed with a boom. We laughed, and he held my hand as we returned to the sports car, and drove to eat BBQ and fried okra.

I heard a faint, "Mom?" and slowly opened my eyes. Both girls stared at me.

I shook off the daydream and shrugged, "Well, I won't push the friend thing. I'll just be happy to get to see him." But we all knew better. Once something was in my head, it was nearly impossible to get it out.

Ren squinted at me, "Mom, I asked what the movie is about."

"Oh, it's called 'Crude Town' and is going to be a romantic comedy set in the heyday of Tulsa's oil industry in the 60's."

"Doesn't sound very funny to me," said Ree, making a face as she picked up the comics section from the floor.

I conceded, "I know, but with Aaron as the star, it's bound to be adorable." I pointed my finger at them, "You know he is nominated for an Academy Award this year – for the movie you didn't watch today?"

Ren said, "Yes Mom, we know. We helped you film your Oscar spoof. Remember?"

I shrugged. "Well, anyway they're having a casting call in 45 minutes and they need me! I should get ready!" I gave a pout, "Could one of you fix a sandwich for me to take and the other feed Iggy, Harriet and Edgar? Please, please, pretty please?"

My sweet 13-year-old perked up with hopeful eyes. "Can I be in the movie too?"

Ren said, "You can't, Ree. You have school."

"Well, Mom has school too."

She offered a valid point and I piped in, "True. But I have all of my personal days left and this seems like the perfect time to use them. Besides, they only need adults now." I felt a little bad she couldn't be involved and sweetened the pot, "I tell you what, fix your own lunch and I'll leave money so you can order pizza for dinner, in case I am late getting home. You can even choose the toppings."

Both girls smiled, then promptly started arguing over what kind to order.

I skipped from the room. "OK. I've gotta get ready." In my bedroom, I dialed Lin and put my phone on speaker while changing into a fresh top and jeans. "Lin, I'm about ready. I'll pick you up in ten minutes."

"No. I have to go to Mom's for Mack's birthday today. Besides, I can't take this week off. I have to do three houses by Thursday."

Lin is a decorator and most of her business is staging homes for realtors. I held my mascara wand away from my face, frozen in disappointment. "But I can't go without you! I mean, we've already been in one movie together and I need my bestie there."

She scoffed. "If you can call that a movie."

That was true. We were extras in a boxing movie; possibly the worst movie ever. Thankfully, it never made it to the theaters. Years later, we found the DVD of the film at a garage sale and watched it.

Within the first five minutes of "Boxed Up", we were cringing and prayed our faces wouldn't be shown in the film. Our prayers were answered when the close-ups of us as spectators were left on the cutting room floor. The camera only focused on the bloody faces of boxers or ring girls in skimpy bikinis. Some scenes were so crude, they verged on porn. We never admitted to anyone we were involved with that flop.

I felt certain that this upcoming movie would be much classier. All directors, actors, and producers had done acclaimed movies.

Lin said, "You'll be fine. But I want all the details. And let me know if they need anyone next week!"

"You got it." I took a deep breath and looked in the mirror. It was all up to me to get chosen as an extra. I told my reflection, "Go get 'em, Pity."

Back in the living room, I said, "Sorry I'm ditching you guys. I'll text you if I'm going to be later than six. Here's 20 bucks to order Mazzio's. Save some for me and don't forget to finish your homework."

Ree ran up, hands behind her back. "I made this." She handed me a little lunch bag with my name written on it and a bottle of iced tea. Her dimpled smile always made me melt and there it was.

"Thanks, Sweetie Pie! I appreciate that." I smiled back. "Wish me luck!" I grabbed my coat and walked to the garage door.

"Good luck, Mom." the girls said in unison. They really are sweet girls.

I got in Liesel, my VW bug, and headed to the Tulsa fairgrounds for the audition. Just as I entered the expressway, my phone rang. I answered before looking at the caller I.D.

"Hi Honey, this is your mother." As if I wouldn't recognize her voice after 45 years.

"Hi, Mom. How are you today?" I asked in a peppy voice.

"Just fine. We went to church and had a nice dinner at Applebee's. I'm calling because your father wanted to make sure you saw the article about the movie filming here this week."

"Yes! I'm on my way to the casting call now! Can you believe Aaron Winston will be in Tulsa?"

"That's nice, but I still don't know what you see in that boy. His hair is always messy and his nose is crooked."

"Mom. He's adorable. You know he was nominated for Best Actor, don't you?"

"Oh, yes. We saw that "Swerve" movie and liked it, except for some of the language. The little boy was darling."

I agreed. "Just darling." At least someone else saw the movie.

She said, "We were surprised that the director wasn't nominated too. I'll bet he wasn't too happy."

I considered that and answered, "Well, Joel Mason has already won an Oscar. And Mom, Aaron's nose gives him character. Besides it's not his looks as much as his carefree personality that I love."

"Now, Pity, don't get your hopes up," she said. "He's used to those young, skinny Hollywood types."

"Mom!"

"No need to be offended. You are lovely and deserve to find a nice man. But I've just seen the types of girls this guy dates and I don't want you to be disappointed if he isn't interested in you."

"Mom, I'm not planning on marrying him. I may not even see Aaron, and if I do, he probably won't even notice me."

"Oh, I have no doubt you'll get noticed, Pity. Just don't expect too much." I heard the door shut and pictured her going out to her garden. She continued, "Speaking of movies, are you ready for your big day?"

"Not really." I frowned. "I still have one video to make and I haven't even watched that movie. I can't spoof it until I've seen it. And I need to e-mail my invitations soon." I made a mental note to work on the invites when I got home. "Are you coming this year?"

"No, Honey. We'll just watch the Oscars at home and use our own ballots. Oh, how did your blind date go this weekend?"

"Well, the guy was kind of boring, but he sure seemed to like me. He said he wants to go out again, but I don't know."

"That's interesting. Well, you had better focus on driving, Dear. Good luck!" She hung up the phone before I got the chance to say goodbye. That's the way my mom rolls. When she's done talking, she's done. Or maybe she was distracted. That happens a lot with ADD people like us.

I shrugged and took the Sheridan Avenue exit. I was chewing a bit of my sandwich when my phone rang again with a number I didn't recognize. I pushed the green phone icon on my VW infotainment touch screen and said with a mouthful, "Hello?"

"Hello, Kitty?" It was a male voice and obviously someone who didn't know me well.

I swallowed. "Yes?"

"I just wanted to make certain that you are having a nice Sunday. It was such a pleasure meeting you last night. You have been on my mind all day long."

Ugh. It was the boring guy from last night. What was his name? Oh yeah. "Is this Kenny?"

"Why yes, it is." He had a lilt in his voice.

"Um, Kenny, I'm driving now and can't talk. Could you call back this evening?" I took another bite as I maneuvered the left turn onto 21st street.

"Oh certainly. Is seven an appropriate time for you to receive a call?"

"Uh…yeah sure. That's fine," I said, thinking he was awfully formal.

"I will count the minutes until I hear your voice again."

I said goodbye and pushed end, thinking he was kind of odd. Those thoughts evaporated when I saw the entrance to the fairgrounds. The Expo Square appeared like a beacon of hope. A sign reading, Casting Call Parking, beckoned me to stardom.

Movie Watching Tip #2
Sometimes a film doesn't live up to its hype.

I breathed faster as I parked my car. Before getting out, I left the crust of my sandwich on the plate and gulped some tea. Looking in the rearview mirror, I realized my maniacal smile was somewhat psycho, so I toned it down to a mere grin.

Trying to be calm, I followed the arrows leading to a building where a line of people had formed. I got in the queue with my driver's license in hand. The guy in front of me was dressed in a suit and felt hat as if he walked out of the "Mad Men" TV series. He even carried a slim briefcase. Then, a woman walked by with a beehive hairdo and empire waist dress. I frowned, wondering if I should have dressed in 60's attire, but relaxed when I noticed most people wore everyday clothes.

I took a deep breath and exhaled slowly to curb my enthusiasm.

When it was my turn, I walked to the desk where a handsome man in his twenties took my papers and ID and looked them over. Without glancing up, he said, "Have you been an extra before?"

"Well, sort of."

"What was the name of the movie?" He continued to look down, pen poised to write my answer.

I didn't want to admit to the boxer porn, so I said, "It was a long time ago and really small production. I wasn't even seen in it." He kept his eyes down. I wondered what I had to do to get him to look at me, a tap dance?

The guy jotted something down and continued, "We'll need you to complete these forms, then step over there for a photograph." His eyes still down, he handed me papers and pointed to a lively girl who snapped pictures of people. Wasn't there a rule you must look into someone's eyes for at least a second when speaking to them?

A bit flustered, I sat at a high-top table equipped with pens and measuring tapes. What was I supposed to do with a tape measure? I began answering the questions.

Name – Kitty Kole (Pity)

Age – 45

Height – 5'10"

Weight – 150 (why did they need to know that?)

Vehicle – silver 2019 Volkswagen Beetle - the last year they were made (I scratched out that fun fact since it wasn't relevant.)

Dates available – Anytime (I hoped they wouldn't expect me for long term since I only had 3 days)

Special skills – knitting, writing songs, photography, swimming and shopping at garage sales (none of which was probably needed in this movie, but I listed them anyway)

Hat size – (seriously?)

The next spots were for waist, arm length, etc. Other people were using the measuring tapes to get their sizes, so I picked up the numbered ribbon and immediately got it tangled in my hair trying to measure around my shoulders.

A tall pretty redhead I guessed to be in her early 20's appeared and said, "I'll help you measure if you'll help me."

I sighed with relief and said, "Whew! I'm such a klutz, I was about to give up."

We set forth measuring waists, chests, hips, shoulders, head circumference, and arm lengths. I felt like a tailor, but without the pins in my mouth. It was odd to poke around on a stranger and vice versa, but we jotted answers in each space on the form.

The girl's eyes flitted around the room, but I couldn't see what distracted her. I just hoped she was doing a good job with the measurements in case I needed to wear a costume. When we finished, I was surprised at how closely our numbers matched. Both of us were tall and slender. Of course, there were a few big differences; my bland brown hair contrasted with her long shiny, auburn locks. My 34 B bra size couldn't compete with her ample chest area, and my extra 20 years made me feel matriarchal. Compared to the girl, I looked downright homely.

Always ready for a new friend, I said, "Now that we know each other so intimately, I'm Pity. I live in Broken Arrow but grew up here in Tulsa. And you?"

"Kat."

She didn't elaborate and continued to search the room, so I did my thing and took up the slack in the conversation. "Pity's just a nickname," I explained. "My real name is Kitty and you're Kat? That's funny. This is so exciting. I really love movies. I go to two a week and am dying to get on as an extra just to say I'm in a movie. Sorry, I babble when I get excited."

Kat didn't seem to pay attention to my chatter. I scanned the area to see who or what she tried to find.

She finally spoke, "Well, I just need a job. I got laid off at the Dairy Queen in Jenks and saw this online."

At least I got a little info out of her, but now I felt like a braggart. She actually needed the job and I hadn't even thought about being paid for this. Although being a single mother with two jobs, I could sure use the extra money. But mostly, I was here to meet a movie star.

I said with a smile, "Well, good luck to both of us!" I stood to hand in my paperwork.

Kat looked at someone and said suddenly, "Um…what's your name again? Pity?" Her eyes finally met mine.

"Yes?"

"Would you mind if I hang out with you? I'm a little nervous about this."

Although she looked at me with puppy dog eyes, something seemed off. She certainly didn't have any reason to be nervous since she already looked like a movie star. But I said, "Sure, come on." I motioned for her to accompany me, figuring it would be good to have a friend.

We went back to the table to hand in our forms. The guy who wouldn't look at me stared directly at Kat and told us to wait until they called our names for pictures. Hmmm. Yeah, I'll never get a part with people like her getting the attention.

All the seats were taken, so we leaned against a wall. I probed further. "Did you go to school in Jenks?"

"No. Just moved here from Alabama. I followed a boyfriend, but he's gone now. I'm on my own."

"Yikes. That's the pits. You don't want to go back home?"

Her head lowered dramatically. "No. There's nobody there for me anymore."

I felt sorry for this girl and decided to take her under my wing. Trying to think of something to say, I offered, "So, did you go to college?"

"Nope." She scoffed. "Never had that opportunity."

I waited for her to continue with more information, but nothing came, so I said, "I'm divorced with two teenage daughters and I'm an elementary school music teacher."

She said, "Hmm," and seemed distracted as she looked around. When her expression switched from sad to disinterested to pissed off, I thought maybe she was already an actress.

I continued, "My daughters are 13 and 16. They're real characters. They have nicknames too – Marie is Ree and Lauren is Ren. Do you have any siblings?"

"I had a twin sister," she said.

My mouth opened wide and I blurted, "I always wanted to be a twin, but that didn't work out, so I figured I'd just have twins. But I didn't get that wish either." I laughed. Then the word she'd said sunk in and I asked more seriously, "Wait, did you say, had?"

She let out a sigh and said, "I don't see her anymore."

Relieved to hear her sister hadn't died, I said, "I'm sorry you lost touch with her. I couldn't live without my sisters. I have one who lives here that I talk to every day. My oldest sister lives in Los Angeles." I chewed my lip, realizing I might sound like I was bragging again, and tried to be more sensitive. "Maybe someday things will work out and the two of you can get together again."

She gave me yet a different expression; a strange chilling stare that unnerved me so much I changed the subject. "Look at that guy." I smiled and nodded towards a cute older man wearing boots, a cowboy hat and a western shirt.

Kat looked at him and said in disgust, "Well, I guess he thought the call was for old farts. What an idiot."

Did she seriously say that? I turned my head so she wouldn't see my disappointment. I guess people see things differently. To me, the guy was adorable. Maybe she isn't the person I wanted to hang out with after all. Oh well, in a few more minutes I'd be leaving and probably wouldn't see her again anyway.

As if on cue, someone called, "Kitty Kole." I breathed a sigh of relief and stepped up to get my picture taken. The bubbly girl photographer had been replaced by a surly-looking man. He shoved a card at me and I stood where he directed for my shot. My head was down looking at the number on the card when I heard "CLICK". He had taken the photo before I could give him my signature Pity smile.

He nodded to the side, and said, "Go on." Then he shouted, "Next!"

I sputtered, "But please... I didn't even smile. I mean...You took it so fast. Can we take another shot? I'll be quick. Please?" I posed with a big smile.

"Nope. One shot per person," he said, looking at his camera with no expression.

My smile dissipated. I shook my head as I moved to the next table and handed my card to a dark-haired woman of about 60, whose nametag read, 'Rita'. She looked directly at me with blue-gray eyes and said in a friendly voice, "We'll contact you tomorrow if you are going to be needed."

I perked up with the actual attention and pleaded, "I sure hope I can do this. It would mean a whole lot to me. My dad worked in the oil industry and he would be thrilled if I got to be in this movie. Is there anything I can do to better my chances? Can I give you another photo?"

She smiled and chuckled. "You're fine. We'll let you know tomorrow…oh and if we call, it will be an 818 number." She adjusted her glasses and read my name, "Kitty." Was that a little twinkle in her eyes? Maybe she knew someone named Kitty, or perhaps really liked cats. If so, wait 'til she saw the next girl's name.

I turned to give a quick wave back to Kat. However, she didn't notice because she was too busy flinging her long red hair from side to side in assorted poses while the grumpy photographer smiled, snapping shot after shot.

Wait a minute! What about the one photo rule? That was more like an entire photoshoot! Hmph. Downcast, I headed out the door, got in Liesel, and drove back to Broken Arrow.

Arriving home earlier than expected, I grumbled to the girls about my experience. "Guess I'll just have to settle for watching movies because apparently, I don't even have what it takes to be an extra." I put my head in my hands.

I could sense my girls looking at each other probably with eyebrows raised. Shaking off my disappointment, I brightened. "I'm sorry. Just being overly dramatic. But don't worry, I'm OK. Hey, Ren, go ahead and order the pizza to be delivered. I'll run up and finish my invitations."

With the girls happy and pizza in the near future, I was back to my perky self. I climbed the stairs to our all-purpose room.

Ree yelled after me, "Don't forget to invite Caitlyn."

"Not to worry! She and Jennifer are always on my list." I couldn't forget my girls' best friends.

I sat at my computer and opened the e-vite and proofread.

GET YOUR GLAM ON
You are invited to the 5th Annual Oscar Party
Sunday, March 2
Red Carpet Arrival 6:00–6:30 p.m.
Pre-Awards Show/Dinner 6:30-7:00 p.m.
Awards Ceremony 7:00–10:00 p.m.
Presentation of Pity-ful Prizes 10:00 p.m.
*Formal Attire-featuring Goodwill designers optimal
*Menu - Gourmet Pizza, Popcorn, Movie Candy
Please RSVP by responding to this e-mail
We hope you can attend this upcoming Pity Party!

I checked my list of regular invitees: Caitlyn, Jennifer, Kim, and R.A. (my sister and brother-in-law) Lin, and my three best friends from school: Becca, Jules, and Jana. I invited a few others and included courtesy invitations to my parents and sister Kay in California. I gave a big sigh when the invitations were finally sent.

Before heading downstairs, I checked on Iggy, Ree's 4-foot iguana who lives in the temperature-controlled aquarium. Iggy's eyes rolled around to look at me as she munched on the remaining lettuce from her bowl. I waved and said, "Good girl, Iggy."

The doorbell rang and there was a stampede to the door. After getting drinks, we sat at the dining table and ate while discussing my disappointing casting call.

"Maybe that Kat girl is trying to get a lead part," Ree suggested, as she dipped her cheese pizza in ranch dressing.

I shook my head. "I'm pretty sure they have the major parts cast."

Ren wiped her mouth and said, "That thing about her twin sounded pretty weird. Are you going to buddy around with her if you see her again?"

"Not if I can help it. She doesn't seem like a very nice person."

"Show us again how you looked in your picture," Ree said, smiling in anticipation.

I bent my head down and made a stupid face, causing them both to giggle.

After dinner, the phone rang with a local area code, so I assumed it was Kenny. I wasn't in the mood to talk to him, so I let it go to voicemail and called Lin to fill her in on my disappointing audition.

Monday morning, the girls and I donned jackets and set out for our respective schools. Ren dropped Ree off at the middle school on her way to Broken Arrow High where she is a sophomore. I drove the short six blocks to my home away from home, Arrowstar Elementary.

I carried my bag of supplies into the school where I had taught for 12 years and stopped by the principal's office to drop off my lesson plans so they could be scrutinized by my tyrannical boss. Barry Love was our new principal and had only been at the helm for a semester, but it seemed like an eternity. When his name was first announced, I just knew he'd be an awesome guy; maybe a cross between a sexy soul singer and a friendly clown. The whole staff was dying to meet him. So, being elementary school teachers who always do cutesy things for new staff members, my buddies and I decided to decorate his office.

We made a big sign adorned with hearts that read, "Welcome Barry Love! You're going to LOVE it here." We taped it on his door to make him feel welcomed on his first day. He tore the sign down immediately and told his administrative assistant, "I won't have any of this tomfoolery in my office. And do let the staff know that I go by Dr. Love."

When we heard the name Dr. Love, we giggled. Maybe he had a sense of humor after all. But, NOPE. As time went on, we realized the man had been born without a happy gene. In fact, he should have been named Dr. Dark. Why this grumpy guy ever chose to be in education was beyond me.

To make matters worse, Dr. Love chose me right away as his target, no doubt because I'm more vocal than other teachers. He harassed me from day one – giving me the worst duties, singling me out for petty mistakes, and turning down almost all the purchase requests I submitted.

Once I had made it to my cozy pre-fab, I prepared my sets of xylophones, metallophones, and glockenspiels in rows on the floor for the hundreds of kids who would soon be tapping and singing their way through my music classes this week.

After everything was set up, I walked to the art room to meet up with my buddies. I decided not to tell them about the audition, since I probably wouldn't get called to work based on my photo.

Entering the art room, I was hit with the familiar smell of crayons, paint, and glue. The teacher, Jules, our very own Rembrandt, sat at her desk. Her long hair was pulled up loosely on her head and held in place by a paintbrush. I have no idea how she does that. She looked up and joked, "So…did you go to the dance hall this weekend?"

"Shhh. Don't you dare tell the other girls about that." I shook my head as a warning, but before we could discuss it, the door opened. In walked Jana, the gifted and talented teacher, dressed in a conservative blue top and knit pants. She breathed heavily lugging a huge stack of notebooks. When she dumped them on the table, the books slid across in an avalanche.

I winced. "Journal grading time?"

"You guessed it. I just hope the kids actually followed directions this year."

Last but not least, Becca made her entrance. Becca always makes an entrance; this time she wore a pink bejeweled t-shirt with 'Fitness Princess' stretched across her abundant chest. Her body was strong and athletic. If there was ever a good example for fitness, it was this PE teacher.

Once in our usual seats, we discussed our weekends. They told stories of their kids and pets. I described my boring blind date with Kenny, but made a face at Jules, warning her not to say anything about our secret. I asked my three buddies, "Are you guys coming to my Oscar party Sunday?"

"Are there gonna be any single guys there?" Becca asked with eyebrows wiggling.

"Sure, if you bring some."

She shrugged and looked away. "If you're not providing any hotties, why should we come?"

I squinted, "Hello? So that you can win prizes and see my new Oscar video."

Becca laughed, "I guess. It's actually worth the drive just to see you act a fool."

Jana looked up from a notebook. "Are you finished with this years' masterpiece?"

I answered, "No. Once I see my last movie, I'll record the spoof and edit. Then I'll be done."

Jules turned her head away from the chalkboard and said, "You gonna invite the weasel to your party?"

"Are you kidding? I wouldn't allow Dr. Love into my home even if he came with an armload of free puppies."

Jana shook her head while she opened a journal. "If I were you, I wouldn't even tell him about the party or he'd forbid it."

Becca held her nose in a nasal impression of Dr. Love, "Being up that late on a school night will interfere with your teaching. I won't allow it."

We laughed, then Jules winked at me, "Speaking of Dr. L...."

I squeezed my eyes shut in anticipation of her spilling the beans, but in a stroke of luck, she was interrupted by a loud crackle. I sighed in relief, as we all stared at the speaker on the wall as if we could see the announcer. Maybe it's good that our antiquated school still doesn't have televised announcements or we would have to watch our annoying principal on a monitor.

On came his familiar whiny voice, "At this time, all staff and students should make your way to the cafegymatorium for the weekly assembly."

We made a collective groan.

I gathered my music and headed that way followed by my team. As we entered the large noisy room that smelled like bacon, my feet stuck to the floor. The substitute custodian must not have done a very good job mopping after the pancake breakfast, but the poor children sitting on the syrupy floor didn't seem to notice.

Small faces of all colors stared at us adoringly. They waved and patted our legs as we walked by. Who wouldn't love this job? We are treated like rock stars.

Becca leaned close to me, tickling my shoulder with her long earrings. She whispered in my ear, "Go work the weasel."

We laughed until I saw the principal scowl at me. My smile faded and I scooted over to the piano and sat on the bench where I belonged.

I led the opening of the assembly, as usual, starting with the pledge of allegiance, the school pledge, a patriotic song, and ending with this month's character song, 'Compassion.' Then, it was Dr. Love's turn. He stood and cleared his throat into the microphone, just one of his many annoying habits. Then he started on his weekly announcements. I wondered what he had come up with to destroy the happiness of our school this week.

Since Love started in August, he had already downgraded the school atmosphere from cheerful to glum by imposing new rules. As a result, our long-time secretary retired early, numerous students transferred and four teachers moved to other schools. Of course, he didn't think any of it was his fault.

As he cleared his throat I thought, please just get it over with. Put us out of our misery. Pull off the Band-Aid, dang it, and tell us what we're in for this time.

Movie Watching Tip #3
Avoid sitting near annoying people.

When Dr. Love put his hand on the microphone, it made a horrible squeal, causing the children to cover their tender ears and me to cringe. He finally spoke in his annoying voice, "As I'm sure you are all aware…" He looked around the room, pausing for some sort of effect that baffled me, "…the attire of this school has become far too lax."

I noticed the dazed expressions of the kindergarteners. Poor innocent things had no idea what the word attire meant, or what was coming next, but I had a hunch it wouldn't be good.

He continued, "I have decided to impose a set of guidelines that will make our school environment free of distractions and more productive for all."

My gaze flew to Becca, Jules, then Jana – each of which wore a similar expression to mine: wide-eyed terror. Panic began to spread throughout the crowd like a wave - well, among people older than ten, anyway.

He leaned to the side and turned on a projector that displayed the new 'guidelines' on a large screen behind him. He read each rule aloud and showed a photo example of each one.

1. **"All children must wear khaki pants or skorts with solid white shirts."** The pictured children wore said uniforms and stood in line as if awaiting execution by firing squad.

2. **"All staff members will wear khaki pants or skirts with solid white shirts. Hosiery must be worn with**

skirts." The accompanying photo could have been torn right out of a 1960s Sears catalog. I would have laughed if he wasn't serious. Wait. Did Dr. Love actually say the staff would have to wear uniforms? I gasped. He couldn't do that!

3.   **"Only closed-toed shoes are allowed."** My heart raced as I studied a photo of an ugly pair of clunky shoes.

4.   **"No sleeveless tops, tight-fitting clothing or printing on any shirts."** This picture was downright disturbing. It was a little girl in a flowered top with a giant red circle around her and a line going straight through like a no-smoking sign. I started to hyperventilate more and more with each change. I wasn't given enough time to grieve my loss of choice, because he kept talking.

5.   **"Clothes must be clean and worn without wrinkles. Permanent press fabric is advisable."** The next photo was even worse because it showed one of our own students, a boy from a large family, wearing a wrinkled shirt. Dr. Love had gone too far this time! The murmurs in the crowd grew louder. Disgusted, I stopped looking at the photos and closed my eyes, but unless I put my fingers in my ears, I couldn't escape the grating sound of his voice.

6.   **"Males must wear collared shirts."** I just stared at my lap in horror as he droned on.

7.   **"No colorful hair accessories or jewelry will be tolerated."** My eyes flew to Becca. Even across the enormous room, I could see the whites of her eyes.

8.   **"The new dress code goes into effect next Monday, so you have one week to gather your new wardrobe."**

9.   **"A note will be sent home with students today to inform their parents of these changes."**

The entire cafegymatorium was silent, as if a bomb had gone off. Everyone was too stunned to move. I half expected teachers to start screaming and running about frantically – at least that's what I wanted to do, but everyone just sat frozen as the principal's ludicrous words sunk in.

Was this even legal? Could a principal impose such rules on his own? I had read statistics stating that some schools with uniforms had better-behaved students, but the thing is, our kids already behaved. And I'd certainly never heard of any staff in our area having a uniform policy. What worried me most was his abrupt decision to make the changes without input from staff or parents.

I couldn't even look at the creepy man with his comb-over hair and thick glasses, partly because I was mad, but mostly for fear he would want me to play a peppy song to break the silence - something I knew I couldn't do in my current state of mind.

"It is at this time," he said with a head tilt and slight smile, "that I'd like to recognize the student of the week, Jesse Jacobs."

I observed the boy sitting in the middle of the gym and relaxed a bit when his classmates patted him on the back. Jesse was a nice boy. At least one good thing came from this assembly.

I smiled at Jesse as Dr. L went on, "Jesse has shown exemplary behavior by turning in a student who wrote on the bathroom mirror. That student was reprimanded for making such a poor decision. Jesse was wise to let us know who had defaced school property. Jesse, come forward for your award."

Oh, no! Poor Jesse was being rewarded for being a snitch. I watched as the boys sitting around him made faces and scooted away as if he had just passed gas. Kids - they'll turn on you for any reason and this was a doozy.

The 4th grader slowly stood up, head hung low, and made his painful way to the stage steps. This day would probably haunt him for life.

I placed my elbows on the piano and rested my head on my hand. Would this assembly ever end? After a small spattering of applause for the humiliated boy, the screechy, high-pitched voice of our leader continued, "At this time we will disperse to our classrooms for a day of education. Ms. Kole, can you play the school song as we exit?"

I had no choice but to do as he asked. However, I did play the song at a somber tempo. Usually, the students sang along, but this time, only a few exuberant little ones sang. Those babies didn't know their freedom of choice had just been taken away.

When the song ended, I motioned to Mrs. Johnson's class to follow me. I led the 3rd graders through the halls and to my prefab. When in my classroom, the kids bombarded me with questions about the dress code. I wasn't in the mood to discuss it, and deferred it to their teacher, Mrs. Johnson, before starting the music activity du jour.

The morning classes continued, and everyone seemed to enjoy playing instruments. Every 30 minutes, between classes, I checked my phone to see if I'd gotten a call from the casting agency but I had no messages. When the last class left, I rushed to the art room with my sandwich and Diet Dew.

Becca arrived at the same time, carrying a protein drink and an arm full of hula hoops complaining, "This is the most ridiculous thing yet!" She plopped herself down on the round stool attached to the table. "Who does he think he is to change OUR dress code? I don't think it's even legal."

Jules stood at the chalkboard and drew something with green chalk, "My theory is…that Dr. L. hasn't gotten ANY in a long time or for that matter, ever. He's punishing women for his lack of sex. I mean, we only have one male teacher and I'm sure Jonesy would be thrilled to wear the same thing every day, so the Weasel is doing this to us. Plain and simple."

I hated to even think of Dr. Love in that scenario, but who knew his motivation? I shook my head and asked, "How are parents supposed to get uniforms in one week? Some families won't be able to afford them at all." I picked up my phone and searched for a number and said, "I'm going to call the Broken Arrow Teachers' Association and find out if he can even do this."

"I beat you to it," Jana said as she entered. "Jeff, at BATA, said a principal can't make that decision on his own. Requiring students to wear uniforms has to be voted upon with parents' involvement. And staff dress codes are set by the district school board, not the school." She smirked as she sat next to Becca, who was wrapping green neon tape around hula hoops, probably for a game in her P.E. class.

I nodded happily. "We finally have him on something." Then I frowned, "But, who is going to confront him about it. Will the district office take care of this?"

Jana frowned. "Only if we file a signed complaint." She opened a student journal and started reading reluctantly.

I said, "Becca, you do it. Dr. L likes you. You won't get in trouble."

"Ha! If he still liked me, he wouldn't have added the part about the jewelry." She cocked her head showing off her bright pink earrings.

Jules turned and gave me a triumphant look, "How about you, Pity. He asked you to go out dancing Friday. He must really like you." I glared at her. Dang it. I knew she couldn't keep her mouth shut!

"What?" Jana and Becca shouted, mouths agape.

I scowled at Jules, then gave in and explained to the others what had happened. "Yep, the worm called me into his office on Friday and asked if I liked to dance. I told him, 'Sure, I love to dance'. I just thought he wanted me teach a dance unit to my students. Then, he dropped the bombshell and said, "Good. I'll pick you up at 8:00 on Saturday so we can go to the new Cowboy Country Dance Hall!"

"No way!" Becca covered her mouth, trying to suppress her snorts of laughter.

Jana's eyes were wide as saucers and asked, "What did you do?"

"Well, I was flabbergasted, so I stammered and said I was busy, and even added that I was dating someone."

She said, "But I thought he couldn't stand you! He's been picking on you since August."

I shook my head. "I know. I guess I was next on his list, after all his advances towards Becca failed." I made a face at Becca then turned my head back to Jana. "You're probably next since you're one of the only other single gals left in the school."

Jana turned a deep shade of red. Never having been married or even dated much, I knew she would just die if he approached her.

Becca said, "Lucky you, Pity. It took me months to shake the leach and convince him I wasn't interested," She took a drink, still smiling uncontrollably.

"Maybe the dress code is his way of getting back at you," Jules said as she moved away from the board, revealing the picture she had drawn. I gasped. There was a hilarious caricature of Dr. Love, kicking up his heels at a country bar. Unfortunately, I was pictured too, standing a head taller than him, wearing cowboy boots and horseshoe earrings. The two of us were just dancing away. I turned even redder than Jana. When Becca saw the picture, she snorted protein drink out of her nose, causing us all to crack up.

Once we calmed down, Jana asked, "So, what are we going to do now?"

I snapped a picture of Jules' silly but amazing artwork with my phone and said, "Personally, I think we can just sit back and watch the drama unfold. The other teachers won't stand for it. I mean, can you imagine Mrs. DuPont being forced to wear solid colors? She's so colorful. She's ready to retire and would have nothing to lose by rebelling or complaining."

Jules added, "And the parents? Mrs. Morgan for instance – her twins have colored bows to match every outfit. She wouldn't want to give those up. There will be an uprising without our help,"

Jana smiled as she returned to her journals. "Yeah, you're right. We probably don't have to do anything,"

I gave a sly smile. "You know what would be fun? Before the 'onset of khaki', let's play with his head a little. How about we all wear tight, colorful clothes with sandals and ultra-big earrings the rest of the week?"

Jana scrunched her nose, "I'm not sure I want to wear sandals in February or tight clothes ever, but I'm good for the rest of it."

Becca asked, "How's this for tomorrow's earrings?" She held two of the wrapped neon green hula hoops up to her earlobes.

I laughed. "Now, that's what I'm talkin' about."

My phone buzzed and I did a double-take when I saw the number, thinking it was a local 918 number, but it was 818! I jumped up and ran from the room feeling the eyes of the girls on my back. "Hello?" I answered as soon as I stepped out onto the porch. It wasn't the best place to stand since it was cold and I could barely hear anything above the playground noise.

A woman's voice said in a friendly tone, "Is this Kitty Kole?"

"Yes, it is."

"This is Rita Carone, from Big Sugar Creek Productions. Will you be available to work on "Crude Town" starting tomorrow?"

"Oh, yes, yes, yes!"

"Good." I could imagine her smile through her voice. "You must arrive at the fairgrounds by 6:00 a.m. and be available to work a minimum of 10 hours tomorrow. If possible, bring several outfits that might work for the 1960s. If you don't have anything, we'll send you to wardrobe for clothes. Come with clean hair and light make-up."

"Oh, thank you! I can't wait."

She added, "Oh, and Kitty, you're being considered as a stand-in for Ms. Baxter, which pays a little extra."

"Oh, okay?" I had no idea what being a stand-in entailed, but it sounded cool. "Do I need to bring my lunch?" Oh gee, that was probably a stupid, uncool question. Why do I always worry about food? I must get my act together by tomorrow.

She chuckled and said, "No. Craft services will take good care of you, but you might want to bring a book for down times."

"Will I see you there, Rita?"

"I'm sure you will. I'll probably check you in – bring your ID again."

"Great! I'll see you bright and early!"

I hung up and realized I was jumping up and down with excitement or maybe from the cold. Did she say to be there at 6:00 a.m.? Jeeze Louise, that was early. I scooted back into the room in time to hear the girls complaining about the new 'Narc of the Month' Award. I rubbed my arms to warm up and tried to decide whether to interrupt with my news or to jump in on the current subject.

Jana was tracing the letter D hard on a journal as she spoke. "I just feel so bad for poor Jesse. Dr. L shouldn't have made a spectacle of him."

Jules bent down to pick up some stray crayons from the floor and said, "The kids will be able to get away with murder now. Nobody will ever tattle after what Dr. L did to Jesse."

Becca turned to me, "Was that phone call from the "boyfriend" you told Dr. L about?"

I straightened with my newfound confidence. "No, but I won't be able to help you annoy him tomorrow with a crazy outfit after all, because I'm taking the day off…" I imitated a drum roll and shouted, "to become a movie star!"

Jules raised her eyebrows. "Are you going to be in that new Aaron Winston movie?"

I nodded, beaming.

Jana's head swung up from her notebooks. "Isn't Alison Baxter going to be in that? And the director is Joel Mason?"

I nodded as Becca stood and gave me a high five. "You go girl!"

Jules said, "I read that Alison just broke up with her football player boyfriend."

"Really?" I hadn't heard that, which was strange because I kept up with all the entertainment news. With faux superiority I said, "I'll let you in on any first-hand gossip I hear, Jules." I winked.

I addressed them all again. "So, I have to take a couple days off to do it." Then in almost a whisper, I said, "I'm not telling anyone but you three why I'll be gone. If the weasel finds out, I'll get in bigger trouble than usual, so keep it quiet, please."

Jana said, "Mum's the word. Even though our personal days can be used for any reason, I doubt Dr. Death would agree."

Becca gave me a sly smirk. "You're going to try to hook up with Aaron Winston, aren't you?"

"Who me?" I gave her a coy smile and then rolled my eyes knowing a date with the megastar wasn't a remote possibility.

The bell rang, and the girls hugged me and wished me luck. While Jana gathered her notebooks, Becca walked out with me. "If you become Mrs. Winston, you'd better introduce me to some of his handsome single friends."

"It's a deal," I laughed and walked to my room, imagining myself, Aaron, and my girls sunning by a pool at our Hollywood mansion.

It was difficult to focus on teaching that afternoon, being so fired up about the next day. While a class of fourth-graders clapped rhythms from my flashcards, I realized if I was discovered, I may have to give up teaching. I frowned at the thought since I love my job. Just then, a boy punched another kid and I had to settle the skirmish. Okay, so if I was a star, I doubt I'd have to deal with that kind of behavior. That made me smile.

After school, I spent an hour making lesson plans for a substitute; then filled out my leave paperwork. I put 'personal' as the reason for my absence and dropped if off with Melanie, our school's admin.

On my way home, I stopped at QuikTrip to get gasoline, so I wouldn't have to stop at zero dark thirty in the morning. I pulled up to the pump and hopped out, thinking all the while about running inside to get a large mango iced tea for myself and slushies for the girls to celebrate.

As I lifted the nozzle, a familiar voice growled, "Well, look at that. You finally got that VW you always wanted. How were you able to afford this?"

Oh brother. What was he doing out in the middle of the day? I slowly turned to see my ex-husband, scuffing his boots on the concrete and sashaying toward me with a walk he thought looked like John Wayne. Truthfully, he looked like he was cleaning cow dung off his heels. His enormous, black pick-up truck towered at the pump behind me.

I quipped, "None of your business, Todd."

In his smug, obnoxious way, he smirked. "Oh, I know…" he nodded slowly, "…probably insurance money from wrecking the van, and from that little extra job of yours, huh?"

I sighed. "Well, it certainly wasn't with any help from you." Why wasn't he working? Probably got fired from another job. I didn't want to prolong the conversation by asking, so I just stared at the nozzle hoping he would leave before my tank filled.

"I heard you were going to a garage sale when you totaled the van. I told you your little addiction would bite you in the ass someday," he said stifling a laugh.

I answered in a huff before thinking. "It wasn't a garage sale; it was a thrift store."

Todd took his ball cap off and slapped it on his knee, laughing. Apparently, my correction was even more hilarious than what he had heard. When my pump turned off, I quickly replaced the nozzle and got in my car. Why did he always fluster me?

"OK, darlin'." He could hardly get the words out he was laughing so hard. "Tell my girls I'll see them on Wednesday."

Our house was only a few blocks away, so I barely had a chance to calm down on the drive. When I got home, I asked the girls if their dad still had his newest job. Ren answered, "I guess so. He works different shifts, so we never know when he's off."

"Well, I just saw him. He said he'll see you on Wednesday."

The girls shrugged and I shook my head trying to get Todd out of it. Then I told Ren and Ree about my exciting phone call.

Ree said, "So your freak-out yesterday was all for nothing?"

I nodded and then led the girls to the garage so we could scan my costume stash. I found bellbottoms, a leather purse with fringe, and great stiletto heels that might work for some part of the '60s. I wasn't sure that was enough, so I announced, "Let's look through Grandma's old clothes."

While driving the 15 minutes from Broken Arrow to Tulsa, I called my sister, Kim, and asked her to meet us at Moms. Then, I called my boss at Tulsa Opinions, to say I couldn't work for the next few days. My part-time job at the market research company improved greatly once I was promoted from working in the call center to becoming the hostess for focus groups.

I pulled into the driveway of the red brick house where I grew up, and parked behind Mom's Camry. I waved at Dad, now in his 70's and as tall and handsome as ever. He stood on the porch ready to greet us. The girls ran ahead, got their hugs and disappeared in the house. When I reached the steps, I saw Dad wore his usual threadbare Dockers and one of his button-up dress shirts. I breathed in his Old Spice cologne as he hugged me. The warm embrace was as welcome as his gentle kiss on my cheek.

Mom stood inside the door, smiling and wearing a navy-blue wildflower sweatshirt. In her typical no-nonsense manner, she said, "Well, come on. Let's see what fits"

Kim appeared behind me on the porch just as I stepped inside. We definitely look like sisters; both of us with Mom's brown hair and dark eyes. In contrast, our oldest sister, Kay got Dad's fair hair and eyes. I always say, she barely looks like a neighbor. I gave Kim a hug. We are a real huggy family, well except for Mom.

The five of us girls crowded into the sewing room that used to be my bedroom. Kim and I sat on the bed while Mom and the girls looked in the closet. I rubbed my hand over the colorful bowtie quilt our grandmother had made. Why didn't I have the aptitude or patience to make a quilt?

Ren pulled out a royal blue empire-waisted dress that looked just like one Jackie O. might have worn.

Kim nodded. "I'll bet they'll let you wear that one if it fits. It's awesome."

Mom, who recently gave up hair dye and traded the boxed color for a gorgeous head of natural white curls, held the dress up against her body and said, "I remember wearing this." She sighed. "I wish I still could."

I was struck by how pretty she looked and said, "Well, you should definitely wear that color. It looks great on you."

She smiled and slipped the dress over my head, tugging it over my broad shoulders and zipping it shut. It fit better than I expected it would. I marveled at the high waist while I studied my reflection in the full-length mirror.

Ree said, "Is that the same dress?" She pointed to an old photo of Mom and Dad on the bookshelf.

I looked at the picture and nodded to Ree. "Wow. Mom, you were a knock-out."

She shook her head and changed the subject. "Here, try on these." Mom handed me a pair of off-white, low heeled slip-ons and a high heeled black patent leather pair. I slipped on one of each, posing awkwardly, thanks to the difference in heel height.

Dad walked by and saw me in the dress. He said to our group of girls, "A wife, daughters, and granddaughters - all such beauties." He stepped into the room and took my hand. "You look lovely in that dress, Pity." He kissed the top of my head and made his way down the hall, whistling. The floor creaked under his feet, making me smile. Memories flooded back of a lifetime of that creaky floor and Dad giving his sweet praise. Oh, and how I love to hear him whistle.

Ren said, "Grandma, did you make this?" She looked inside the waistband of a red skirt for a label.

"Yes, Lauren. I did. I probably still have the pattern." Mom walked over to a bin and dug through to find it while I changed into another dress.

Kim pouted. "I wish I could go with you, Pity. Darned library meeting. You'd better give me a full report and let me know if they need anyone after tomorrow." Since Kim is the head librarian at the Brookside Library, she couldn't ditch the meetings, but maybe she and R.A. could join me later in the week.

"You bet I will!"

Mom found the pattern, sat by Ren, and they discussed how the skirt was made. That oldest daughter of mine loves any kind of needlework so she soaked up every word. Unlike my mother, I only used my sewing machine to make curtains or costumes. I steer clear of confusing patterns.

Ree popped out of the closet surprising me, and said, "Mom, you should take this coat with you. It looks vintage to me." I took the tan leather jacket from her and tried it on, wondering how a thirteen-year-old would even know what vintage was? But, once I put it on, we all agreed with her and it went in the stack to take.

By the end, we had chosen three complete outfits. I even got cool accessories: vintage shoes, fake pearls, white gloves, a jacket and a purse.

After we finished, we sat at their long cherry dining table and ate a piece of Mom's yummy lemon meringue pie while Dad told us one of his long, but fascinating stories about when Tulsa was an oil boomtown.

Before we left, Dad said, "Pity, have fun reliving the past tomorrow. I hope they get it right." I did too.

That night, I tried without much success, to get a good night's sleep before my big day.

Movie Watching Tip #4
Pay attention to the technical side of the film.

A shower, coffee, and a bowl of Life cereal boosted me back to the living after I woke up at the ungodly hour of 4:30 a.m. I squeezed into Mom's blue dress. Then I pulled on a pair of pantyhose for the first time in years. I can't believe I would have to wear these to school every time I wore a skirt if Dr. L got his way. I added white gloves and the pair of off-white patent leather shoes that were too big but more comfortable than my other choices.

When I tried to pin up my hair the way Mom showed me, it looked like a bird had nested on my head so I brushed it out and left it loose, hoping a professional could do something with it.

I stopped by the girls' rooms to make sure their phone alarms were set to ring on time and gave them each a kiss on the cheeks as they slept.

Harriet met me in the hallway, bouncing with excitement. Our silly girl had no sense of time and thought we should play. I tousled her hair and threw her stuffed elephant across the room a few times, watching her bound over to retrieve it. I gathered my additional costume choices, a paperback book, and remembering what the weatherman said about the forecast, I made sure I had Mom's jacket.

Since Liesel took a while to warm up, I shivered as I drove through the dark streets of my neighborhood. Accelerating onto the Broken Arrow Expressway, I was surprised to see so many people up at the ridiculous hour. Were they all going to Tulsa to be extras in the movie? The answer became clear when only a few cars pulled into the fairgrounds. Where were all those other people going so early in the morning?

By the time I parked, my car was toasty warm and I dreaded getting out. But seeing others walking in the building in their 1960's attire got me so excited, I forgot completely about the cold and marched up to the building. A warm shudder went through me when I realized I could see Aaron Winston at any moment!

A long line of people dressed in period garb snaked around the hall. I giggled, feeling like I had gone back in time. I peeked around a girl in white Go-Go boots and saw Rita sitting at a table checking people in.

Luckily, the line was moving pretty fast. Just as I neared the table, I heard someone yell out my name, "Pity!"

I turned and saw Kat, dressed like a 1960's stewardess. She pushed her way past the line towards me. Oh brother. I had to admit she looked amazing in her tall, black patent leather boots, mini skirt, and a little shiny cap. With no enthusiasm, I said, "Hi Kat. So, they called you too?"

"Yes, they called me first thing yesterday. I'm going to be a stand-in." Her head was lifted so that her nose was actually in the air, just like she sounded.

I tried to act cool and confident. "Oh. They told me I was being considered for a stand-in too…for Alison Baxter." I refused to admit to Kat that I still didn't know what a stand-in was.

Her smile disappeared and she stepped away from me as if I'd announced my leprosy diagnosis. In a flat tone she said, "Well, I guess we're going for the same part."

I shrugged. "I'll just be happy to be involved in any way." I turned around, and found myself next in line. "Hi Rita," I said as I handed the friendly woman my driver's license.

"Kitty?" She said with a sweet smile, not bothering to look at my I.D.

"That's right – or Pity. Either is fine" I smiled back. "I'm sure glad we'll be inside today, 'cause it's dang cold out there."

Rita raised her eyebrows. "Well, you are actually filming outside, but not for a few hours. It should warm up quite a bit by then."

She must not have checked out the weather, since it wasn't supposed to get over 40 degrees today.

When Rita scanned my outfit, she nodded. "Very nice. No need to go to wardrobe. Go straight to Hair and then over to Make-up. Give them this." She handed me a small pink paper and a three-part carbonless form. Then she pointed to the room down the hall. "Hang on to that voucher if you want to get paid."

"Thanks." I folded the voucher, stuffed it in Mom's purse, and headed to the room labeled Hair.

As I walked away, I heard Kat ask Rita in a superior voice, "Where do the stand-ins go?"

Rita replied, "They'll decide who the stand-ins are later today. For now, join the large group."

A cloud of hairspray hit me as I entered a crowded room, labeled Hair. I couldn't help but cough with all the fumes. After lining up behind a few girls who waited for a spot at one of five hair styling stations, I watched in awe as hair was transformed from today's styles to that of the 1960s.

After standing for 20 minutes, I was very glad I wore the comfy clunky shoes instead of the heels.

A young woman wearing combat boots, cargo shorts, a flannel shirt and a cowboy hat flew into the room. She whistled so loud I covered my ears. She bellowed, "OK, background, listen up!"

I took my hands down. Background? Who are they? I figured even if she wasn't talking to me, I would listen. But the girl with the cowboy hat spoke so loud and fast that that I couldn't ignore her if I tried, "After Hair and Make-up if you want a quick breakfast, go to Craft Catering in the next building." She pointed to her right. "Background holding area is in the lobby of the Pavilion. Stay there and listen for instructions... and remember..." She held up one finger, "Keep quiet." Then she held up two fingers, "Don't talk to or take any photos of the stars". Then with three fingers up, she said, "And stay out of the way of the crew." The girl left just as quickly as she had entered.

I turned to the young girl behind me and asked, "Are we background?"

She said, "I guess."

I heard, "Next!" and a stylist with pink hair motioned me over to her station. She took my slip of paper with an outstretched arm that had a tattoo of scissors. I hoped she wouldn't cut my hair, then rethought it. A free haircut might not be such a bad idea.

I couldn't resist asking, "What are you going to do to me?"

She put the paper down, turned her head from side to side examining my boring brown hair. She said, "Oh, I have a plan." She combed, teased, and sprayed for at least 20 minutes. I usually love to have my hair brushed, and at times have even fallen asleep while getting a haircut, but her pulling, poking and spraying was anything but relaxing.

When she finally stopped and turned me around so I could see myself in the mirror, I practically choked. I looked like a cartoon character. My signature bangs were poofed up and I had a huge flip at my shoulders. I turned my head but my hair didn't move. It looked like I wore a huge plastic wig. I started laughing and couldn't stop.

"You might want to calm down." She said with a smile. "They can't do your make-up if you're crying."

I wiped away my tears of laughter and controlled myself as best I could before standing up to go to Makeup. I felt a little guilty for not leaving the girl a tip.

In the next room, a quiet girl transformed my face into someone I didn't recognize. The eyeliner was so thick and heavy that it made me sleepy, but her magical make-up made my boring brown eyes stand out in a good way. I just may have to shop for more cosmetics.

A man with dreadlocks and a Polaroid camera stopped me on my way out and took my picture for what he called 'continuity'. Then I was off to check out breakfast. The large room was filled with rented white plastic tables and chairs. The smell of bacon made my stomach growl, even though I'd eaten cereal before leaving the house. I stood in line behind a man who looked like Sean Connery and wondered if I could now pass as a Bond girl. I was about to strike a sexy pose to try it out, then gave up, snickering at the thought. I filled my plate with bacon and a muffin, then grabbed a cup of coffee and sat at a long table with a bunch of other "background."

It hadn't been five minutes before Kat arrived with the exact same hairdo as mine but in her auburn shade. She wore a more subdued outfit than before and didn't seem happy about it. I watched as she pulled on her shirt and fidgeted while she walked. When Kat saw me, she gave me a dirty look and sat with flair at another table. Fine. I really didn't want to be her friend anyway.

Not long after, CowboyHatGirl announced in her high-speed voice, "All prospective stand-ins come with me." I stood and tossed my paper plate and coffee cup in the trash and tried to keep up with her. Upon entering a new room, I stood next to two guys who matched each other in size and dress. Kat came in and walked to the other side of the men, avoiding me.

One of the men was undeniably handsome. He was in his mid-30's, had black hair with denim blue eyes, but he exuded an aura of supremacy. His lip curled as if he was an expert actor and we were scum. When our fast-talking leader explained that she was going to put us with a partner to try out, he rolled his eyes. I quickly dubbed him, "SmugGuy".

The other more average-looking man was probably late 40's, had thinning brown hair, and a warm smile complete with dimples. I named him "NiceGuy".

CowboyHatGirl led us down some maze-like hallways and out a door to a crazy scene that stopped me in my tracks. There must have been 50 crew members with cameras, poles, carts, lights, and cables. I had just entered a different world. I was pretty sure people shouted in English, but I had no idea what they were saying. I looked around but didn't see Aaron or Alison.

Despite the rising of the sun, it had NOT warmed up at all. I was freezing and wished I had brought my mom's leather jacket from the car. At least I wore her gloves and I had to admit the hose helped a little bit. Only the crew was dressed warmly, wearing coats, scarves, and even earmuffs. Oh, wait. Maybe those weren't earmuffs, but headphones. Whatever. All the extras or background were like me, dressed in period attire, and not winter 1960's clothes either. I shivered as I tried to focus on CowboyHatGirl's directions.

She said SmugGuy and I were to stand by a pillar. When we heard the word Action, we should start walking down the sidewalk then stop at the red tape 20 feet away.

When she said, "Action" we did as told and stopped at the red tape. Then she repeated the move with Kat and NiceGuy. When she said "Action" to them, Kat sauntered down, swinging her hips. She grabbed the arm of NiceGuy and laughed as she walked.

"What the hell was that?" asked CowboyHatGirl. "You're not the stars. Just walk. Do it again." I smirked as Kat pinched her lips together and walked back with poor NiceGuy, whose face turned pink. They got in position for the next try. Upon "Action", they walked again. This time she was more stoic, but I did notice her hair swinging more than mine.

CowboyHatGirl, I was beginning to like my nickname for her, said, "The first two, Kitty and Sean? Come do it for real now."

A man shouted, "Team 2 in!"

Shouts came from all around: "Quiet" "Set" "Pictures up" "Camera team ready?" "Rolling" "A Mark" "B Mark", "Background!", none of which made sense to me except the first word.

As soon as they had yelled, "Background", a group of extras walked and pretended to talk. Then a man with thick-rimmed, black glasses made a loud sneeze. I stood, watching everyone else until SmugGuy grabbed my arm and spat, "Come on! Move!" I walked with him to the end spot and heard "Cut – Reset."

The crew members buzzed about, fiddling with gizmos and moving equipment. Some stood in groups around cameras, some watched monitors. Everything was so chaotic I wasn't sure what we were supposed to do. SmugGuy turned around and walked back to the beginning mark, so I followed him and whispered, "I didn't even hear him say Action. I just heard him sneeze."

He looked down at me with furrowed brows. "What?"

"So, what do we do next? You don't think we have to jump off buildings, do you?"

When SmugGuy wrinkled his nose, I explained, "We're stand-ins. Don't we have to do dangerous stuff to protect the stars?"

With an annoying scoff, he said, "Did you just fall off a hay truck? We're not stunt doubles. We're stand-ins." He shook his head rudely.

"But then, why do they need us?"

"Seriously? What is this, Stand-in 101?" He huffed, but then began to explain, "We're the same size as the stars. The crew practices with us to set the lighting and camera angles before shooting Team 1."

"Oh." I nodded, feeling stupid. Then I put two and two together. The stars must be Team 1 and we were Team 2.

He shook his head and mumbled, "Dumb Bitch."

My jaw dropped, but before I could react, I heard the same loud "Achoo!" I realized the director was really saying "Action!" and not sneezing. We took off walking again. I wondered why they didn't call Kat and NiceGuy to have a turn, but I sure wasn't going to ask my rude partner anything else.

We repeated the routine a few more times after hearing the weird sounding "Action." It was so cold. I wished I had worn a long-sleeved dress. Standing as far away from SmugGuy as I could, I rubbed my arms to warm up, waiting for more directions.

Then, someone called out, "Team 1 in." Like glowing beacons of light, Aaron Winston and Alison Baxter stepped out of a trailer! I froze, but this time not from the cold. The two stars were more beautiful than I had ever dreamed they would be, and in their costumes, they might as well have stepped right out of the '60s. Aaron Winston looked like a blonde Cary Grant with his hair slicked back and she could have been Audrey Hepburn. I'm pretty sure my mouth hung open as they glided toward me.

Seriously, the megastars walked right up to me. The sexy actress, whose hair was styled like mine, raised her eyebrows and crooned to me, "I think it's our turn now."

I stared at her and blinked. Oh my. I was supposed to move off set. I said, "I'm sorry. Here, please take my place." I stepped backward and Aaron gave me a curious look just as I backed into a guy with a big long microphone on a stick. Aaron reached out his hand to catch me, but I righted myself on my own. I stammered some nonsensical excuse and quickly turned around, covering my face in embarrassment as I fled the scene.

My heart pumped abnormally fast as I rushed toward the background holding area. What a klutz. I had just stood in the way of two major stars. When I approached the pavilion, Kat stood outside, apparently waiting for me. She said, "Aren't you special being a stand-in, 'Miss I'll Just Be Happy to Be Involved.'" Then she smirked. "We'll see how long that lasts." She left in a huff.

Gee, that girl had issues. She must really want my job.

SmugGuy stood smoking by the door of the pavilion, shaking his head at me as I passed. I sure wasn't making any friends here. I shivered at the thought of being so goofy and friendless, but the warmth of the beautiful Art Deco building hit me as soon as I entered. The intricate tile architecture surrounding the lobby made me smile. I poured hot coffee from the snack station urn and took a drink to warm my insides. Holding my Styrofoam cup, I ran my free hand along the smooth tiles in awe of the designs.

As I was trying to forget how foolish I had been, a low voice asked, "Was it fun to stand in for Alison Baxter?" I turned to see NiceGuy holding a water bottle.

I smiled. "I guess. But I was an idiot. She had to ask me to move because I was too dumb to realize they were supposed to take my spot."

"Ha! I wouldn't worry. We're not professionals. And on the bright side, maybe they'll remember you now."

"Maybe they'll replace me!" I shook my head and shivered.

He said, "That Kat girl is a real piece of work. She cussed up a storm when they chose you. I've never seen anyone sound so vindictive. She's a ticking time bomb if you ask me."

I held out my cold hand. "My name is Pity."

"I'm Pat."

"Ha! Kat and Pat. You two could have been quite a couple – if only you liked her."

He shrugged his shoulders. "That's not possible. Besides, I'm married to Penny."

I thought about making a comment about the names Pat and Penny, but CowboyHatGirl barged in and pointed to a large group. "You and the stand-ins, come out front."

I turned to NiceGuy. "Back to the cold." I sighed, dreading the frigid air.

CowboyHatGirl's rapid-fire directions continued as we tried to keep up, "Go around the Expo building. I'll meet you where they are installing the fake oilman statue." She peeled off in another direction as our group made its way around the enormous building.

Did she say a fake Golden Driller? I smiled at Niceguy and said, "I love the Golden Driller."

"Hm." He nodded.

"No. You don't understand. He's been my boyfriend ever since I was little. I even wrote a song about him called, "I'm in love with the Golden Driller."

He lifted his eyebrows and chuckled. "Well, there you go!"

High above the parking lot, a giant crane slowly lowered a huge replica of Tulsa's famed golden oilman. We craned our necks up to see the enormous reproduction. I was surprised he looked so much like the real one, a massive golden man with incredible muscles wearing a giant hard hat.

Beneath him, orange cones and caution tape lined the area to keep people away from the equipment. Movie cameras filmed the fly-in, but apparently, it wasn't necessary to be quiet on the set for this, as people were talking while the cameras rolled.

CowboyHatGirl gave a loud whistle that pierced my ears. My hands flew up so fast to cover them that I hit myself in the head with Mom's purse. Lucky for me, it was practically empty – my purse not my head. I uncovered my ears just in time to hear her say, "You guys can hang out in this alcove until we call you."

NiceGuy and I made our way into the small indoor area, where I found a lone stool and sat on it. I was happy I didn't have to sit on the ground in my dress and hose. NiceGuy joined other extras who sat on the floor or leaned against the wall. Most of the other women wore slacks, so I didn't feel too bad grabbing the only seat. The small area had large windows so we could watch the activity outside while staying warm. SmugGuy stood in a corner wearing earbuds, probably to tune out our lowly group of amateurs.

I searched the area for Kat and was surprised to spot her standing outside talking to a tall man who appeared to be a crew member. She pointed up to the giant oilman in the sky and the man nodded.

As I gawked at Kat, trying to figure out what she was doing, NiceGuy interrupted me. "Why don't you sing your song?"

"What?" I laughed and looked around the small crowded room. "No. I wouldn't want to subject these people to my singing."

A woman with a beehive hairdo overheard and said, "What song?"

Pat (Now that I knew his name, I should probably call him that instead of NiceGuy) said, "She wrote a song about the Golden Driller."

Since he answered louder than I would have liked, we now had everyone's attention.

The woman cocked her head. "I want to hear it."

The sun glinted in an old man's eyes. He held up his hand to shade them and said, "What else have we got to do?"

That was true, but seriously? Yes, I'm a music teacher and I sing all the time for my students, but my voice is not performance quality by any means. I explained, "I'm not a great singer so…"

At that, people began to coax me, "Come on." "Do it." and "We're not judges on the Voice."

My face flushed. "Well, it's just a fun country song I wrote about being single in Tulsa."

All eyes, except SmugGuy's, were upon me. I wished I wasn't sitting on the stool for it made me feel like I was on stage and that they were truly my audience. But I cleared my throat and went over the lyrics in my head. I opted to only sing one verse then opened my mouth and sang,

"Of all the men in Tulsa, and believe me I've met a few,
From doctors, policemen, and cowboys
I've met an interesting crew.
I've been picked up for a date in a pick-up truck,
A Jeep and a Lexus too
But I'll drive myself across the town
to meet one man so true.

I'm in love with the Golden Driller.
He's the tall and silent type.
A hard-workin' man, watching over Tulsa
Every day and night.
I'm in love with the Golden Driller.
He's always there for me.
No expectations, no broken hearts
The perfect man indeed.
He's the perfect man, the perfect man
If only he could dance with me!!

When the song was finished, I took a deep breath as the group clapped and laughed. I felt hot all over and I was sure my face was red. How odd to be so embarrassed. After all, I speak in front of the whole school quite regularly. I guess singing for strangers is a whole new, nerve-wracking ballgame.

"That's so cute!" said a woman from across the room.

A young girl said, "Carrie Underwood should record that."

A few others had nice comments about my voice not being bad and such, but SmugGuy shook his head and rolled his eyes at me.

Pat said quietly, "I've never known anyone who could write songs."

I said, "Well, I'm a music teacher, so it's kinda my thing. And Pat, what do you do?"

He said slyly, "I own a portable toilet company."

I opened my mouth wide. "Well, I've never known anyone who collected pee." I winked and guessed, "So tell me, do you call it Pat's Porta Potties?"

He smirked and said, "No. We actually call it Pat and Penny's Party Poopers."

Movie Watching Tip #5
Be open-minded and try to watch all genres.

Not long after my somewhat embarrassing performance, CowboyHatGirl stormed in to the alcove. "Background, wait here 'til I give you directions. Stand-ins, come on out." She sped out of the room so fast I wondered if she was actually on speed.

Outside, I shivered and waited for directions while SmugGuy continued to listen to something through earbuds. The giant statue had stopped moving once it had been positioned directly above the oil derrick. CowboyHatGirl said, "Team 2" up. She motioned for us to duck under the caution tape and get to our spots next to the oil derrick. On my way, I hopped over a large rack in the sidewalk and took my place. CowboyHatGirl put a hard hat on SmugGuy's head and had me stand next to him.

"I'm so excited, I hardly feel the cold anymore," I said to SmugGuy, forgetting for a second that he was a jerk.

Through clenched teeth, he said, "Would you just shut up, already?"

I couldn't believe my ears and strained again to think of a good comeback, but an important-looking blonde man wearing sunglasses, a grey sweater, and skinny black jeans strode over to us. He said, "In this scene, it's early April of 1966. Aaron's character is helping set up the Golden Driller for the International Petroleum Exposition, but Alison comes over and distracts him."

He explained further to SmugGuy, "On "Action", you'll look up, then after counting to three, turn to watch her come toward you." He took me to a spot about 20 feet away and said, "Stand here until you hear 'Action', then walk, keeping your face toward that camera." He pointed to my right.

"OK," I said and stood in my starting spot. This man was patient, friendly, and not in a rush like CowboyHatGirl. Was he Joel Mason? Before he left, I asked him, "Is it safe to stand underneath the statue?"

He lifted his sunglasses, revealing warm amber eyes. "We had to have a fake statue in order to recreate its dedication. We couldn't move the real one even if we wanted to. This one is made of Styrofoam and is held up by industrial-strength cables, so it better be safe." Then he winked and walked away.

I took a moment to admire the real Golden Driller that stood a block away – all 43,000 majestic pounds of him. As a kid, I wanted to know everything there was to know about the statue. I even memorized his stats: He stood 76 feet tall, with his left arm on his hip, and his right hand on a real oil derrick that came up to his chest. His belt was 48 feet long and his hardhat was size 128. My giant boyfriend was built to withstand 200 mph tornadoes. And to think, he stood alone in front of the I.P.E. building my entire life. The name of the building has changed so many times, I can't keep up, so I just use its original name from 1966 when it was built for the International Petroleum Exposition.

I turned and focused on the instructions I had been given. I heard "Action", which this time actually sounded like the word, and moved toward SmugGuy. I was careful to step over the crack in the sidewalk and took my place beside him. I was so glad I didn't have to remember lines too.

The director had us repeat the scene a few more times. Then, as cameras rolled yet again, I plainly heard, "Team 1 in!" Upon "Action," I hesitated because we were Team 2. When I realized the stars were nowhere to be seen. I finally started walking toward SmugGuy, who shook his head at me as though I was an idiot for taking so long. Since I was distracted, and maybe because of my loose shoes, I tripped on that stupid crack in the sidewalk. I fell hard, landing on my knees. My upper body flew forward as if I was performing a tumbling routine, and I landed, scraping my hands across the cold hard concrete. Someone was laughing. Through my pain, I managed to look up from my prone position to see SmugGuy's obnoxious open smile directed right at me.

Suddenly, I heard a loud crack and watched in horror as the giant Styrofoam Golden Driller came loose from its cable. As it fell toward SmugGuy, I shouted, "Look out!" to warn him, but he was still laughing so loud he couldn't hear me.

The oilman's enormous boot hit SmugGuy smack on the head, essentially stepping on him, and smashing him to the ground. The statue creaked, wobbled, and fell back to land against the building. SmugGuy was trapped underneath the enormous oilman's weight. It may not have weighed 43,000 pounds, but at 76 feet tall, the Styrofoam replica had to be extremely heavy!

The sound of screams was deafening, and it was hard to tell exactly what was going on with all the commotion. Medics rushed to the scene. Men struggled to pull the oversized driller off of SmugGuy. I sat up, covered my mouth with my bloody hands, and wondered how anyone could survive being stepped on by a size 393DDD shoe. I doubted the hard hat CowboyHatGirl had put on SmugGuy's head helped to protect him at all.

Once the large group of men had tipped the fake oilman to the side enough to uncover SmugGuy, the medics took over. After a uniformed E.M.T checked his vitals, she shook her head slowly; the universal sign that it was no use. He was gone.

My heart skipped a beat. How horrifying! I couldn't believe my acting partner, albeit a mean one, was dead! And I saw it all happen. My head felt light and dizzy. Still sitting on the ground, I put my head between my torn pantyhose-covered knees to get air and hoped I wouldn't faint.

Once I caught my breath, it occurred to me, if I hadn't tripped on that crack, I would have been under the boot too! There was a sour taste in my mouth and I began to shiver uncontrollably.

CowboyHatGirl yelled through a megaphone for everyone to go inside the Craft Catering building. I couldn't get up. I couldn't move. I just sat by myself, frozen to the ground in shock. After a few minutes, Pat came over and asked if I was alright. He helped me to my feet and walked me to the warm building. "Can I get you some coffee or hot tea?"

"Maybe some tea?"

He led me to a chair and left me to assess the damage to my skin.

Kat walked up and smirked, "You're lucky you're so clumsy."

I didn't even try to think of a comeback. Why she was so cruel to me and so disrespectful to SmugGuy.

I dabbed my palms and knees with a napkin I found on the table and realized I should find out SmugGuy's name since that isn't a very nice thing to call someone who had passed. I felt a sudden urge to vomit, but Pat returned with my drink, and thankfully, just holding the warm cup gave me comfort. I closed my eyes and tried to block out what had just happened. I heard the fast-talking CowyboyHatGirl approach and I looked up to see her pointing me out to a male medic.

He came over to me, bent down, and said softly, "Mind if I clean up those hands?"

I tried to speak, but words wouldn't come. I nodded, set my tea down, and turned my hands over. Gently and silently, he cleaned and bandaged my hands. When finished, he tipped his head down and said, "Looks like your knees could use some attention too."

I shook my head and said, "That's okay. I'm wearing hose. I'll just take care of them at home."

He shrugged and gave me a package of bandages. I put what I could in my small purse and left the rest on the table.

When the blond director entered the room, somebody whistled and the room grew quiet. His voice cracked as he spoke, "I'd like to suggest we have a moment of silence to honor Sean." The director dipped his head and closed his eyes.

I followed suit, praying for Sean's family and then giving thanks that I had been spared.

The director stepped forward, "Due to the accident, we will suspend filming for the rest of the day. Please turn in your vouchers. We'll let you know when we will resume shooting and if we'll need you. Thank you very much for your cooperation."

The mood was somber as people gathered their belongings and started for the door. I sat a few more minutes, still shaken. Pat said, "Do you think you're alright to drive?"

I nodded. "They're only superficial wounds." But I knew he meant my mental state, not my physical one. Pat's forehead crinkled with worry. I took his hand and said, "Thank you for being so kind."

He helped me up, saying, "I hope I'll see you again."

With a slight smile, I limped over to give my voucher to Rita.

Her face was drawn and she looked as though she had aged years since morning. Rita pointed to my knees and said, "You may not be interested, but I'll call you when we start shooting again and you can decide if you want to join us again."

I thanked her and hobbled to my car, still in disbelief.

I arrived home just before noon. I was still upset and unusually tired, so I took a pain reliever and trashed my torn hose. After cleaning and bandaging my scraped knees, I climbed into bed and fell into a deep sleep.

As I slept, I dreamt that a giant shoe hovered over me. As I turned to run, it followed me, all the while descending closer to my head. Finally, I froze in one spot and closed my eyes as the boot knocked me down and smashed me to the ground. I lay helpless between the sole of the boot and the pavement. Trapped, I panicked, unable to breathe as the weight of the oilman continued to crush me.

The heavy boot shifted, and I awoke sweaty and disoriented. When I opened my eyes, I found my big hairy dog sprawled across my chest. I pushed her off me and gasped for air. "Harriet, you nearly scared me to death."

When I regained my composure, I apologized to Harriet and snuggled her tight, thankful to be alive.

After a few hours, I dragged myself out of bed, fixed a plate of nachos, and munched on them while reading the Broken Arrow newspaper, hoping to get my mind off the accident. I found a letter to the editor from an Arrowstar parent, complaining about Dr. Love's uniform decision. Oh, baby, it was just beginning.

Harriet nudged my hand causing it to land on an ad for "The Next Temptation", the only nominated movie I hadn't yet seen. It was finally showing here, but I was in no mood to see it.

I had an hour before the girls would get home from school, so I decided to go upstairs and edit my annual Oscar video. A few years ago, I started filming a short scene from all the films nominated for best picture. The spoofs are stupid, the acting is awful and the production quality is way below amateur, but my videos still entertain friends at my Oscar Party each year.

I left the living room intent on going upstairs but caught a flash of red out of the corner of my eye. "Edgar, have I been ignoring you?"

I walked over to my large African Grey parrot, stuck my fingers through the bars of his cage, and ruffled his soft feathers. His large yellow eyes blinked as he climbed to the top of his huge cage. He flung his gorgeous red tail at me and then he swiftly moved to the other side and got a peanut from his bowl. Effortlessly, he climbed all the way back and cracked the nut, never taking his eyes off me. Edgar loves to have an audience while he eats.

I said, "How long have you been waiting to eat that nut, you nut?" Then, I ascended the stairs to my Music/Computer/Sewing room and turned on the computer.

I pulled up the spoofs I had already filmed for my Not Quite the Oscars video. First, I reviewed my silly version of the film, "Wild Hearts of Mystic Canyon," where I wore full cowgirl attire, and rode a stick horse. Then for "The Forbidden Place", I donned Dad's fishing waders and climbed into my pond in the backyard for the drowning scene.

Outfitting myself for the skits is never a problem because I have quite an extensive costume collection; in fact, a third of my garage and a large closet in my schoolroom are filled with costumes. Most wigs, hats, and props were bought at garage sales. Other costumes, I make myself.

Even though the movie, "Swerve", wasn't nominated for best picture, I spoofed Aaron Winston's character as a presenter in my fake Oscar video since he was nominated individually. I watched on my computer screen as I walked to a fake microphone. I wore a ball cap, and my face was scuffed-up ala Aaron's character. I carried my enormous dog, Harriet, and smiled when she stared straight at the camera as I announced this year's nominees for best picture. Hopefully, viewers would catch the irony of Harriet being 20 times bigger and hairier than the tiny Chihuahua in "Swerve."

Only one more skit to film and I'd be finished. I felt much better since I had eaten, so maybe I could go see the last movie on my list this evening after all. I'd see if Lin would go with me.

I worked a bit longer adding sound effects and music, then went downstairs to call Mom.

"You won't believe what happened today. I went to the set…"

She interrupted, "Someone died. Your father and I heard it on the noon news. Please tell me you weren't in any danger, Pity."

How does the woman do that? She always knows what happens before I can tell her. "Well…Mom," I stammered, not knowing whether, to tell the truth, or sugar coat it, but blurted out, "I was actually supposed to be right beside the man who was killed when the accident happened, but I tripped, and didn't make it to the spot-on time. It was horrible."

The silence on the phone was disturbing. Had she fainted? She finally spoke. "Which shoes were you wearing?"

That was an odd response, but I answered, "Your clunky low heels that are too big for me."

In her matter-of-fact way, she said, "I guess it was a blessing you wore those." Then, in an uncharacteristically sweet tone, she said, "How are you holding up, dear?"

"Well, when I got home, I took a nap then I tried to keep my mind off of the day by working on my Oscar video. It was awful."

She said, "Would that be your video or the incident on set?"

I chuckled. "Well, you know my video is awful. I meant the accident."

My mother actually sounded worried when she said, "You're not going back there, are you?"

"Um. I don't know." I hadn't even thought about whether I'd want to go back and answered, "I'll see if they even call me."

"Well, you know what you can handle. If you do go, take care of yourself."

"OK. Thanks, Mom, and tell Dad hi." I decided not to tell her about how I had scraped my knees and hands. She never was very sympathetic for my injuries and would expect me to tough it out.

After I hung up, I checked out the movie times and texted Lin to see if she wanted to go at 7 p.m. I saw the dot-dot-dot on my phone and waited for her reply to pop up.

I waited a full minute, but nothing appeared on my phone. I wrote again 'Well, do you want to go?' This time she responded.

"What in the world is "The Nest Repression?""

I read the message I had sent and sure enough my predictive text had gone haywire. Instead of 'Do you want to see the "The Best Temptation at seven?"', it read, 'Do you want to see the "The Nest Repression at seven?"' Actually, that title sounded almost as good as the real one for a movie.

I imagined the plot and spoke in my deep announcer voice, *"In a world - where most live on the ground, A young macaw sits high above the rainforest repressing memories of falling from his nest. How long can he keep his feelings bottled up before flying off the handle?"*

Haha. Someday, maybe I'll read my texts before sending them.

I quickly retyped my message and sent it to Lin. She responded immediately, "See you there at 6:45, Goofus. How was today?"

I wrote, "I'll tell you about it tonight."

I sank down on the couch and turned on a local channel to see if there was a news report about the tragedy on set. There wasn't, so I watched a rerun of "Judge Michael." Michael was in rare form when he reprimanded a girl for loaning her car out and not noticing for two weeks that it had dents when it was returned. He held up a picture and barked at the girl, "Are you blind? Did you even look at the car?"

Turning to the guy with missing teeth, Michael glared, "Did you damage Miss Gray's car?" The guy's long greasy hair shifted as he shrugged and said, "I dunno."

"Well, either you did or you didn't! Which one is it?"

The redneck blinked and answered, "I guess so."

"Did you show her the damage when you returned the car?"

He shrugged. "I figured she'd see it and she owed me a hundred bucks anyway."

The judge shook his head. "Mr. Loban, were your parents first cousins?"

A special report interrupted Michael's rant. The local reporter's hair was so perfect, I wondered if my pink-haired stylist had fixed it. She wore a KOTV jacket and stood in front of the fake Golden Driller, who casually leaned against the building as if he was on a smoke break. I sat up and focused on what she had to say next.

The somber gal gripped her microphone and looked straight at the camera. "A local debt collector died today in a tragic movie accident." A photo of SmugGuy appeared with the name Sean Marco displayed. She continued, "The filming of the highly anticipated movie, 'Crude Town', was halted in its first day of shooting, after a 76-foot replica of the iconic Golden Driller fell from a crane, crushing Aaron Winston's stand-in to death."

Captioned photos of Aaron Winston, Alison Baxter, and Joel Mason popped up as the reporter explained the accident in detail.

I nodded. So, Joel Mason was the director with thick-rimmed glasses who yelled "Achoo!" and barked orders. I guess he wasn't the super nice director after all.

As the reporter finished the news brief, she knitted her eyebrows and said, "An investigation into what caused the cable to break continues. Stay tuned to KOTV for updates. Reporting live from the Tulsa Fairgrounds this is Molly Simmons."

Judge Michael returned, reaming out a landlord for his lack of safety standards on a garage door. From what I could guess, his renter's car was smashed. That made me wonder about the safety standards of the crane holding the fake Golden Driller.

The station went to a commercial and there on TV, dressed as George Washington, was Smelly Shelly, Todd's girlfriend. Ren and Ree had given her that nickname because of her strong perfume. Shelly has been starring in commercials for her father's Big Jack's Cadillac Company since she was a little girl. Back then, she was cute dressed in costumes. Not so much anymore. I about died when the girls said their dad was dating that ditzy blonde.

I rolled my eyes and muted Shelly before calling Kim. She wasn't home from work yet, so I talked to my brother-in-law, R.A.

"Well, how's our little actress?" I could hear his warm smile through the phone.

I commenced to tell him about the day.

"Woah. That's really bad. Are they investigating? What would have caused the cable to break? You said you heard a crack? Describe the crack. Do you think it was really an accident?"

"Uhm. I dunno." I realized I just sounded like the trashy punk from Judge Michael, so I quickly amended my answer, "It sounded like something breaking, like a really loud snap or crack. The whole thing happened so fast; I can't really explain it. They called it an accident on the news, so I assume it was."

After a few more questions, R.A. told me he'd have Kim call me and that I should be careful if I went back to work there.

A bit later, the girls walked in the house. They stopped abruptly in the foyer and stared at me as if I was a ghost.

"What?" I asked.

Ren said, "Oh my gosh! For a second, I thought we were in the wrong house."

"Why?"

"Your hair!" squealed Ree.

I lifted my hand and touched the hard shell surrounding my head. I forgot I still looked as if I stepped out of the musical, "Hairspray". I said, "Oh yeah, they sure did me up, didn't they?" I patted the seat next to me. "Girls, come sit down. I have something to tell you."

They joined me on the couch, staring at my hair the whole time. Ree reached out and touched the bouffant hair and pulled her hand back as if stung.

I casually covered my bandaged knees with my bandaged palms and began. "OK, you know how I went to the movie set today?"

"Mm-hm?" They both said, smiling, probably expecting a far funnier story than I had was about to tell.

"Well, I got to be the stand-in for Alison Baxter." Their eyes grew large, but I continued before they got too excited. "That was really cool, but there was an accident on the set and…" I winced, "the other stand-in was killed."

Ren's eyes darkened. "What happened? Were you in danger?"

I shrugged. "I was about 20 feet away from him when I tripped over a crack in the pavement and fell on the ground. Just as I did, I heard a loud sound and this enormous, fake Styrofoam Golden Driller – almost the size of the real one, fell from a crane that held it. Its boot literally stepped on Aaron Winston's stand-in and crushed him to death. It was awful."

Both girls cringed in horror. Then Ree's face relaxed. She nodded and said, "Sure Mom. What really happened?"

"I know it sounds crazy, but it really happened."

Ren asked, "Did you know the guy?"

"We worked together all morning, but I didn't know him well."

She shook her head. "How horrible!"

When Ree realized I wasn't kidding, she said softly, "Mom, I'm glad you're so clumsy." She gave a sob and I rubbed her small back.

"Me too, honey. Me too."

With my hand lifted, Ren saw my bandages. "Are you hurt?"

"Just a little. They are only scrapes." I turned my hands over to reveal all four of my bandages.

"Ooh." Ree took my hand and lifted the corner of the dressing to peek underneath.

Ren said, "That must have been scary. Are you going back?"

"Maybe? I don't know when they'll start filming again."

To lighten the mood I said, "When I came home, I took a nap and feel better but I still need to get my mind off the accident. So, tonight I'm going with Lin to see 'The Best Temptation' at 7:00. Do you girls want to go? It's supposed to be pretty good. Or do you have too much homework?"

Ree said, "I want to go."

That's my Ree, the girl who never wants to miss anything.

"Me too," said Ren, "I mean, Jolie Marks is in it, so I'm thinking I need to see it."

"Good. Then you can help me choose which scene I should choose for my last spoof. You know I have to finish my video by Sunday or the whole party will be ruined." I winked. "Well, hop to your homework while I start dinner."

The girls stood and Ree literally hopped over to her backpack to get her homework. Having just turned 13 last week, she was thrilled to finally become a teen, but I was happy she could still be a silly little girl at times.

I was relieved the girls weren't too upset about my close call and headed to the bathroom to tackle my hair. Looking in the mirror, I was surprised to find my hair hadn't been smooshed during my nap. It was too stiff for a comb to go through and I didn't want to take a shower yet, so I settled for washing my face.

I fried hamburger patties, made a salad, and heated a can of beans while Harriet sat patiently in the kitchen waiting for something to fall her way. When I "accidentally" dropped a carrot, she scarfed it up like it was candy. I caught sight of my reflection in the window and had to snicker. All I needed was an apron and I'd be a model 1960s housewife – well minus the cigar-smoking husband, of course.

🎥

Movie Watching Tip #6
Bring your own snacks to save money.

When we met Lin in the theater parking lot, she was in her ever-chipper mood.

"Ooh, check out that do!" Lin ran over and touched my hair. "So, did ya meet Aaron Winston?" she asked as she automatically handed over money for her portion of the popcorn. We had gone to so many movies together, our routine was routine.

"Umm. Kinda?" I forgot all about my brief run-in with him once everything else happened. "I'll tell you in a minute."

As we walked up to buy tickets, Ree exclaimed, "Mom, you're leaking!"

I looked down and saw that my purse was indeed dripping. Oops. I had put a cup of iced tea in my purse and the lid must have come loose. That's the problem with movie contraband. I quickly hid behind Lin so the gangly teen ticket seller wouldn't see me. I attempted to put the lid back on, but Lin moved aside just at the wrong time and I was busted.

"Ma'am, you can't bring your own food or drink into the theater." The boy's voice modulated from low to high.

"Oh, I know." I nodded and struggled for an explanation. "I always buy popcorn here and usually pop, but I was really in the mood for iced tea and you don't sell it so…" He folded his arms and frowned. I gave up on my lame attempt to justify my smuggling, and walked, defeated to the trash can.

As I paid for tickets, Ren told Lin, "That's nothing. One time, Ree and I met Mom at a movie, and during the show, I saw her munching on something. I asked what it was and without taking her eyes off the screen, she said nonchalantly, 'Fried Alligator.'"

I caught up with them and piped up, "In my defense, I had just had lunch at White River Fish Market and I couldn't finish my meal, so I got a take-home box. It was 102 degrees and the alligator would have been ruined in the car, so I had it for a movie snack. I mean, it was expensive." Lin shook her head, but I knew she would have done the exact same thing.

At the concession stand, I got a stack of napkins and stuffed some in my purse to soak up the mess. Then I ordered two drinks and a large bucket of popcorn. I asked the girl behind the counter, "Can you put butter on the first half and then more on top? And I'll need 2 extra cups of ice. Oh, and salt, please." As usual, we paid more for the snacks than the movie tickets.

My Junior Mints were stashed in my soggy purse. (shh) I know…I shouldn't do it, but come on, if I bought their candy too every time I went to a movie, I'd be bankrupt.

Since this wasn't a mainstream movie and it was a Tuesday night, we got perfect seats in the center of the theater with nobody in front, beside, or behind us. Lin sat on one side of me and Ree sat on the other so we could share a drink. I spread six napkins on my lap and poured popcorn on top and passed the bucket down the row. After salting my stash, I pulled out the Junior Mints and I started on the feast. There is nothing better than that sweet/salty combination to get you in the mood for a movie.

I leaned over to Lin and whispered, "So, I got to see both Aaron and Alison today. Problem is, they think I'm a dork."

"Yeah?" She said nodding her head.

"Well, you don't have to agree with them."

She turned and made a face at me. "And who just got caught trying to smuggle tea into the theater?" She shrugged trying to prove a point. "So, did you talk to them?"

"Sort of. I had to apologize for standing in their spot. But then I backed into a crewman and almost knocked over a boom mike."

Just then the screen lit up with a talking popcorn box telling people to turn their phones off and go visit the concession stand. I whispered to Lin, "But the worst thing that happened today was that someone died on the set! It was awful...and it could have been me!"

"What?" she asked, in a voice way too loud for a theater. She practically poured the whole bucket of popcorn on her lap as she stared at me. Then she stopped pouring and shook her head and said, "I thought you said someone died on the set?"

I pointed to her mess and spoke loud enough so Lin could hear me over the animated Coke cup telling people not to talk during the movie, "I did! It was Aaron's stand-in. It could have been me too! I was the stand-in for Alison, but I tripped before reaching the spot and the Golden Driller fell and stepped on him."

She screeched, "Wait, the Golden Driller stepped on him?" Unfortunately, the commercial had ended, replaced by a preview for a tense but quiet drama, so everyone heard her.

Ren, Ree and a lady two rows behind us all said "Shh!"

Lin whispered, "What did you put in your drink?" She leaned over to sniff for alcohol, obviously thinking I had made up the whole story.

I sighed and put my napkins full of popcorn on Ree's lap. "I'll be right back." I stood and motioned to Lin. She followed, dropping popcorn down the aisle like Hansel and Gretel as she followed me. Ren shook her head as we passed. In the hall, Lin got the quick version.

Her voice rose as she responded to my story. Just as a couple walked by, Lin said, "I can't believe your true love killed somebody." The two turned to us open-mouthed.

I shook my head and explained, "My boyfriend didn't kill anyone. The Golden Driller did it." They scrunched their faces and made a wide berth around us as they entered our theater.

After answering a few more of Lin's questions, we returned to our seats. I repositioned my popcorn, reclined my chair and turned on the seat warmer. Ahh. Lin continued to shake her head as she took in my incredible story.

Once I had eaten my fill of popcorn and Junior Mints, and the previews were almost over, I made a mad dash to the bathroom, hoping I would get back in time for the movie to start. I did.

When I returned just in the nick of time, Ree whispered, "Why do you wait until the last second to go?"

"Because I might not make it through the whole movie otherwise."

She warned, "Someday you're gonna miss the beginning."

I was glad my child couldn't read my guilty face in the dark since I have miscalculated the length of trailers many times before.

I settled into my seat and hoped Lin wouldn't be too noisy. She's one of those people who actually screams when scared or tells the character, "Look out behind you!" or "He didn't mean it. He really loves you." It's kinda funny to watch but distracts from the film. I have to be selective in which ones I see with her.

The movie started and I waited for the sound to go up before taking care of my last detail. I dumped the extra cup of ice into my half-empty cup and Voila! My cup was full again and super cold. I'm a self-proclaimed extremist. Cold things had to be cold, hot things hot, salty things salty and I wanted gooey things gooey.

The screen lit up with the words, "The Best Temptation". From what I had read, the film was a modern-day version of Adam and Eve. I was content with my family around me and a full belly. I just hoped I could forget the accident for a few hours.

The characters were named Adam and Eve – go figure. Adam was the caretaker of a botanic garden and Eve worked at the local zoo. Clever! Of course, like most Oscar nominees, the film was artsy. The cinematography was celestial and ethereal (Okay, so I may have read that description in a critic's review).

Just as I was fully engrossed in the story, bright lights flickered. Had someone set off fireworks under a seat? I looked around but nobody else stirred. The lights twinkled again briefly. Was I having a stroke? I closed my eyes and breathed evenly, hoping to identify anything internal that might be wrong.

When I felt nothing out of the ordinary, I opened my eyes and there were the lights again. I squinted to the right. Aha. There was the source – a little kid sitting just past Lin was kicking his feet. His light-up shoes blinked with each kick.

I shook my head and leaned back, trying to ignore him, but it was no use, my ADD had already kicked in and all my senses were affected. I couldn't focus on anything except the multi-colored flickers and the boy's incessant giggling.

I whispered to Lin, "Why is that little boy here anyway? This isn't a kid's movie."

She turned and said, "What are you talking about?" Apparently, she was oblivious to the obscenely bright lights.

Unfortunately, the boy's mother didn't seem to notice either or maybe she didn't care. The boy kicked and blinked, then kicked and blinked and giggled more. I finally leaned across Lin and said, "Psst", trying to get the mom's attention, but she was too engrossed in the movie, which is exactly what I wanted to be. The kid kept kicking, so I hunkered down and crept over to the mother. "Could you please ask your son to stop lighting up his shoes?"

Despite the blinking lights and darkness of the theater, I could distinctly read her expression of disgust. "You're kidding, right? He's only 4. He can't keep still."

"I understand that, but his shoes are distracting me from watching the movie."

She whispered, "Sounds like you have a problem then."

I was incensed but didn't know what to do aside from throwing popcorn at her, so I sat back down and shielded the lights with my hand. I could still see the reflection and hear the boy's giggles so I reached over and offered my box of mints to the lady for the boy. She grabbed the box rudely but her child instantly stopped kicking, distracted by the candy. Whew!

When I finally focused on the movie again, I was a little disappointed. I had looked forward to seeing Jon Masterson wearing only a fig leaf, but darn it, in this modern-day version, both stars were fully clothed. The coolest character in the film was actually the serpent, who didn't talk, but somehow had a fascinating personality.

Despite the uplifting message at the end, it was a pretty weird movie that only open-minded people would enjoy. Of course, that description fits many of the films nominated for Oscars.

As we left the theater, the lady with the blinky kid gave me a scowl. She could have at least thanked me for the candy. I'm ashamed to say it, but I got a kick out of seeing the little boy's face and hands covered in chocolate.

Then, the couple who overheard our murder conversation scooted by us quickly as if our crazy might rub off on them. To keep them from calling the police or funny farm, I yelled, "Watch the news tonight. You'll see what we were talking about."

The four of us discussed the film as we walked to our cars. I said, "I liked it, but I wouldn't buy it." Forget the stars or thumbs-up rating system, I have a 'Would Buy It' or 'Wouldn't Buy It' system. Simple as that. Lin and the girls agreed with my critique.

Ree spoke up, "Ooh, Mom, you should spoof the dinner scene." Ren and Lin both nodded.

Ren said, "That would be perfect. You could do the apple pie part."

Confused, I said, "I don't remember a dinner scene."

They all stared at me. After a beat, Lin nodded, "Oh. You were probably in the middle of your shoe confrontation."

A little embarrassed, I said, "Maybe? I guess I'll do a serpent scene instead. Lin, why were you so quiet during the movie?"

"Because I kept trying to picture the Golden Driller stepping on someone."

A slight wave of nausea came over me. "Well, I'm tired of picturing it."

We got home just before the 10 o'clock report and the girls left to get ready for bed.

I called Kim and told her all the details of the day and just as I hung up, my phone rang. "Is this Kitty Kole?"

"Yes?"

"This is Rita from Big Sugar Creek Productions. We're going to start filming again tomorrow morning. We've taken extra measures to protect everyone involved. I know what happened was very upsetting to you, but would you be able to help us out and work as Alison's stand-in?"

Decision time. I always have a hard time telling anyone no. I did still have two personal days left and the sub was already scheduled. Rita was so nice, but most importantly, I still wanted to see Aaron Winston in action. Without any more thought, I said, "Well if you're sure it's safe."

"Oh, thank you!" Rita exhaled as if she had been holding her breath. Then she continued, "Yes, they have anchored the fake Golden Driller and rewritten the scene. And, if you know anyone else who might be interested in being extras, let me know their names and numbers. We need more people since some chose not to come back."

"Actually, I do know someone. My sister and brother-in-law, Kim and R.A. Ross might be available tomorrow." I gave her their phone numbers.

"Thank you so much. Oh, and make sure to wear the same outfit as today, in case you are shown in a scene. And, you don't need to be there until 6:30."

"OK. I'll see you then." I wasn't sure how to feel about going back but thought it would be fine and I'm always up for an adventure. Plus...I'd get an extra half-hour sleep this time.

I stood between the girls' rooms and said, "Well, it looks like I'm going back tomorrow. They assured me everything would be safe. I might get home late though. Do you want to watch the news? The story of the accident will probably be on first." We all moved into the living room. I could tell the girls were a little anxious because Ren was biting the inside of her mouth and Ree chewed the ends of her hair.

As expected, the leading story was the death on the set of "Crude Town", but they didn't report any new details. Apparently, the primary cable holding the statue had simply broken. They interviewed several witnesses, each of which explained exactly what I had seen and heard. Joel Mason made a statement on behalf of Big Sugar Creek Productions. "We are investigating this tragic accident further and our condolences go to the family of Sean Marco."

Then, the camera moved to of all people, Kat, who began to shed the biggest fake tears I'd ever seen. "That's Kat!" I yelled and sat forward in my chair.

As expected, Kat overacted and made it all about herself. She sniffed, "It was just horrible watching the giant oilman smash down on my good friend, Sean. It was the most devastating thing I've ever experienced." She wiped her eyes. I shook my head in disgust. As far as I knew, Kat had never even spoken to her "good friend, Sean." Interesting.

Ree sat on the arm of my chair and leaned her head on my shoulder. "Are you sure you want to go back?"

I stroked her hair. "You know. It was a freak accident. I can't live my life in fear of a giant statue falling on me."

Next, the weatherman reported that by Thursday, the temps would rise to 65 degrees and it would be humid. Nice. Typical Oklahoma, it's freezing one day and hot the next."

I went to the kitchen for some milk, but Ree called out, "Mom, your school is on TV!"

I ran back and saw a male reporter standing in front of the Arrowstar sign. "This Broken Arrow elementary school is in the middle of a dispute after the principal, Dr. Barry Love, took it upon himself to change the school's dress code, creating a strict uniform policy for both the students and staff. Before the controversial change takes effect, some teachers are enjoying their last days of fashion freedom."

The segment cut to clips of teachers wearing brightly colored clothing in their classrooms. I perked up when I glimpsed Jana wearing a Renaissance costume while teaching her annual Shakespeare unit. Jules wore a wild artsy outfit with a number of elaborate pins on her top.

Then the camera zoomed in on Becca, bright as ever, standing with the reporter at the track. She wore huge earrings, leopard skin pants, and silver running shoes. Her hot pink long-sleeved shirt had a cartoon violin running across her big chest, reading "Fit as a Fiddle and Ready to Run."

Becca told the reporter that she was just wearing what she normally wore. "I encourage kids to be themselves and to keep healthy and fit." She flashed her magnetic smile at the camera. The male reporter ogled over her and nearly drooled on his microphone.

Ree said, "Looks like Ms. Marshall is still the same." I chuckled.

Next, they interviewed a few outraged parents. They reacted just as we thought they would.

They cut back to the reporter who said, "The big question is whether a principal can do that on his own? Although Dr. Love refused to comment, Broken Arrow School officials are looking into the situation as to whether Dr. Love overstepped his authority. They will make a decision as early as tomorrow. John James reporting from Arrowstar Elementary in Broken Arrow."

Ren said, "Teachers in uniforms? Is your principal a dictator?"

I had to bite my tongue to keep from saying something rude and just nodded.

I should have been there to fight the fight with my cohorts, but they were handling it fine without me. I wasn't surprised the cowardly Love didn't make a comment, but good for the rest of the world for not having to see or hear the pompous jerk.

I patted Ree on the head. "Time for bed, especially for me since I've got to get up at the crack o' dawn. I guess I'll see you when you get back from your dad's tomorrow night. Love you both forever and ever."

After kisses, the girls said in unison, "Night Mom," and went to their rooms.

I was about to turn off the TV when they showed a video of Alison Baxter coming out of a popular downtown pub. She held the arm of a man I vaguely recognized.

My favorite female news anchor announced, "Ms. Baxter has been seen around town, enjoying Tulsa's nightlife." Then she turned to her co-anchor with casual banter, "I wonder where Aaron Winston is? Aren't they an item?" The man shrugged, totally uninterested.

I hadn't realized Alison and Aaron were an item and shrugged just like the newsman had. I must be very tired not to care about Aaron Winston's love life.

Once I climbed into bed and when my head touched the pillow, I was out.

Movie Watching Tip #7
Sometimes you have to watch a movie again to catch what
you missed.

Wednesday morning it took 20 minutes to wash the hairspray
out of my hair. I wore precisely the same outfit as yesterday, but
with new pantyhose covering the bandages on my knees.

As I drove to the film site, I wondered if I was making the right
decision to go back to the scene of the crime, or in this case, the
scene of the accident.

That phrase, "scene of the crime", made me wonder: What if
it was a crime? Who could possibly gain anything from killing
SmugGuy? Of course, if he treated other people like he treated
me, I supposed someone could wish him harm. But wait a minute.
I could have been underneath that boot too. What if I was the
target? I gulped. The only person I could think of who might want
me out of the way was Kat. She was furious that I had been chosen
as the stand-in. A chill went down my spine but I remembered I
could remedy that with my new car's seat warmer, so I turned it
on and felt better right away. I should keep my wild imagination
in check. But as I got closer to the fairgrounds, I vowed to pay
closer attention to Kat if I saw her, just in case.

It was still dark when I parked. As I exited the car, I was glad
the weatherman was right again. The temperature was already
warmer than yesterday. I looked forward to a better day all around.

I found Rita at her table and was thrilled to see my sister and
brother-in-law standing by her. Kim wore one of Mom's dresses
that was too short for me. How darling. Rita was explaining to
R.A. that his white beard would not be appropriate for the '60s

unless he wanted to be a member of the Hell's Angels club that would roll through town in an upcoming scene. She said apologetically, "It's either that or shave."

His eyes lit up at the mention of the motorcycle gang and said, "Hell yeah; I'll be a biker." I knew there was no way he would shave off his signature "Santa beard".

R.A. gave a little hop and wave as he headed to wardrobe.

Kim and I picked up our vouchers and went to Hair together. As we stood in line, I told her more about yesterday and she said she couldn't believe it. "I'll show you, Kat, if I see her. She was on channel 6 news last night. Did you watch?"

"No, we always watch channel 2."

The same pink-haired girl who had fixed my hair the day before waved me over. "Are you Alison's stand-in again?"

I sat in the tall chair. "I guess so". The girl rifled through a stack of papers until she found the photo they had taken yesterday. She stuck it on the mirror and started replicating my earlier look. While she pulled and sprayed, I caught a glimpse of Kim's hair and yelled, "Love those bangs, girl! And the ringlets!"

Kim could only move her eyes towards me since there was a curling iron next to her head. Without moving she shouted, "Did she use a whole bottle of spray to get your hair to do that?"

"Yep." I pointed to my hair. "This could withstand a tornado."

Afterward, we giggled the entire time our make-up artists worked on us. When our faces were rendered unrecognizable, I snuck my phone from Mom's purse and took a selfie of Kim and me, then slipped it back. Then I showed Kim the background holding area and Craft catering. While we were getting a donut, a scruffy guy wearing a black leather jacket and leather pants walked up. It was only a second before I realized it was R.A.! His beard had been darkened and he was wearing a bandana, both of which disguised him well. Wow. He sure looked rough.

In a gravelly voice R.A. said, "Hey Chicks, wanna go for a ride?" He sidled up to our table.

"Sure, Biker Boy," Kim said batting her eyes.

He scanned Kim up and down. "Ooh baby, you do look groovy." He kissed her with mock passion. What a cute couple – married 30 years and still crazy about each other.

It was times like this that I wondered if I would still be married if I had chosen someone other than Todd. I smiled at the two of them, hoping someday I'd find that kind of love.

When R.A. released Kim, she asked, "Do you actually get to ride a motorcycle?"

"I hope not, 'cause I've never been on a big hog."

I tried to picture R.A. on a huge Harley. He's only about 5'6". But he's very strong so I felt sure he could handle it.

CowboyHatGirl zipped in. Thankfully, she wore her cowboy hat or I wouldn't know what to call her. She didn't have her camo shorts but still wore her army boots, just like most other crew members. I wondered if they had a uniform policy here. Boots and shorts would sure be more fun than Dr. L's plan. After giving her signature whistle, she shouted, "Background, follow me."

I leaned over to Kim and R.A. and whispered, "You guys are background." Just then, Kat strode in, wearing a totally different outfit from yesterday. I pinched Kim.

"Ouch!" she yelled and turned to me. "Why did you do that?"

I whispered, "Sorry, but that's Kat," and pointed.

Kim nodded and said, "I'll keep an eye on her." Kim and R.A. followed the group of background outside.

I was left alone in the large room until I spotted Pat getting a cup of coffee. I waved him over and said, "I hoped you would show up today. Will you be my partner?"

He raised his eyebrows. "It looks that way. I hope I don't get killed off like your last one did."

I cringed. "Eew, don't say that!"

He smiled. "Sorry. I wasn't sure if you would come back. "

CowboyHatGirl entered again and rushed over to us. "The AD is organizing background. Just follow the script to see what to do." She turned to leave.

I spoke up, "Wait. We don't have one."

Annoyed, she turned around. "Where's your copy?"

I said, "Where were we supposed to get one?"

She huffed, "Yesterday, I gave the pages to that tall redhead to give you to study last night in case you came back today."

That explained it. Pat stepped up. "Well, we never got them."

"Just a minute." She sighed heavily and hurried off. Everything CowboyHatGirl did was in a rush. Her job must be very stressful.

Pat scoffed. "I think Kat is bound and determined to sabotage you to get your job."

I nodded and my stomach tightened as I wondered if it was true. Would she go as far as murder just to be a stand-in? That was ridiculous, but the thought continued to nag at me.

It wasn't long before our leader bolted back in with two small stapled sections of scripts. "Find your character and do what it says on page two. You need to be on set in five."

We scanned the scene. It was nice to know in advance what we would be doing. Once our five minutes were up, we made our way to the giant I.P.E building. According to the script, the scene was to take place a month after the Golden Driller's dedication.

I knew the huge building well since I'd been inside for many events. The 10-acre structure was built in 1966 specifically for the International Petroleum Exposition, which my father helped organize. The event was attended by 350,000 people from around the world. Oil was big business in Tulsa for years.

My jaw dropped when I entered the huge building. It had been transformed to look like the brochures my dad kept. All kinds of exhibitors showcased their "new-fangled" 1966 oil industry products. Had I just stepped back in time?

There were booths with actual oil derricks, life-sized oil rigs and according to the posters, the "world's largest pipe layer" on display. I stared at a Chevrolet exhibit introducing the Turbo-Titan III. What in the world did that do?

I said to Pat, "I can't believe how much money these Hollywood production companies spend to get things to look authentic." He nodded and I wished my dad could see this. I guess he would have to wait and see it on the big screen.

CowboyHatGirl flagged us over and showed us where to stand. In the scene, Aaron was to act cool and show off for Alison by pretending to know how to work the simulated oil pump. But he would pull the wrong lever and accidentally spray oil everywhere, drenching them both in the black crude. The scene should be funny, but of course, in our takes, there would be no mess.

When we took our places, Joel Mason made his loud "Achoo" and we pantomimed the scene. Then he shouted, "Team 1 in!" Again, I saw my idols walk towards us, looking amazing. To my delight, we were allowed to stand to the side and watch them perform. Mesmerized, I watched the pros get ready for the scene.

On "Action", Kim walked right by Alison. How cool that she might actually be in a scene of the movie. Lucky sister!

When Aaron and Alison acted, I had to cover my mouth so I wouldn't laugh at Aaron's ridiculous faces. It wasn't until the third take that they actually sprayed the black gunk all over them. It was so funny, I almost wet my pants.

Joel yelled "Cut! Print!"

Two assistants ran to the slime-covered stars and gave them towels. What had they used for oil? When Aaron licked his black gooey lips and smiled, I figured it must be chocolate syrup. The two giggled as they walked to their trailers to shower. The blond director told us to get ready for scene six. We grabbed snacks from the craft stand and sat down at a table. I started reading the new scene and asked Pat, "Do we have to run downstairs?"

"Looks like it."

Kim joined us at our table and I said, "You're definitely going to be in that scene. How cool was it to walk right by Alison?"

She smiled. "Pretty cool."

Then we watched the workers set up cameras in front of the long flight of stairs for the new scene. When R.A. walked up, I introduced him to my new partner.

Pat nodded at RA. "Have you gotten to do anything yet?"

"No. My scene is later today. I met a cameraman who let me watch him work. Wen I grow up, I want to be a boom operator."

"You'll never grow up," said Kim with a sweet smile.

R.A. turned to Pat and me. "I hope you two don't have to do any scenes like the one in Kim's favorite movie." He smirked.

I made a face when I figured out what he meant. I said, "Love Actually? Ha! I hope not!" I guess that was a good example of what stand-ins do, but yikes.

Apparently, Pat knew the scene too, for he said, "Yeah. A nude scene would sure be hard to explain to my wife."

We all laughed as we nibbled on snacks.

Since both actors had to shower off the goo and become beautiful again, I figured we had a bit more time before they needed us, so I said, "Hey R.A., will you come here for a second?" I stood and nodded to the door.

"Sure." My sweet brother-in-law followed me without question.

I turned back and said, "Kim, will you call me if CowboyHatGirl comes for us?"

She nodded, and R.A. and I went outside. "I want you to see the scene of the accident." We walked around to the 21st street side of the IPE building, where crime scene tape surrounded Tulsa's huge murderous oilman. The crane was still in its exact spot with the broken cable still dangling from it."

We looked up, shaded our eyes from the sun, and studied the scene. I asked, "Do you that could just break?"

"Well, a cable like that should be able to hold several tons. Do you think the Styrofoam driller weighed more than that?"

"I don't know. Look at him."

We both walked over to the giant man who stood with one hand on his waist. The chiseled features of his face reminded me of an invincible Greek warrior. He had a slender waist, with ripped muscles on his chest. I sighed. Who wouldn't love this guy? I still couldn't believe he stepped on someone yesterday.

R.A. inspected the cable from afar and said, "I think it's a 3/8" 7 x 19 stainless steel cable – probably type 316. If so, it shouldn't break at under 11,000 pounds. And the winch seems to be the appropriate size."

I stared at him in wonder. How did he know any of that? R.A. always amazes me.

He continued, "There's no way this Styrofoam man weighs more than five tons, even if he is 7 stories tall. Which means..."

I finished his sentence, "It might not have been an accident?"

He looked up with hands on his hips. "Yep."

My phone buzzed, and Kim's face popped up on the screen. We ran back to the IPE building and slipped into our seats as CowboyHatGirl barked, "Motorcycle gang, come with me." R.A. winked at us and followed her.

I told Kim what R.A had said about the cable. We were discussing it when Kat walked up. "Hey Kitty, I mean Pity. Is this your sister?"

I narrowed my eyes, not trusting myself to speak.

Kim took up the slack and held out her hand. "Yes. I'm Kim."

Kat took it and said sweetly, "I thought so. You look so much alike. I'm Kat. Mind if I sit with you two?"

I looked at Kim and back at Kat, wondering what the catch was, but said. "Sure?"

She sat down and bragged, "I just saw Aaron changing clothes outside." She flung her hair back and said, "He dropped his shirt and I picked it up for him. He said I had the prettiest hair he'd ever seen." Kat leaned in closer and whispered, "Then he asked if I was a "real" redhead. I told him there was only one way to find out." She lifted her shoulder in a provocative manner.

My eyes narrowed, even more, this time not in confusion, but in disgust. In contrast, Kim's eyes widened so much I thought they might pop out of her head.

Kat went on, "He told me he'd sure like to find out, and then he asked if we could meet after shooting tomorrow."

Thankfully, I heard CowboyHatGirl yell, "Team 2 is up now."

I excused myself, feeling bad for leaving my sister with that skank. Why did she tell us that story? Was it even true?

As I rushed to catch up with Pat, I overheard a deep voice from behind me whisper, "Not my fault. They announced it wrong."

Another voice growled, "We'll try again when things calm down."

I started to turn to see who uttered the odd phrase, but Pat distracted me by saying, "That sure is a long staircase." I looked up to see where we would soon be standing. Wow. It was a very long staircase. When I finally glanced back, there was only a short man in a ball cap carrying equipment beside a pile of oil cans. What was that all about?

I felt a little jittery when I realized we were to chase a man down the stairway from the second floor to the main level. As we climbed the stairs, my knees were stiff, probably from my fall yesterday. There were cameras stationed above, below, and to both sides of the open stairway. I must remember to hold in my stomach. Wait a minute. Nobody cares what I look like. I'm just a stand-in and will never be seen on film anyway.

Someone called out, "Team 2 in", followed by the usual jargon. When the word, "Action" came, we ran down the steps. I was pleased that I didn't fall, but they needed us to do it again. And again. And again. After doing the scene four times, I was glad we weren't running up the stairs because I was getting really winded just walking back up. Just before the next take, I saw Alison and Aaron standing at the bottom of the stairs watching us. That made me so nervous that when they called "Action," I grabbed the rail to keep from falling. I tried to keep my feet as steady as I could with my jelly-like legs and descended the steps.

Somehow, perhaps due to my tired legs or maybe just because I'm clumsy, I missed the bottom step entirely and flew spread eagle into the arms of Aaron Winston!

There I was, smashed up against his chest, my head to the side. His shirt was soft and smelled very good. I recognized the aroma from one of the cologne samples in a People magazine but I didn't know if it was Polo or Prada Sport? My senses were so overloaded that humiliation didn't set in until I realized Aaron Winston was holding me under my armpits. He said, "Well hello, Darlin'", in his southern drawl, melting me even more than I already was.

Managing to push myself away and stand on my own feet, I grabbed his hand, shook it awkwardly, and said, "I'm so sorry, Mr. Winston. Thank you for catching me. I'm a real klutz." Without thinking, I added, "But then again, tripping yesterday did save my life." I pointed to my knees as evidence and continued to babble, "See, I only got a scratch."

I turned to Alison. "Ms. Baxter, watch out for that bottom step. It's a doozy!" When I saw the blank stares of my reluctant audience, I added sheepishly, "Remember that line from… oh never mind."

As if my ridiculous rambling wasn't enough, I continued to shake Aaron's hand. Finally, I let go, moved away, and turned a deep shade of red. At least this time I didn't hit a boom operator as I backed up.

Pat came over, took my hand, and escorted me away from the den of embarrassment. I hid behind a large pillar and shook my head, not believing I had just made a complete idiot of myself - again. For some reason, when I get nervous, I just can't stop talking.

I turned to Pat and said, "Thanks."

He smirked as he shook his head. "You looked like you needed rescuing. If it makes you feel better, I thought your reference to "Groundhog Day" was funny. And now you can tell people Aaron Winston held you in his arms."

I brightened. "That's true." I peeked out from behind the pillar to watch Team 1 do their thing. Alison was so graceful running down the steps - in high heels, no less! Why in the world was I, a total lummox, chosen as her stand-in?

Movie Watching Tip #8

Turn off your phone while watching a movie.

Just as I typed a text to Lin describing my very close and humiliating encounter with Aaron Winston, a deep voice growled, "Put it away!" I stashed my phone and looked up to see who had spoken, but he was gone.

I watched Aaron and Alison do the staircase scene again, but this time Aaron ran down the stairs in front of her and when she reached the second to last step, she tripped and fell into his arms, just like I had done. I couldn't believe how funny it looked. Everyone laughed, even the crew.

"Cut!" Joel Mason stormed over to them and said, "What the hell was that?"

Aaron chuckled. "It was so funny when the stand-in did it that I thought I'd add it to the scene."

Mason's eyes bulged and his lips pursed. I marveled at the sight of his beet-red face. He barked, "And just who is the director?"

A hush fell over the set as everyone's eyes widened wondering what would happen next.

Mason waited for a beat and then added with a quieter gruff voice only people nearby could hear, "You are not going to take over this movie, Winston!"

Aaron held up his hands in surrender. "Whoa. Relax Joel. We'll do it your way. Just wanted to try something different."

The crew began setting up for the scene again, cutting the awkward tension. When Team 1 performed the scene the correct way, Mason yelled, "Cut. Print." He left the building taking giant strides and shaking his head.

Kim walked over and joined us. "Drama on the set, huh?"

I blew out a big puff of air. "Yeah."

She said, "Hey Sis, that was sure a slick way to get close to Aaron."

"It was an accident!" Then I changed the subject, "What did you think of Kat's story?"

She made a face. "Ick. After you left, she went on bragging about Aaron. She also let it slip that she took a bunch of pictures of the stars. Hasn't she heard all the announcements telling us not to do that?"

I scoffed, "Kat doesn't think rules apply to her. But I, on the other hand, get in trouble just for sending one text." I grabbed Kim's hand. "You know, this morning I had a crazy idea. What if Kat tried to kill me to get my job? I mean she was furious about it and I can't think of any other motive for someone to hurt Smug Guy or me. Please tell me that's ridiculous."

"Killing? Are you serious? Well, she's definitely delusional, but I don't think she would kill someone...at least I hope not. You always have had quite the imagination, Pity."

I let out a sigh of relief, but couldn't shake my uneasy feeling. As we watched the crew pack up for the next scene, I searched for the guy with the ball cap I had heard grumbling earlier. What if he was talking about the incident yesterday? Was he responsible for it, and would he try again? I considered anyone else who could have been involved. I scrutinized Pat's pleasant face as he watched the action. No way he could hurt anyone.

As Kim, Pat, and I started back to the holding area, Kat stormed over to me and scowled, "I heard how you grabbed Aaron. Are you trying to steal him from me? You're such a bitch!" She stomped away.

The three of us froze. I laughed incredulously, "Oh My Gosh. Now, what do you think, Kim?"

Kim shrugged and said, "Maybe?"

I was still shaking my head about Kat's outburst as we walked to Craft catering for lunch. I wasn't sure how they would handle the meal since yesterday's shoot was cut short before we got to eat. We stood around with the rest of the background waiting for instructions. CowboyHatGirl appeared and called for the crew to line up first. She said background had to wait to line up until the crew had been served. We found seats in the large makeshift cafeteria and waited our turn. I didn't realize how hungry I was until I saw how many crew members were ahead of us.

R.A. joined us, beaming, "They'll shoot my scene after lunch!"

I gave him a high five. "Woohoo!"

Pat nodded, then pointed to the line, "Check her out."

I followed his gaze and saw Kat standing in line with the crew getting food. She sure had nerve.

On the table in front of me, someone left a copy of the "Tulsa World". I picked it up and read the main headline. "Crude Town Death." I skimmed the article and my stomach churned as I took in information about Sean Marco's life.

Skipping ahead, I read aloud, "Filming commences today on 'Crude Town', despite the ongoing investigation of the accident. This is the 7th film directed by Joel Mason and the second one with Aaron Winston.... The production will take a break this weekend as Mr. Winston heads to Los Angeles for the Academy Awards. He is vying for an Oscar for his nominated role in the recent movie, 'Swerve'. Filming will resume in Tulsa next Wednesday when Winston returns."

Kim nudged me, "Sorry, but I doubt you'll have time to get to know Aaron well enough to be his date to the real Oscars this weekend."

I laughed. "Yeah, probably not."

A bald guy with a plate of food walked by and stopped when he saw R.A. He smiled. "The food looks pretty amazing. Fried Shrimp from White River."

Yum. I wondered if alligator was on the menu too.

R.A. smiled and said, "Can't wait." The guy moved on to sit with some other crew members.

I asked, "Is that your new cameraman friend?"

"Yeah."

I brightened. "Do you think he has access to the accident footage?"

"The police probably took that for their investigation."

I frowned. Of course. That made sense and said, "How about the shots leading up to it? Maybe we could see something interesting." I tried to think like a detective would on CSI.

R.A. shrugged. "He just works the camera. I doubt he has the clout to access any footage at all."

"Can you just ask him though?" I pleaded with a pouty face.

He sighed, knowing I wouldn't take no for an answer. I smiled when he stood and walked to the nearby table to speak to his new friend."

While he talked to him, I found the City/State section of the paper. There was a picture of Dr. L standing, arms folded, wearing his typical scowl. The caption read, 'Dr. Barry Love, principal of Arrowstar Elementary, didn't follow district protocol when setting dress codes.' I couldn't control my smile as I read further, 'Broken Arrow school officials deemed the new rules inappropriate, and regular dress codes will remain in place.' Yay!

"Kim, did I tell you about this? Look." I held the paper between us and pointed at a photo of smiling teachers and students wearing their normal clothes. Beside the photo was a cartoon picture, obviously drawn by Jules, that depicted the same group wearing drab uniforms, but with solemn faces. Perfect. Dr. L will be furious, not to mention how he'll react to Becca's earlier TV interview. Gotta love my bold friends.

Kim read the article and said, "Your principal truly is a jerk. Too bad you're missing out on all the school drama by being here. Looks like Jules, Becca and Jana have it under control though."

I felt a little bad that I wasn't needed, but really just wanted to join the celebration. I forgot all about it when R.A. returned.

He whispered, "He doesn't have access to anything. Once he films it, everything has to be turned in, so that idea is a bust. But…" he looked at me with a twinkle, "he told me a sound technician, who happens to be my friend Jesse from Dowell, recorded some scenes on his cell phone. He probably didn't turn that in to the police since personal phones are forbidden on set. Maybe he still has the video? I'll keep a lookout for Jesse."

"Thanks, R.A." With renewed hope for my own investigation, I scanned the crew members. Where was that short guy with the ball cap I had overheard earlier today?

I was startled when a loud voice boomed, "Background can now get in line. You have ten minutes."

You would think I hadn't eaten for a month the way I bolted for a plate. Sadly, they had switched out the fried shrimp for tuna salad, the chocolate cake for cookies and the iced tea for powdered lemonade. Guess we lowly extras just don't rate. Oh well, I filled my plate anyway.

Within minutes everyone was herded outside, where the temperature had risen considerably and the air had turned muggy. I spotted R.A. standing alongside a bunch of undesirable characters with big motorcycles in the parking lot.

Joel Mason walked to the gang, turned and yelled, "Why isn't Team 2 in place?"

CowboyHatGirl rushed over to apologize. "I'm sorry, Mr. Mason. I'll get them."

I hurried to our spot and Pat joined me, saying, "Jeeze, this guy is grumpy."

Mr. Mason stomped over to us and ordered, "When you hear Action, run to the 4th motorcycle and act upset. Wave your arms around like you're angry."

Then, he pointed to R.A. and said, "You, the one without a bike, when you hear Action, storm over, grab her arm and pull her away while he's distracted with the other bikers."

Excited that R.A. had a real part, I nodded goofily at my brother-in-law. I didn't mind him grabbing me. How fun! After a few more instructions were given, Joel Mason yelled "Action."

Pat and I did as we were told; we went to the motorcycle gang and acted upset. Then, a familiar hand grabbed my upper arm. I looked up and saw my sweet brother-in-law wearing a ferocious expression as he yanked me backward. Wow, he was a good actor. I would have been scared if I hadn't known him since I was twelve.

"Cut! Perfect! Do it again."

We did it a few more times and then it was time for Team 1 to step in. I was giddy just thinking of R.A. grabbing Alison Baxter.

"Action!" The stars, all dressed in new outfits, walked to the bikers and yelled about how they were disturbing the peace and that they were so loud, nobody could hear the dedication of the new statue. It was funny how everything was being shot out of order. We were back to the christening of the Golden Driller.

I watched R.A. walk up and tap Alison on the shoulder. He gently took her arm and escorted her backward with a smile.

"Cut! What the Hell? Where is that rough demeanor you had a minute ago? You are a Hell's Angel, not a prom date." shouted Joel Mason in a very rude manner.

"I didn't want to scare her," R.A. said with his sweet smile and a shrug.

"She knows you are coming. Just do what you did with that stand-in."

The second time, R.A. did it just right, but afterwards, he had the same apologetic face I'd seen him make when he forgot Kim's birthday once. Of course, the sweet guy didn't want to hurt Alison. With me, it was like he was horsing around with his kid sister.

The actress whispered something to him and on the third take R.A. actually looked scary when he grabbed Alison.

"Cut! Print!"

In the next scene, R.A. had to heave Alison onto a motorcycle with another biker who took off with her. How cool! I couldn't wait to see R.A. on the big screen.

We did a few more scenes out of order, so it was impossible to follow the storyline. I sure hope someone saved poor Alison. The day progressed without anyone dying or any other mishaps for that matter. I was exhausted when someone finally announced, "That's a Wrap" and we were released to go home. I told Kim and R.A. goodbye. When I handed my voucher to Rita, I asked, "Will you need me again tomorrow?"

"Absolutely. We'll need you all week. Plan to come at 6:00. And we can use more background if you know anyone else."

"Oh, I only have one more day. I have to go back to teaching Friday."

"Hmm. That might pose a problem, but at least we'll have tomorrow to find someone to take your place. Maybe that redhead, Kat?" She looked at me with eyebrows raised, as if waiting for my opinion.

As much as I wanted to tell her about Kat, I held my tongue and forced a smile. Casting wasn't my business.

While walking to the car, I heard some men speaking in loud whispers. I turned toward the sound but with the sun so low in the sky and positioned directly behind the men, I could only see their outlines - one man was very tall and the other was short and wearing a ball cap. I stopped walking and bent down to fiddle with my shoe as I strained to hear what they were saying. There was the same gruff voice I'd heard earlier. "Saturday's our last chance. It has to happen before then."

Last chance for what?

When I finally got home, the girls weren't back from their dad's house yet. Despite my exhaustion, I set up my scene to spoof the final movie for my Oscar video. I went to the costume section of the garage and found a wig that might fit the part for the modern Eve and tried to stuff my 1960's hair doo inside it, but it was too stiff. I decided to shower to get my normal hair back. As I neared the living room in my bathrobe with wet hair, I was hit by a strong odor. It kind of smelled like rum and pickles, but I couldn't imagine my daughters with either. So, it could mean only one thing: Smelly Shelly was in our house.

Why was my ex-husband's Big Jack's Cadillac girlfriend here? I turned the corner and there she stood, clad in a mini skirt, high heels, and her fake boobs. Oh goodie.

I sighed. "Hi, Shelly. What brings you here?" I gave a stilted smile as I held my robe shut.

She gave me a once over, then did the same for the living room. Both resulted in a wrinkled nose. This was her first time to be in our house and I was just sure she would tell Todd how ghastly my decorating was and that I greeted a guest wearing a robe.

Shelly glared at the birdcage as if it was disgusting and said in her whiny irritating voice, "Lauren had to stop by her friend's house for something and I offered to bring little Marie home,"

Little Marie? Who was she kidding? She doesn't even like the girls. She walked to the couch and brushed off the cushion as if it had a layer of dirt, then sat down on the very edge. It didn't take a genius to figure out the reason for her visit.

"So, the girls tell me you've been working on the movie shooting in town?" Her fake eyelashes fluttered with excitement.

Bingo. Proud that I was able to resist rolling my eyes, I said, "Yes, I've been acting as the stand-in for Alison Baxter." I hadn't said that to impress her, but it sure worked.

Shelly's mouth dropped open and it remained agape as she breathed heavily, as if in a trance. Then, her questions bubbled out, "What is she like? Tell me everything. Did you meet Aaron Winston? Is he really funny in person?"

Oh brother, next she'll probably want me to introduce her to them. "Well Shelly, I don't really work with them. I only spoke to them briefly." I didn't mention that both times I spoke to them was to apologize. I said, "They seem nice, but I don't know any more about them than you do."

"Are they taller than they seem on TV or shorter? Is she really beautiful? I just know that Alison and I would be best friends if I only got to know her."

Here it comes. I braced myself.

She scooted so close to the edge of her seat, I thought she would tumble over. "You wouldn't mind letting me come on set with you tomorrow just to meet her, would you?" And just like that, Shelly acted like I was her BFF. In reality, this was the first time the woman had ever spoken directly to me.

I shook my head. "I'm sorry but nobody is allowed to talk to the stars and you can't be there at all unless you're working on set."

Her eyelash extensions blinked slowly and her head sunk dramatically, making her look so pathetic that I did the unthinkable; I said, "If you want to call, they may be able to use you as an extra, then you might catch a glimpse of Alison." I cringed as soon as I said it and backpaddled, "But I doubt you can take off work on such short notice." I hoped it was true.

She perked up. "Oh, Daddy lets me off anytime I want."

But, of course he did. He adored his little Shelly Welly. Besides being the TV spokesperson for Big Jack's Cadillacs, Shelly worked as her father's "secretary". I could only imagine her spending the day filing and painting her fingernails, like Mrs. Wiggins on the "Carol Burnett Show" reruns.

She brightened and asked, "Will I get to work directly with Alison? What should I wear? How do I get in the inner circle? How many lines do you think I will get?"

I tried to ignore her as I wrote down Rita's number, already regretting what I had done. "Here is the phone number for Rita. You'll have to ask her those questions, but I'm pretty sure you'll just be an extra, or what they call background, with no lines at all."

She grabbed the paper from me and simultaneously called Rita - impressive. I watched in wonder as this prissy blonde spoke non-stop into the phone. I caught her saying, "I've been a television actress for years."

It was true she had been in TV commercials since she was little, but the term "actress" was a real stretch. Her job was to wear costumes for every holiday sale while standing beside cars, or sitting in SUVs. Her pat line was, "You'll get the max from Big Jack's Cadillacs."

Then she added, "My good friend, Pity Kole, told me I just had to get involved."

I wanted to snatch the phone away and deny that statement, but I let it fly. I would have to explain to Rita tomorrow. To my dismay, Shelly nodded and said she would see Rita in the morning.

"Looks like you are in?" My smile had turned even weaker, but she didn't notice.

She squealed, "Oh yes. I can't wait! I asked if I could bring my own make-up girl, but she said they will have someone to do it. It's too late to call my costumer, but apparently, they'll have something for me to wear."

"Yes, they have it all. But Shelly, this job is not at all glamorous and you must remember, nobody can take pictures of the stars."

She jumped up and said, "We'll see," and left with a flourish – wafting her gross perfume throughout the room as she walked.

I could have sworn I heard Edgar cough as she left, but I may have imagined it. His feathers were definitely ruffled, as were mine.

As soon as the door closed, Ree emerged from her room. She whispered, "I was hiding in my bedroom."

"I can't blame you. Hi, Sweetie."

"I get so sick of her. Why did she come inside our house?"

I took a deep breath and rolled my eyes. "Oh, she wants to be an extra and thinks she can be Alison Baxter's best friend." I said with a smirk.

"There is no way Alison Baxter would be friends with Shelly. She's awful. Do you know that tonight she told me that if I knew what was good for me, I would put away my book, apply some make-up and get a boyfriend?"

I laughed, "Seriously? What did your dad say to that?"

"He wasn't around."

I put my arm around my youngest daughter. "Well, I say, keep your nose in a book as long as you can, girl. Books make you smart. Boys just make you dumb. As for me? I get to see Shelly on set tomorrow. Oh joy."

"Let me know how that goes," she said with a laugh.

Just then, Ren walked in and I filled her in on Shelly's visit. Then with a flick of my wrist, I crowed, "Oh, I forgot to tell you that Aaron Winston held me in his arms today."

Ree lifted her eyebrows in anticipation while Ren's eyes narrowed skeptically.

"Well, I actually tripped down some stairs and he happened to catch me."

"How embarrassing," said Ree, with a half-smile, half look of horror.

"Mom, you have to stop being so clumsy," Ren said.

I lifted my shoulder. "I'm not so sure I want to stop. My clumsiness saved my life yesterday and today enabled me to hug a movie star, so I think I'm on the right track.

Both girls shook their heads at me.

I said, "Ree, can I borrow Iggy for my skit?"

She tipped her head to the side, then asked, "Are you going to pretend she is your serpent?"

"Yes, Ma'am. And I could sure use some help."

Both girls followed me upstairs and we filmed my final skit for my video. Of course, it took us about 20 minutes to film the 20-second scene mostly because Iggy the iguana wouldn't cooperate. Then after all that, I realized a green iguana wouldn't show up in front of the green screen and had to change the background and do it all again,

30 minutes later, we sat and ate ice cream, then went our separate ways to bed.

Harriet was already on my bed snoring. I snuggled under my covers next to her and turned on the TV. There was no new news about the accident, but there were more photos of Alison out on the town. I wondered if Aaron Winston actually went out with Kat as she claimed, or if she had made it all up.

Apparently, Arrowstar's uprising wasn't newsworthy anymore, so I texted my school buddies and said, "Good going, girls! I see you stopped the worm. Thanks for fighting the fight so well!"

Jana wrote back and said, "It was all your idea."

My phone pinged again with a text from Jules, saying, "We missed you!"

Becca chimed in, "You better have good stories to tell since you ditched us."

I smiled as I wrote back, "Oh, believe me. I have some doozies!" I added a winking emoji.

Movie Watching Tip #9
Watch your step in the dark.

My final day of filming began much the way the first two had, except I could hear Shelly's whiny voice even before I entered the building. There she stood, dressed in her mini skirt, blingy top, and huge hair. Poor Rita was trying to explain to Shelly that she would need to stand in line and have her hair and make-up re-applied. From what I've heard, Shelly would never stand in line like a commoner. Her horrified face proved that theory right.

I mouthed, "I'm so sorry" to Rita while I picked up my voucher and scooted past Shelly without her seeing me. After getting dolled up, I found Kim in the pavilion, this time dressed in a pantsuit. "Where's R.A.?"

"They didn't need him today, but he's still going to try to reach his sound guy friend for you."

I nodded. "You won't believe it, but Shelly is an extra today."

Kim snickered, "I thought I smelled something. Maybe they can have her wear a George Washington suit and pose on top of a car. She had a lot of experience doing that."

In the corner, we watched as Kat whispered in some tall guy's ear.

A friendly voice said, "Back for one more round huh?"

I turned, relieved to see Pat. "Yep, you're stuck with me for another day."

"Any plans to jump in Aaron's arms?"

"No, but I will if I have to." I winked. I didn't mention my real plan - to watch for anything unusual that could lead to information about the "accident".

Our morning was spent creating two fun scenes outside. The temperature had warmed so much that I was actually comfortable in my dress. I watched to see if Alison and Aaron showed signs of being in a relationship, but they barely spoke to each other. I didn't notice anything suspicious and believe it or not, I didn't do anything embarrassing all morning. By 11 a.m., the cloudy morning had turned muggy and it was hard to breathe. I was glad the next scene would be inside. Leave it to Oklahoma to go from 50 to 80 in two hours.

Suddenly, the smell of putrid perfume wafted through the air and I looked for Shelly. All I saw was 4 fake nuns carrying bibles.

While waiting for the next scene, I headed to the bathroom in the old brown building where we would be shooting. I peeked in the door, but there was a long line, so went to look for another bathroom. I walked down some stairs and followed signs to find a nice empty ladies' room. After I had washed my hands, I stepped into the hallway. Suddenly everything went black.

I figured I hadn't fainted since I was still upright. The electricity had clearly gone off. Since I was in the basement, there were no windows and the old building didn't seem to have any emergency lights on backup batteries. It was impossible to see anything. To make matters worse, I'd left my iPhone with Kim, so I didn't have my phone flashlight. I used my hands to feel along the wall as I made my way back toward the stairs.

I'd only gone a few feet when sirens started to wail. Great - a tornado warning. In response, I did what every Oklahoman is conditioned to do in the situation; I hunkered down on my knees, put my arms over my ears, and laced my fingers behind my neck.

As I crouched down uncomfortably, I heard sniffling and lifted my head to discern the source of the sound. It was coming from the nearest room, so I stood up and started inching my way along the wall to find the next door's jamb. It sounded like someone whimpering or even crying and the sound was getting louder.

I said gently, "Hello? Are you OK?"

A throat cleared, then a low voice said, "Um. Yes. Just nervous about the siren."

"Oh, it's probably nothing. Are you from out of town?" That wasn't hard to deduce, since most native Oklahomans don't get that upset when hearing a tornado siren. Of course, we have a respectful fear of the destructive vortex, but once you take cover there's not much else you can do.

The voice, definitely male, answered, "Yes."

I continued my dark journey toward the sound, talking as I inched along, "We have tornado warnings all the time here but rarely do they touch down. I wouldn't worry."

I found the door and made my way inside, carefully shuffling my feet so I wouldn't step on anything or anyone. I added, "We're very lucky to be in one of the few basements in Tulsa. And it's even better that there are no windows down here. We learn early on to find a room on the bottom floor and stay away from windows during a tornado warning, so we're in the best place possible."

"How can you stand it?"

"The tornadoes?" I crouched and felt around to make sure the floor was clear. "Oh, you just get used to it. But, to be extra safe you might want to get on your knees, face the wall and cover the back of your neck with your hands." I got in my disaster drill position again.

"Oh. OK." I heard him rustle around, presumably getting in the awkward position. I gauged him to be about 3 feet away from me on my left.

"So, where are you from?" I asked from under my self-made cave.

"L.A.," he said with a muffled voice.

"And you are worried about this? I could never live in California. I'd be terrified of earthquakes. After all, I've seen the movie, San Andreas."

He chuckled. "They aren't an issue until the big one hits."

My face scrunched up at the thought. "Well, the chances of a tornado hitting our spot are slim."

As if rebuking my statement, the winds picked up, emitting ominous creaking and cracking sounds. The moan of the old building sounded sinister, even to me.

"Oh my…" the man's voice quivered, "how often do you have these?"

I swallowed and tried to stay calm. "We have watches weekly during tornado season, but few tornadoes actually make it to the ground. This is early. They usually don't appear until April."

"Lucky me."

I changed the topic, "I assume you are here working on the movie?"

"Uh-huh. Do the sirens always go off?"

I guess he wasn't ready to change the subject. "Only if it's a warning." I didn't add that a warning meant one had touched down in the area. No point freaking him out even more.

The winds whistled and loud creaking and thumping became louder outside. I hoped the real Golden Driller wasn't blown over.

He said, "Oh my…how long will this go on?"

"Oh, they move through pretty quickly. Usually no more than 15 to 20 minutes."

He cleared his throat. "Do you worry about your family?"

"Yes, but there is nothing I can do about it now. As soon as it's over, I'll check to see if there was any activity near my parents' house or my daughters' schools." Dang it. Once he brought it up, I started worrying about my kids. We've been lucky forever, but you never know.

The stranger's voice cracked as he said, "You have a pretty good outlook. I can't believe you're so calm. What's your name?"

"It's Kitty, but my nickname is Pity."

"Pity, with a P? What a great nickname. How did you get it?"

"When I was born, my sister was only two and called me 'Baby Pity'. I'm just sure she was trying to say, 'Baby Pretty', but my family says, 'No, she just couldn't say her K's and besides, you really weren't that pretty.' So, I've been Pity ever since."

"I wish I had a cool nickname."

"How about Crouch? For your first time in this position." I laughed at my stupid suggestion.

He snickered. "Keep thinking – there's gotta be a better one."

"Give me time to get to know you and I'll think of one. I give nicknames to everyone – including my car."

"Which is?"

"Liesel. She's German. So, what's your name, so I can start thinking of a good nickname?"

Just then, the lights came back on. I blinked, trying to get used to the bright glare, then blinked again when I saw the guy crouched on his knees right next to me was Aaron Winston! After taking in my surroundings, I realized I was in his dressing room!

I started to yell, "Aaron Winston?" but somehow, despite my shock and quickening heartbeat, I had the wherewithal to play it cool. Still in my unflattering position, I pulled my short skirt down and turned sideways, hoping he hadn't seen my underwear.

"Is it over now?" he asked, still in the tornado position.

"I think so."

From under my arm, I stared at his golden curls and wanted to pinch myself to make sure I wasn't dreaming. Why hadn't I recognized his voice? But in my defense, he was pretty freaked out and his voice was muffled most of the time.

The siren finally wound down and stopped. Aaron let out a deep breath. "Now?"

"Yes. It's really over. See, we're all in one piece." And I was three feet from my favorite movie star. I said, "We should wait a few minutes to make sure it's safe to go up."

I unlocked my fingers, turned around and leaned against the wall with my legs outstretched. I stared as Aaron Winston smoothed his soft-looking curls, stretched his arms and sighed. Then he turned around to position himself like me.

He looked over at me and smiled. "To answer your question, my name is Aaron Winston."

"Yeah, I got that once the lights came on." I nodded with a nervous smile.

He narrowed his eyes and said with a tilt of his head, "Hey, aren't you the stand-in that jumped into my arms yesterday?"

I blushed. "Yep. Well, I'm kinda clumsy. Sorry about that. I didn't mean to come in your dressing room either, Mr. Winston. I was just on my way back from the bathroom and the lights went out then I heard you. I'm so sorry."

"Are you kidding? You got me distracted from a pretty scary experience. Thank you."

I smiled and said, "I thought all you actors had trailers. Why is your dressing room down here?"

His demeanor changed and he relaxed. "It's kind of a funny story. I'm an active guy, right? I'm pretty fearless. I even do most of my own stunts because it's so exciting, but the one thing I'm terrified of is tornadoes. When I heard we were filming in Oklahoma, my only stipulation was that they provide me with a sturdy dressing room. So, when everyone else got a trailer, I got this place down here. Pretty sweet, huh?"

I nodded, thinking that made sense and said, "You're in the right place today anyway."

He looked at me again and said, "So speaking of me being fearless, I'd really appreciate it if you would keep it quiet that I was a sniveling mess."

"Oh, of course. It's our little secret." I made the little twist with my fingers to lock my mouth shut then added, "But there's no need to be embarrassed. I'd expect anyone new to the area to be nervous."

"Yeah, but if it got out that I was bawling like a baby, it might damage my tough guy image."

I laughed because I never thought of him as a tough guy. "Oh, come on. You weren't that bad."

"Are you kidding? You just couldn't see my tears."

"Just proves you're a good actor. Ooh, speaking of acting, are you so excited about Sunday's Academy Awards? I'd just die if I were you.

"Yeah. It's a real kick being nominated. I don't deserve it."

I shook my head vehemently. "I disagree. I've seen "Swerve" four times. You were amazing!"

He opened his mouth wide. "Gee, you must have some stamina to sit through it that many times. And thanks, but I'm really just a romantic comedian, at least that's what Joel says. I think he's sore that I got nominated."

"Joel Mason? Why isn't he proud of you? I mean, he directed you in it, right?"

Winston picked at a fingernail. "Well, to be honest, we had some artistic differences and I sort of did my own thing at times. Honestly, I was surprised he would work with me again."

"So, he's not a fan of ad-libbing?" I ventured.

He nodded. "Definitely not."

"I kinda figured that when he got on to you for replicating our scene." Our scene? Did I actually say that? I corrected myself, "I mean when I fell." I scrambled for something else to say. "I'll bet he's just grumpy that he didn't get nominated for best director."

"Maybe? No telling with that guy. I didn't really want to work with him again, but my agent told me it was the right move. Why am I telling you all of this?" He held his hands up. "You don't need to hear me whine about all this crap."

"I'm happy to be your personal bartender, minus the booze. Are you enjoying Tulsa?"

"Aside from this weather scare, which could drive a guy to drink, and that awful accident? Yeah. It's been fun working on Crude Town, but I haven't seen any of the actual town. Every night I go back to the hotel, study my lines, and chill."

Suddenly I remembered my daydream of taking him all around town and smiled but kept that to myself. "Well, our local news keeps showing Alison out and about so I figured you would be too. Tulsa's a great city with lots to do. But I guess it's nothing compared to LA."

"Well, Alison's nice but I don't really like the bar scene as she does and ..."

"And you have your eye on certain redhead?" I baited.

He raised one eyebrow. "Redhead? No. What?"

"The beautiful statuesque extra?" I teased. "She said you asked her out."

He squinted his eyes and cocked his head. It's one of the faces I just love to see him make in movies. He looks like a puppy who just heard a new sound. "No. I don't remember a redhead..." then nodded slowly, "well, one girl picked up my hat when I dropped it the other day, but we didn't speak."

I shook my head and smirked. I should have known. "Figures. She's been telling some tall tales about you. "

"Hey, you're not a reporter for a gossip magazine, are you?"

"Me? No." I laughed. "I do have a nice camera and would be pretty good at stalking stars if I ever had the chance." I sighed, "So, today is my last day on the set. Back to school tomorrow – I used my only three personal days to get this experience."

"You're a teacher?"

"Yep, elementary school music"

"Really? I'm terrible at music."

I chuckled. "I know, I've heard you sing...but I love you anyway." My face went slack. Did I just tell a major movie star that he was a bad singer and that I LOVED him? I cleared my throat and continued as my face grew hot. "Well, you're not THAT bad of a singer. And I LOVE to watch you in your movies."

He laughed as he watched me squirm. I continued as my face grew hot, "I nearly peed my pants when you got sprayed with crude oil yesterday. That was so funny."

"Yeah, that was fun, except washing the chocolate syrup from my hair."

So, I guessed right. He narrowed his eyes at me. "Too bad you won't be on set Saturday when I get to climb the big oil derrick. Next week's scenes are going to be pretty cool too."

I sighed. "Guess I'll have to wait 'til the movie comes out to see all that. Speaking of the Oscars, I portrayed your character from "Swerve" for my Oscar spoof video."

"Seriously? I want to see it. Is it on YouTube?"

Why did I tell him that? I never dreamed he would want to see it and sputtered, "But...it's not ready yet. I'd show you last years' ridiculous video, but my sister has my phone and we probably couldn't get service down here anyway."

"I have one!" He pulled an iPhone from his pocket, handed it to me, and scooted closer. "And I'm already hooked up to WIFI."

I blushed and trembled as I sat shoulder to shoulder with my favorite actor and pulled up his YouTube app. When would I ever learn to keep my mouth shut?

"Let me warn you. This is really bad on all levels." I found last year's video then added another disclaimer, "It's really just a joke for friends to watch at my annual Oscar party."

He took the phone from me and pushed play. He grinned and read aloud, "Not Quite the Oscars?"

I shrugged and peeked over his shoulder, noticing the faint smell of cologne I had enjoyed inhaling yesterday. He laughed out loud when I "floated" by in a spacesuit for my scene in last year's Academy Award winner, "Way Beyond.'"

I said, "That was my first attempt using a green screen. I made the space helmet out of paper mâché."

I watched his bright eyes as he stared at the tiny screen. He chuckled as he viewed each of the skits.

A female voice came from upstairs. "Mr. Winston, are you okay down there?"

He yelled. "Yes! I'm good." The woman continued to shout in other areas of the building until her voice faded away.

I said with a laugh, "We should go. Can't watch any more of that." I grabbed his phone from him and quickly turned it off. "It sounds like we are free to move back upstairs." I was glad he didn't see the scene from a western where I wore a handlebar mustache.

"You did all that by yourself?"

"Yes, and it shows. My daughters help with the filming sometimes. You know these are big-budget productions when they cost me about $30 per year for props and costumes. You should have seen me in Avatar when I was painted blue"

"I may have to look that one up. Give me your phone number and I'll let you know if I watch some others."

At that, I was almost too stunned to speak but managed to read off the numbers as he punched them into his phone. I said, "I can't believe I showed that to you." My hand hit my forehead.

He stood and brushed off his pants, then held out his hand to help me up. "I think you are pretty amazing, Pity. I'll look for you on set this afternoon."

Yes, Aaron Winston actually said that to me! I so wish I'd gotten a recording to prove it to my friends. I found my knees were wobbly, maybe from sitting on the floor so long but more likely because a movie star called me by my name! I wanted to shake his hand, but that seemed formal. Hugging him would be out of line, so I just said, "I'll look for you too." I cringed at my stupid reply.

"Hey and thanks again for your..." he winked, "help."

"Sure, Mr. Winston."

He held up his hand and shook his head. "Nope. Nope. Nope. Call me Aaron."

That was the icing on the cake. I felt shaky but I played it cool as I walked out the door. When I was safely out of his view, I did a happy dance at the foot of the stairs.

Movie Watching Tip #10
Avoid scary movies.

I floated up the stairs, elated from my encounter with Aaron. I was happy to see everything above ground was intact. When I returned to the holding area, I spotted Kim and ran up to her and asked, "Are you okay? Have you heard from Mom and Dad?"

"I'm fine. Mom and Dad are okay and there was no activity in Broken Arrow. Only one twister touched down and it was about four blocks from here. No real damage." I sighed with relief as Kim took a breath. "Where were you? I've been worried sick."

I watched her eyes widen as I told my story about being in the dark downstairs. But when I got to the punch line as to who I was with, her jaw dropped. As promised, I didn't mention that Aaron was scared or worse yet, crying.

CowboyHatGirl came in and yelled, "Since you already ate, we've gotta book it. We're behind schedule thanks to this Oklahoma weather." She rolled her eyes. "Team 2 follow me to the restaurant scene."

Sad that I'd missed lunch, but still giddy from the bizarre time with Aaron Winston, I headed with Pat to yet another building. As we walked, I noticed downed tree limbs and a bent light pole that curved so far it nearly touched the car beneath it. Yikes.

We entered a fake retro diner, that was so realistic it had a checkerboard floor, vintage coke signs, a neon clock and an old cash register. The two of us sat where directed, at a booth by a window. Out of habit, I opened the fake menu. My stomach growled and I salivated when I saw the daily special was a hamburger, fries and coke.

I pouted to Pat. "Did you get to eat? I was stuck underground during the tornado, so I missed lunch."

"Yeah. Once the worst of the storm was over, they said to grab something, so I had a sandwich. Sorry you didn't get anything."

I shrugged. "It's okay. I can stand to lose a meal." We watched the extras as they were seated at other tables around the fake diner. A group of nuns sat in the booth next to us. One particularly grumpy-looking nun opened her mouth and said in a loud familiar voice, "I can't believe they put me in this hideous outfit."

Oh my gosh, it was Shelly! Stripped of all her glitz and make-up, she was completely disguised in a full habit. Nothing but her extended eyelashes and annoying voice gave her away. I studied her and realized she was very pretty without all the goo. I had to stifle a laugh, knowing how upset she must be in the unflattering role. I was pretty sure Shelly would blame me for it.

The nice blond director told us to order the blue plate special and then when the food arrived, we needed to eat. I got very excited at the promise of food. Upon "Action!", a "Flo" type waitress walked up to take our order, smacking gum the whole time. I thought her talking while chewing was a little too cliché, but unfortunately, I wasn't the director.

After we ordered, she put the pen behind her ear, the pad in her apron pocket, and off she went. My stomach growled at the prospect of a meal.

As I looked around the café, I saw two men standing behind the counter, hidden partially by a pillar. They were somehow familiar to me – one tall and slender, and the other stocky and wearing a ball cap. Then it came to me. They looked like the outlines of the men who said, "Saturday's our last chance," but I figured a lot of people fit that description.

I scanned the area further. There were no big oilmen to fall so I felt pretty safe until the taller man took something from his pocket. The counter covered his hands, but he did a movement that looked like he was sprinkling something on a plate. Probably salt or pepper, but why would he carry seasoning in his pocket? What if it was poison?

In a flash, I jumped up, yelled, "Cut!" and ran to the director. I pleaded with him, "Sir, that guy just pulled something from his pocket and put it in our food. It might be poison!"

The director's eyes remained calm. "Did you read your script?"

"Not all of it."

"Well, they are supposed to poison Alison's character. It's part of the plot. Good eye though." He winked and without too much annoyance, he said, "Reset!"

Flustered, I said, "Oh, I'm really sorry."

I walked back to my seat with a crimson face and explained my actions to Pat.

He gave a snort with lips closed. "Paranoid?"

"Apparently." How humiliating. I must read the script from now on. Most everyone was looking at me, including Shelly. She pointed at me and made a face at her fellow nuns.

Pat whispered, "It's a good thing Joel Mason wasn't directing."

I nodded, then heard Shelly squawk, "That's my boyfriend's ex-wife. No wonder he left her." The group of nuns laughed aloud. I felt like I was in the movie Mean Girls, where snooty girls dressed alike and harassed me.

On the second take, piping hot food was served. Did they have a real kitchen back there? I took a bite of the hamburger and knew right away the food had been brought in from Goldie's – my favorite hamburger place. Good thing I didn't order The Goldie's Special in my usual way, or it would have caused a ten-minute delay. The burger was amazing, even with the mustard and onions I always avoid. As soon as I took my second bite, I heard a legitimate, "Cut!". Someone snatched my plate away and left me ravenous after the yummy teaser.

When they called for Team 1, we slid from the booth and stood to the side to watch the stars film the scene. I carefully watched as the actor behind the counter shook something on Alison's food.

When she had eaten only a few bites, she started choking and then coughed violently. Aaron spotted the two men as they left the kitchen through a side door. He immediately grabbed Alison's burger off her plate, smelled it, and yelled, "Poison!" He turned to the waitress. "Call an ambulance!" He jumped into action and ran after the two imposter cooks.

It was exciting to watch the real scene after the disastrous rehearsal. Of course, Aaron caught the bad guys. Once I heard the men's voices, I knew they were not the same had heard earlier.

My stomach growled loud enough I was afraid it would be heard on film, but the action was pretty lively so nobody noticed. Since lunch wasn't on the agenda, I read the next scene in advance to avoid yet another misunderstanding. It didn't look like anyone would try to kill poor Alison this time. I was glad since she had already been kidnapped by a biker gang and then poisoned. It was hard to know the story since everything was filmed out of sequence. But, ooh, in this scene I would get to drive a car!

Before I could finish skimming the script, we were ushered outside where my eyes drew skyward. It wasn't a tornado, but a crane looming overhead holding a huge white screen in the sky.

I asked Pat, "What is that?"

"It's a filter to diffuse the sunlight on bright days."

I wondered how he knew that. When he noticed me staring at him, he shrugged, "I saw it being installed and googled it."

I nodded, thinking the whole day was odd. Only a few hours ago a tornado came through and now the sun was too bright to film naturally? We walked to the parking lot, which was filled with a wide assortment of vintage cars. When we passed an adorable wood-paneled pickup. I stopped and stuck my head in the window. The dashboard looked like it was made from maple. I was tempted to jump in the driver's seat to check out the cool truck, but instead, I ran to catch up with Pat.

CowboyHatGirl positioned me by a two-tone VW that wasn't a bug. I circled back and read that it was a Karmann Ghia, black on top, white on the bottom. It looked like someone had taken my Liesel and squashed her down.

CowboyHatGirl said, "You can drive a stick, right?"

I nodded, wondering why she assumed that, then I remembered checking yes on the questionnaire beside 'Drive a manual transmission'. She told me to get in the car, so I opened the creaky door and sat on the worn driver's seat of the 1960's VW. This car was so cool it even smelled vintage. The dashboard looked like wood, but might have been plastic and just looked grained. I was instantly in love with the vehicle and considered taking it for a joyride.

I forgot all about my joyride when I looked through the squatty window to see grumpy Joel Mason was at the helm of this scene. I'd have to behave for real now.

Nobody gave me any instructions so I just checked out the car. I loved the feel of the huge, but skinny steering wheel. As I turned the wheel back and forth like a 3-year-old pretending to steer, my attention was drawn to Kat who stood off to the side, talking to a tall, balding older man. He certainly didn't seem to be her type. Then I had a flashback of her talking to a tall man earlier. Was it the same man, or even the one I had heard talking to the guy with the ball cap? Of course, it was possible that there were just a lot of tall men on this set.

There was a loud knock on my window and I jumped, then turned to find CowboyHatGirl's face an inch away from mine causing me to jump again. I rolled the glass down manually, which took a while. She said, "Upon action, back up and then drive. When you get to the sign over there, stop and let Pat in."

I nodded, figuring I could do that. Exciting!

When I heard Mason's "Achoo!" I turned the key. The engine was so much louder than my VW, it startled me. I tried to put the car in reverse, but it lurched forward, almost hitting a tripod. I tried again and stripped the gears with a horrible grinding sound.

Mr. Mason yelled, "Cut" and marched to my window and grunted, "I thought you knew how to drive."

I stammered, "Well, I know how to shift in most cars, but…"

He sighed impatiently, "Push the damn knob down for reverse.

I said, "OK. I will. I'm so sorry."

I managed to get it in reverse, back up, and drive to the sign without hitting a thing. I happily relinquished the keys.

When Alison sat in the car, she looked like a movie star; maybe because she was one. I smiled at the scene and looked around the crowd of bystanders. The tall guy who had been standing with Kat held something silver. A foil-wrapped burrito? A cell phone maybe? When he winked at someone across the road, I followed his gaze to see Kat nodding at him. Man, she sure was a flirt.

Alison drove to the sign and Aaron jumped in the car as expected. As she took off, there was a loud bang! I held my ears and expected all action to stop, but filming continued as if nothing happened. I saw the tall man pointing his object at the car. It didn't look like a burrito or phone now. It looked like a gun!

I jumped out, right into the scene, and shouted, "Cut! Stop!"

Everyone stared at me. Joel Mason immediately stormed over and shouted in my face, spittle and all, "Nobody yells cut but me!"

"But Mr. Mason, please! Didn't you hear that gunshot? That man over there is holding what I'm sure is a gun." I pointed a shaky finger in the direction of the crowd, but the man was gone.

He looked that way and growled, "What man?"

"He was right there! I swear!" I ran over frantically and searched the crowd, but the tall man had disappeared.

Mr. Mason shouted loud enough for everyone to hear, "I don't know who the hell you think you are but leave my set now!"

"But what about the gunshot?"

His face was as red as a water balloon I had as a kid. And just like that balloon that burst when overfilled, the angry director exploded at me, "That was the car backfiring, idiot! It was part of the scene. Get OUT!" He jabbed his finger at the exit.

I flinched at his display of fury. It was the car backfiring? I could feel the entire cast and crew, including Pat, Kim, Aaron, and Alison, staring at me. They must think I lost my mind. Humiliated and distraught, I trudged away with my head lowered. Kat sashayed past me and murmured, "You really are Pity-full". As she reached Joel Mason, I heard her say, "I'm supposed to take over tomorrow as Alison's stand-in. Want me to start now?"

Mr. Mason nodded his head and said, "Do it!"

I walked to Rita to relinquish my voucher and wondered how I had become so paranoid. There was no gun. It was all in my imagination. There was no poison in the kitchen and the murderous "accident" was probably really an accident. I was mortified. I was sure my sister was ashamed of me and I had ruined my brief friendship with a big movie star.

When Rita saw me, she said, "Hey, what's up? Aren't you supposed to be in that scene?"

"No. I was sent away by Mr. Mason." I watched her head tilt as I continued, "I kind of yelled, 'cut' because I thought someone shot a gun." I grimaced. "But I was wrong."

She nodded and bit the inside of her mouth, probably trying to hold back a laugh, but then she said sweetly. "Look at the bright side. At least there was no gun."

I relaxed a little. "I guess you're right, but I've never been fired from a job. It was all so embarrassing."

She gave a sympathetic pout. "Well, you weren't going to come back tomorrow anyway, right?"

How refreshing it was to meet someone new who wasn't judgmental? "Rita, you are a good person. Thank you." Reluctantly I asked, "Will I still get paid for today?"

"I'll make sure you do. I've enjoyed getting to know you, Pity."

I shook her hand and said, "Thank you and goodbye."

As I slowly made my way to Liesel, I felt exhausted. It was hard work conjuring up so many murder plots. From the corner of my eye, I noticed men climbing the oil derrick beside the fake Golden Driller. Forget it, Pity. They are just working.

On my way home, I drove through Taco Bueno, got a burrito, and laughed at my wild imagination when I saw the silver wrapped food and devoured the warm burrito within seconds. A few miles from my house I saw a sign for an estate sale. Why not go? I could use some sale therapy to lift my spirits. I followed the signs to a house on a lovely street and parked. It's rare to find garage sales in February, but since estate sales are usually held inside, it's common for them to be year-round. I parked by the sign, walked to the front door, and went inside.

An older woman sitting in a chair asked, "Can I help you?"

"I'm looking for DVDs. Can you tell me where they are?"

The old woman pointed slowly to a bookcase by the TV and said in a shaky voice, "They are over there."

I usually feel sad at estate sales, since it often means someone must have died. In this case, perhaps the old woman would be moving to a senior home and had to sell her belongings. Still Sad.

I picked out a few DVDs from the bookcase as the woman dialed her rotary phone, a painfully slow endeavor. She said quietly, "Yes, I need the police. There is an intruder in my home."

I turned to her in alarm and said, "Where?" I glanced around the space. "Why didn't you tell me?" I was in defensive mode now. My hands went up as if I knew karate, and was ready to pounce.

Instead of pointing to another room, the woman stared at me looking terrified. I scanned the room and it finally clicked. I was the intruder! You have to be kidding! Grimacing, I said, "This isn't the estate sale, is it?"

"No. It is not. Could you please leave?" The old woman's eyes were as round as saucers.

Horrified, I quickly put the DVDs back and pleaded, "I am so sorry, Ma'am. It's all a big mistake. Please cancel the police. I'm leaving now." I backed toward the door holding my hands up, with the universal sign that I was unarmed. I blubbered, "I'm so, so sorry. I just wanted to buy some DVD's and from the signs out front I genuinely thought this was the estate sale."

Her face relaxed a bit and she said something I couldn't hear into the mouthpiece. I quickly opened the door and ran out, shutting the door behind me. What kind of dork was I to just walk into someone's house uninvited! I should have figured it out when there were no price tags or other people around. It just goes to show you not to trust your own judgment when you are under extreme duress. I was lucky she didn't have a heart attack or I would have been haunted by that for years to come.

Once back on the driveway, I caught my breath. There was the sign I thought was pointing at the old woman's house. Instead, people exited the house next door carrying items and bags. I hit my forehead with my palm. Oh, brother!

When I reached my car, I looked at the correct house and twisted my mouth. Could I possibly go to the sale even after my latest embarrassment? Of course, I could.

Flustered as I was, I still managed to find five movies I needed for my huge DVD collection. So many people are getting rid of them now in exchange for digital downloads and streaming. I prefer to own DVDs so I can re-watch movies again and again. Same with CDs. Don't get me started on my LP and 45 record collection.

As I left the sale with my stack of discs, I looked next door, worrying about the old woman. I hoped she had locked her door to prevent any other kooks from entering. I vowed to make amends for my mistake and jotted down her address.

When I arrived home, the girls were hanging out with their best friends, Caitlyn and Jennifer.

Caitlyn said, "Mrs. Kole. Your hair is beautiful. How did you get it to stand up like that?"

Caitlyn has always been my biggest fan. I smiled and said, "Look at it now, because you'll never see it like this again."

I waved and walked straight to the bedroom and washed the hairspray out of my hair and put on jeans. Then I found a blank note card and wrote an apology to the old woman. I gave her my name and number and said I wouldn't blame her if she wanted to press charges. But I also assured her that it really was an honest, if stupid, mistake. I filled in the address and put a stamp on the envelope then stuck it in my mail before I forgot to do it.

Back in the living room I told the four girls about my crazy day but didn't mention the DVD break-in fiasco.

"Mom, you have an overactive imagination," said Ren.

"I guess so."

Ree laughed, "Shelly was really dressed like a nun? That's hilarious." All four girls snickered. Everyone in Tulsa County knew who Shelly was from her commercials.

Changing the subject, I kidded in a hoity-toity voice, "Caitlyn and Jennifer, are your backless strapless sequined gowns ready for Sunday night?"

Jennifer, Ren's best friend smiled and said, "No. I haven't gotten to look for a dress yet."

Caitlyn, answered, "Mom said she'll buy me a beautiful dress. I told her dressing up for your party is kind of a joke and I don't need anything expensive, but she won't listen."

This didn't surprise me. Her mother, Trish, is used to high society life and probably wouldn't understand my silly dress-up party. I said, "Well, we don't have ours yet either. How about we take a trip to Goodwill now and I'll buy you each a dress." I was tired but needed this.

"Yes!" Ree jumped up ready to go.

Ren whined, "Mom, how embarrassing."

Jennifer said, "Come on, Ren. It sounds like fun." Her enthusiasm changed Ren's attitude and they stood, ready to go.

Little Caitlyn clapped. "I've never been in a thrift store, but I want to go!"

"Well, that settles it. Jennifer, call your mom and see if she can meet us there. She probably needs a dress too." That wasn't as weird as it sounded, since Jennifer's Mom is my best friend, Lin.

As I drove, I said, "Caitlyn, just get something you would have fun wearing on the fake red carpet. And if you don't think your mother will let you bring home a second-hand dress, leave it at our house and you can put it on when you get here Sunday."

"OK!"

Ren added, "If you've never gone to a thrift store, get ready for the smell. It's gross. The clothes are OK if you wash them or spray with Febreze right away." She added in a super friendly tone, "Hey Caitlyn, why don't you invite your Uncle Andy to the party!"

Jennifer reached upfront and gave Ren a high five.

I smiled at their request since both Ren and Jennifer had crushes on Caitlyn's handsome uncle who was in his twenties.

Caitlyn shook her red curls and said, "Oh, he can't come. He's on a work trip and will still be out of town Sunday night."

The 16-year-olds let out a defeated sigh in unison.

Andy would have been a great guest, but I prayed Caitlyn's mom, Trish, wouldn't come. It would be disastrous having the high-strung woman at my party - almost as bad as if Shelly were to show up.

We arrived at the thrift store and piled out of the VW bug, like clowns exiting a tiny car. We headed directly to the formal section to look for possibilities. It just happened that all five dressing rooms were empty, so we each took our bargain dresses into a room. Before latching my door, I said, "The rule is, if it fits you at all, you have to model it for us."

Giggles emitted from the rooms as we started trying on the fancy, dated gowns. I tried on a bright green dress with hideous ruffles around the bottom. "Check this out." I stepped outside the door and did my catwalk in front of the rooms. The girls peeked through the door and laughed. "OK, so not this one?"

I heard a "Psst." Caitlyn opened her door a crack and said, "These are all too long for me."

Caitlyn, who is really short and a bit chubby looked sad. I said, "No problem, girl. I can take it up if you find one you like."

She smiled. "You are so wonderful."

Lin snuck up behind me and we squealed together. She quickly gathered a stack of dresses. Since there wasn't a sixth dressing room, Ree and Caitlyn shared one, which worked out since neither was very good with zippers. As if to illustrate their lack of fashion,

Ree came out wearing a dress that fit so badly I had to investigate. It turned out she had put it on upside down.

Ren said, "You're such a dork."

Ree came back with, "We're not all perfect, Ren." Sisters...

Surprisingly, I found a long gold gown that fit my 5'10 frame. At $7.99, I snatched it up after getting a thumbs up from everyone. Back in my jeans, I sat on a bench and waited for the others. Lin came out wearing a crazy purple dress. I said, "I cannot believe you found a formal polka dot dress?" Lin loves polka dots. She squealed, "And it's got a matching jacket!"

"Of course, it does." I smiled at my bestie.

She changed into her regular clothes and sat by me with a thump. "So. How was your last day on the set?"

I put my head in my hands. "Oh, Lin. It was the worst day ever!" Then, I remembered Aaron Winston and perked up. "But it was also the best day of my life!"

She scrunched her face.

I explained the tornado story, sans Aaron's crying. After all, a promise is a promise.

"Wait. Aaron Winston was sitting three feet from you for half an hour and you didn't recognize his voice? You weirdo!"

"I know." I shrugged. Now don't be judgy, but..." I forged ahead and told her about being fired and even whispered, "I also broke into an old lady's house and tried to steal her DVDs."

The look on Lin's face was priceless. After I explained what happened, she shook her head, "I can't believe you just barged into an old lady's house." After she stopped giggling, she put her hand on my shoulder. "I'm sorry you were banned from the set. You usually have pretty good intuition. Are you sure there really isn't something odd going on at the fairgrounds?"

Finally, emotional support! "That's just it, Lin! I still have a feeling there is a plot to hurt somebody, but I don't know who or why?"

Movie Watching Tip #11
Don't base your opinions on critics' reviews.

After we all found something fun to wear on Sunday night, we dropped Caitlyn off at her house. I kept her dress so her mother didn't give it to their housekeeper to use as cleaning rags. Luckily, Trish wasn't home when we arrived, so I didn't have to deal with her. That was never pleasant.

I made chicken tetrazzini for dinner and was surprised by my extreme hunger.

Ren licked her fork and squinted. "Mom, so you really don't think the death on the set was an accident?"

"I don't know, Honey. Maybe I imagined it all. It's a good thing I'm not going back tomorrow or I'd probably just imagine a plot to stab someone with a plastic knife from Craft Catering."

Ree pointed her spoon at me. "If it was murder, do you think Kat was involved?"

"Who knows? At any rate, she got what she wanted - my job."

Ren said, "Tell me you didn't actually show Aaron Winston one of your Oscar videos."

I gave a sly nod then said, "Speaking of which, I need to finish editing this year's film." After cleaning up, I climbed the stairs, worked on it a bit. As I watched the spoof of Aaron's role, I had to laugh. He'd probably get a kick out of this – not that he would want to watch it after he found out I was a movie-set pariah. Once this year's "Not Quite the Oscars" masterpiece was burned to a DVD, I felt lighter. One big project was done. I made a copy for Mom and Dad to watch Sunday night.

Back downstairs, my phone rang, but I couldn't dig it out of my purse before it stopped. Kim had left a message, the second one today, but I was too tired and depressed to be kidded or reprimanded. I vowed to call back tomorrow.

The doorbell rang. When I answered it, our little 80-year-old neighbor, Mrs. Garmin stood there. She wore her pink housecoat and a hairnet. Her face was flushed.

"Ellen, what's wrong?"

"Can you come help me, Dear? My house is too warm again."

I sighed, "Sure, let's go check it out." I followed the 4'10" woman to her house next door as I wondered what she had done this time. Upon entering her house, I could hardly breathe. The heat was sweltering. "Oh Ellen, it feels like a sauna in here. What happened?"

She rubbed her hands together nervously as she led me to the hall thermostat. "It was too warm today, so I turned the heat down, but it keeps getting hotter and hotter." Her New Jersey accent usually sounds adorable, but in this stifling heat, nothing was cute.

The thermostat was set at 95 degrees. My face beaded with sweat as I quickly turned the knob and heard the blower stop. Trying to remain patient, I said, "Ellen, you turned the heat up instead of down again. See the snowflake I drew on here last time? If you want it cooler – go to the snowflake, if you want it warmer, turn it to the sunshine."

"Oh, that's right. I get confused on which way to turn it." She sighed.

I made my way through her house, opening several windows I thought she could reach to shut later. The air rushing in from outside felt like cool water on my skin. I gulped a deep breath.

She gave me a shy shrug, "Can I make you a cup of coffee?"

Although I wanted to be kind, the last thing I wanted was hot coffee in this hothouse. "No Thank you. Why don't you come to our place 'til yours cools down?"

She stood beneath her bell collection on shelves that wound around her kitchen table. "Nah. It already feels much better and it's almost bedtime."

I thought 7 o'clock was pretty early for bed, but my attention was drawn to the new People magazine on her flowered plastic tablecloth. A huge Oscar statue took up most of the cover. The headline read, 'Academy Awards Edition.' There was a small picture of Alison Baxter in a photo box near Oscar's feet. "Ellen, may I borrow this?"

"Take it. I've already read it. And take a piece of candy for Lauren and Marie."

I looked at the bowl of hard candy, and it reminded me of my grandmother's candy dish back in the day. I chose cinnamon balls for my girls. "Thanks. Don't forget to close the windows or you'll get cold tonight."

When I got home, I threw off my shirt and sat on the couch to cool down. Pouring over the magazine, I read every detail about the Oscar contenders.

I turned a page and there was Aaron. In the picture, apparently taken at a recent red-carpet event, he wore a tuxedo and stared directly at me with his famous flirty expression. I smiled back at him, imagining being his date at the real Academy award show. That bubble burst pretty quickly when I remember he witnessed me being a paranoid psycho today. I am doomed to hold my fake Oscar Party at home forever.

The cover story about Alison wasn't related to the Oscars. According to the article, she had broken up with her boyfriend and was rumored to be dating Aaron Winston.

I scoffed, knowing first hand that it wasn't true. I laughed aloud when I realized that I, Pity Kole, a music teacher from Broken Arrow, Oklahoma, knew more about entertainment gossip than People magazine. What a day!

I sniffed the two men's fragrance samples tucked in the magazine and was able to discern that Aaron's cologne must have been Prada Sport. Nice. I breathed it in again, fondly recalling our accidental embrace, then stuck the foil packet in my dresser drawer so I could conjure up the memory later.

Ren stopped short in front of me. "Mom, is that magazine too hot for you? Seriously?"

I looked down at my bra. "Ha! No. Just another trip to Mrs. Garmin's house."

She nodded as if that made perfect sense, then grabbed a piece of candy and continued into the kitchen. "Gross, it's melted to the wrapper."

I enjoyed "sleeping-in" to my normal wake-up time of 7:00. something I never thought I would enjoy. Upon checking my phone, there were texts from each of my three school buddies.

Becca: "Today's wild animal day! Come as you are☺"

Jules: "Wild animal day – don't be boring."

Jana – "Can't wait to hear about your movie experience. Try to find something to wear for wild animal day today."

I dreaded seeing the girls for I'd have to tell them I'd been ousted from the set. And mentioning the estate sale fiasco was a hard no. They would never let me live that down.

Although my closet was packed tight with clothes, nothing was very wild. I found a sweater in a zebra pattern that had to work and I pulled it on over my camisole. When Ren and Ree entered the small space, Ren asked, "Are you okay today, Mom?"

I shrugged. "Got a good night's sleep. That should count for something. I'll be fine." I smiled.

Ree straightened my shirt and said, "Just go to school where you can celebrate beating Dr. L in his evil plot to rule the school and maybe you'll forget all about yesterday."

I hugged them both. "That's right. Let's go get 'em, Tigers. Speaking of Tigers Ren, your swim team is going up against the Jenks Trojans next week. Are you ready?"

She answered, "I hope so. I swam a personal best at practice on Tuesday."

My eyes widened. "Breast Stroke?"

She nodded.

"Good for you! I'm sorry I've been so involved in my own crazy stuff. Next week, I'll try to be a better mom. And what about you, Ree? What have I missed?"

Ree said, "Nothing important, but I don't want to be late for school, we're having a pep assembly first thing."

As I entered Arrowstar, Melanie, called me into the office and said with twinkly eyes, "You received this yesterday."

She handed me a gorgeous bouquet of daisies. Oh my gosh, were they from Aaron? I felt giddy until I realized, duh, of course they weren't. He doesn't know where I teach.

A tall, pleasant woman I recognized as one of the district's permanent substitutes brushed by me and said, "I'll be in the teacher's lounge if anyone needs me."

I smelled the daisies and said, "I should leave more often if I can get flowers when I return."

Melanie said, "No. Please don't. Your substitute was…well… just take a look at your notes. I'm sure she left a book." Her wide eyes told me little, except there was some sort of trouble. She nodded at the teacher's lounge, "Too bad Josie wasn't available to take your classes."

I sighed, dreading what I might find in my room, then thanked her and tried to balance my load as I walked down the hall. I snagged a 3rd grader walking by. "Emily, can you carry something to my room for me? I'm a little overloaded."

"Sure!" The girl's cornrow beads clacked together as she bounced over to me. She beamed when I handed her the flowers and the card. Emily held her head high as she passed a classmate who saw her helping me.

As we walked, she looked up. "Mrs. Kole, where were you yesterday? We didn't get to do anything fun in music. The substitute was so mean."

"I'm sorry, Honey. I'll make it up to you next time you come to Music."

I opened my prefab door and thanked the 10-year-old for her help. She offered to get water for my vase and I said, "Yes. Thank you." My classroom was in good order, but I anxiously went to my desk to see if the sub had left a note. Boy did she! There was a lengthy list of every child who had spoken out of order and a note saying that she had given up on trying to teach "these kids anything". She also apparently decided not to follow my lesson plans after the first hour and showed every class a video about the percussion section of the orchestra. Great, I was saving that to show during my instrument unit.

That is why I don't like taking a day off. It was hard to rely on the students and many times, the subs.

I opened the card that came with the flowers and read, "Pity, I have missed you so much. Could you see fit to go out with me tomorrow night? If I don't hear from you, I'll pick you up at 6:00 - Kenny."

That guy is a little intense, but it was thoughtful of him to send me flowers. If I did go out with him, I'd probably get a good meal and the distraction would be nice. Rather than call him, I would just be ready at six tomorrow.

When Emily returned with the filled vase, I offered her a piece of candy from my giant apple. She took one and gave me a big hug. "I love you, Mrs. Kole."

I patted her back and said, "You are so sweet."

I didn't feel up to going to the art room yet, so I stayed in my classroom enjoying the silence before the kids arrived. I thought back on the past 24 hours and pondered how I had been so wrong about so many things.

As it turned out, I couldn't hide from my crazy trio of friends. They barged through my door, like a herd of wild animals.

"There's our movie star!" squealed Becca. She had gone to great lengths to be noticed – possibly from space. Her tight zebra pants managed to coordinate with a purple wild animal top. To accent that, she wore a wide, tiger-striped bangle bracelet, huge matching earrings, and a purple head wrap of zebra stripes. As if my senses weren't overloaded enough, Becca carried a stack of bright orange caution cones.

I squinted at her wild concoction "Geeze Becca, you're blinding me."

Jules sat down on the choral risers, where my students sit in lieu of desks or chairs. She was wearing black pants and the most beautiful jacket that bore an entire painted tiger from front to back. The lifelike tail wrapped completely around one arm. She said dryly, "Did you even think about your poor friends having to fight the battle without you while you hobnobbed with the stars?"

I ignored her question and inspected her beautifully detailed jacket. "You painted that just for today, didn't you?"

She shrugged. "You know I have to do something while I watch TV."

I shook my head in wonder. "Jules, I hope these kids appreciate your talent. If you ever want to leave teaching, you can sell your artwork and become mega-rich. I was sincere about that.

Jana pointed at Jules and said, "She did that, and all I could come up with was a giraffe scarf I got at the zoo on a field trip."

I walked over and touched her scarf. "It's lovely, Jana. And I see you have a giraffe on your notebook too, which is all better than my lame sweater." I smiled at my three wild friends. "You guys are crazy. I loved seeing you in the paper and news. What a way to get Dr. Dread!"

Jules said, "You guys know he'll find some way to get back at us."

"Probably." I nodded.

Jana perked up. "So, tell us about your adventure! Did you get to meet Aaron Winston?"

"Oh…Yes, I actually did." Like a pride of lions, they leaned forward, ready to devour my story. As much as I wanted to tell them everything, I didn't have it in me. I felt kind of puny emotionally. I admitted, "Please don't kill me, but I really don't feel well. Can I tell you about it later?"

Becca scoffed. "You must be sick if you're not going to brag about meeting your idol." She turned to the others, "Fine. We'll leave and I'll set up my cones, but you better believe we'll get the juicy information out of you one way or another."

"Yeah, we get the hint," said Jules without inflection. She stood and walked to the door, tiger tail and all.

"Thanks, girls. I'll make it up to you, I promise."

As Becca walked to the door, she split the cones in two stacks and held them over her breasts, extending them by two feet. Despite my funk, I cracked a smile.

When the door shut, my mood plummeted even more. I couldn't shake the feeling that something wasn't right on the set. I should just give up since nobody else seemed concerned.

When the bell rang and the first class exploded into my room, I pepped up enough to lead them in the character song I'd written for March. "Perseverance" was a rowdy, cowboy-themed song that included actions. The lyrics spoke to me as we sang:

You gotta keep determination, be stubborn if you please,
Ignore frustration, you can do it with ease
Be a steadfast pardner when others say "Nay"
A diehard cowboy never goes astray
Perseverance - Stay in the saddle today. Yee Haw!

Was my intuition giving me the uneasy feeling? Maybe I should persevere as the song said.

After the next class sang the same song, Shayna, one of my fifth graders, said, "This song would be a lot better if Alabama Shakes sang it."

I had no idea what she was talking about. "Who?"

"Alabama Shakes."

I shook my head and she explained further, "It's my mom's favorite country band."

I said, "OK. Well, if a famous band wants to sing my kid's cowboy song about perseverance, they sure can." Heck, I'd let anyone sing my songs.

I persevered and taught my morning classes, all the time worrying about yesterday. At lunch break, I got a text from Kim, "Why aren't you answering your phone? I need to talk to you!"

I gave up and called her. "Get it over with, Kim. Let me have it."

"Pity, why didn't you call me back?" She didn't sound like she wanted to berate me at all.

"Why do you think? I humiliated myself and everyone who knows me."

"Ah, don't worry about that. You have to hear what happened after you left." She continued breathlessly, "Kat took over your position and of course, she was annoying. Everything was going okay, until…there was another accident!"

My mouth dropped. "Another accident?"

"Yes. A fire broke out in a dressing room." She added quickly, "But nobody was hurt, luckily."

That did it. This was just too coincidental. I asked, "Whose dressing room was it?"

Kim sped on, "I don't know, but there were firetrucks everywhere and they stopped shooting for hours. And of all things, I was stuck in a room with Kat. She acted like she owned the place and believe it or not, she and Alison Baxter are friends!"

I tried to imagine them as friends, while Kim continued, "Poor Pat is miserable working with Kat. Oh, and remember those workers you talked to me about? The tall one and ballcap guy? They hung out all day by the oil derrick. I don't know what that was about."

I remembered them, but thought of the tall guy and wondered if it was the same missing burrito/phone/gun man? I felt a nervous twinge thinking about the oil derrick. Aaron was supposed to climb it on Saturday. When Kim took a breath, I jumped in, "Thanks for the info. And thanks for not disowning me. It's been tearing me up worrying that I embarrassed you."

She said, "Well, you would have known earlier if you had called me back. And FYI, you've always been an embarrassment, but I haven't disowned you…yet." She chuckled.

"Touché. Hey, Kim, has R.A. found his sound guy yet?"

"No. R.A.'s not here today and he can't get hold of Jesse."

I looked at the clock and realized my 30-minute lunch break was counting down. "Look, I should eat my lunch. Text me if anything happens and call me when you leave tonight."

"Sure. I will."

I took a bite of my tuna sandwich and started to hang up, but Kim said, "Oh…I have to tell you one more thing. Shelly got in trouble for trying to talk to Alison today. It was so funny watching her squirm while Mr. Mason reprimanded her."

Now that made me laugh. I hung up, ate more of my sandwich, and woke up my computer to google the Alabama band. I couldn't remember the name and typed Alabama Rocks, Alabama Hits, and Alabama Sings. I got nothing except the 80's band, Alabama. When I tried Alabama Girl, a news article popped up saying a girl had been missing for a month and her twin sister was suspected in her disappearance. I was about to close the site, but the photograph of the missing girl stunned me. She was a dead ringer for Kat, but her hair was short and her face looked thinner.

I double-clicked on the article and read a disturbing story of the girl, named Jenn, who had been missing since January. I zoomed in on two photos and almost choked when her twin sister, Katherine, was the prime suspect in Jenn's disappearance!

My mouth went dry at the notion of Kat kidnapping her sister. I remembered when she had mentioned her twin in Alabama that she didn't 'talk to anymore'. If she could do something evil to her own sister, she might also be the one causing trouble on set. After all, I had seen her pointing at the fake statue just minutes before it fell, and she really did want my job. It was all too suspicious.

I started to panic. I had to tell someone, but who? I called Kim, but it went to voicemail, so I called R.A. I told him about Kat and said, "I have to go back and warn people about her."

"Why don't you just call the police and tell them what you found out?"

"Because I want to know if she was involved in the incidents on the set before I turn her in for kidnapping her sister."

He argued, "But Pity, you were banned. You can't just waltz in there."

My mind worked overtime. "I can if I wear a disguise!" I quickly concocted a plan that might work and said, "R.A., do you still have welding equipment?"

"Yes, but I won't let you use it since you aren't trained."

"Can a welding gun work without the machine?"

"Good. So, if I only borrowed the helmet and the gun thingy, I couldn't possibly turn it on, right?"

"Of course not."

"Great. Can I meet you at your house in 30 minutes?"

"Sure, but wait. What are you going to do?"

"I'll call you on the way and explain."

After changing the date to today on my substitute notes, I left them on my desk, grabbed my purse, and ran to the office.

I scanned the area, hoping to avoid my adversary, Dr. Love, and whispered, "Melanie, I really have to leave. Can you get that sub, Josie, to take my class for the afternoon?"

She furrowed her brow and turned towards Dr. Love's office, looking fearful.

I pleaded, "It's an emergency. Lesson plans are on my desk."

She gave a little nod and I scooted away, but before I could make it to the front door, I heard Dr. Love's grating, sustained voice calling my name.

I held my breath and turned around in surrender.

He sauntered towards me with pursed lips. "I hope you have a good reason for being absent the past few days?" He cleared his throat and continued, "Your substitute called the office far too often while you were gone. You must prepare your students and leave quality plans so that it doesn't happen again."

In a moment of brilliance, I tried my hand at acting. I croaked, "I'm sorry, Dr. Love, but I'm really sick. I can't talk right now." I held my hand over my mouth as though I might vomit. He jumped back in disgust and I made my getaway without looking back to see whether his face was repulsed or furious.

I know…lying is terrible, but I actually was sick. Sick with worry. The situation could be a matter of life and death and trying to explain it to Dr. L. would be a waste of valuable time.

At home, I rummaged through my costume collection and found my blue jr. astronaut jumpsuit. I grabbed an old patch from my patch collection that said "Johnson" and pinned it over the NASA lettering on the pocket. Then, I put on clunky black shoes, yanked my hair up in a high ponytail, and ran out of the house.

On the drive, I called Kim and left a detailed message asking her to get a note to Aaron Winston. After dictating exactly what to write, I said I'd meet her next to the IPE building in 30 minutes.

Next, I called R. A. and explained my plan. When I arrived, my sweet brother-in-law stood on his porch with the welding supplies in hand, shaking his head at me.

I jumped out of the car and into my jumpsuit. I put on the tool belt and helmet he handed me, then held up the torch. "Do I look like a welder?" I asked from under the steamy mask.

"What?"

I lifted the facemask and repeated my question. He squinted as he studied my get-up. "Sort of?" He shook his head and said, "I'll text Kim and warn her that you will be dressed like that."

I thanked him and waved as I drove away. After parking at Expo Square I checked my reflection in the car window. Satisfied with my disguise, I marched past the sign-in table. I got curious glances, but nobody stopped me. My faceplate was down and I carried a torch, so I felt confident people would think I was part of the crew.

It didn't take Kim long to spot me. She rolled her eyes slightly, then walked beside me nonchalantly as if she didn't know me. She whispered "I can't believe you came in here wearing that. Are you crazy?"

I couldn't really hear her while wearing the helmet but caught the last part. I spoke out of the corner of my mouth as we walked, "I may be crazy, but I had to do something to prove there is something malicious going on. Did you get the note to Aaron?"

I lifted my helmet a bit so I could hear her answer.

"Yeah. I snuck it to him and said it was from you. He looked at me strangely, but he took it. I think all the actors are in the pavilion now. What's this all about?"

I explained, "Apparently Kat is wanted in Alabama in connection with her twin sister's disappearance."

Kim turned to me with wide eyes and said, "No way!"

I nodded and said, "I want to see if she'll admit to her involvement in that or more importantly, in things going on here. So, I'm pretending to be a repairman so I can investigate."

As if summoned, a huge guard with a tattoo on his neck appeared and said, "Excuse me. Who are you?"

Kim peeled off in another direction as if we weren't together. I lowered my voice and growled, "Um. Edgar Johnson, from Johnson's Welding. I'm here to check out the 'ol derrick. Heard they's some problems. You never can be too careful, 'specially if people's gonna be climbin' it."

When the uniformed guard wrinkled his eyebrows as if I was lying, my stomach churned with nerves. I began to sweat and could barely see through my foggy helmet window. Finally, the burly man waved me on to pass. I felt his eyes watching my back, so I sauntered as much like a man as I could to the oil derrick. I stood there pretending to inspect it until the guard turned and walked the other way. When he did, I made a quick left and ran to the pavilion, hoping Kat was there.

My sister appeared by my side again and we stood in the shadow of the pavilion. She whispered, "If your idea doesn't work, do you have a plan B or are you going to wing it like usual?"

If I was smart, I'd have a secondary plan because my emotions usually got me in trouble. I pulled Kim behind a big dead tree and lifted my faceplate. "Do you have any ideas?"

She held up her finger. "I was thinking you could...no that won't work." Then her eyes lit up. "How about you go...nope." She shrugged. "Oh Pity, who am I kidding? I don't have any ideas. Kat's not going to just admit that she did anything. Just call the Alabama police and tell them you found her."

I sighed. "I will if I can't prove anything here. I just feel like she's up to something."

We stood silent for a while, thinking and watching, then took in a collective breath when the side door of the pavilion opened. In a stroke of luck, or maybe because Aaron got Alison to do what I had requested of him, Kat and Alison walked out arm in arm.

They giggled as Alison led her down the steps. We inched sideways to hide behind the large trunk. Luckily, we were close enough to hear them, well, once I took off my helmet.

Alison spoke first in a serious tone, "I can't believe you did that to your sister."

I quickly pulled my phone from my pocket and pushed record.

Kat replied, "It was so easy. All I had to do was wait until she was asleep. She never knew what hit her."

In my peripheral vision, I could see Kim's eyes were just as wide as mine, wondering what Kat had actually done. I held up my phone and showed her that I was recording.

Then Alison, who I now revered as a true actress, asked, "So, where is she now?"

Kat laughed, "She's still making sundaes and Blizzards alongside my dirtbag ex-boyfriend."

I let out my breath silently, glad to know the missing sister wasn't dead. We waited while they made plans to go out tonight and discussed what guys might be there. I was amazed that they had become friends so fast. Or was this all an act on Alison's part too?

The door behind them opened and someone yelled, "Ms. Baxter, you're needed on set." Both girls walked back inside. Before the door shut, Alison glanced our way and gave us a nod.

Kim hit my arm. "You are brilliant! How did you know she would ask Kat about her sister?"

I too was surprised and said, "I didn't. I just hoped Aaron would explain to her what I needed. Even a Hollywood starlet can't resist that man." I turned to Kim and announced, "Sis, I'm going to Jenks!"

"Why?"

"To buy a Dilly Bar and find the missing twin."

She looked confused. "Do you want me to come with you?"

"No, you need to stay here. Keep your phone with you and text me if anything odd happens. I'll let you know if I find her."

I drove as fast as I could to Jenks. The suburb is just 15 miles Southwest of Tulsa. Using GPS, I found the only Dairy Queen in Jenks and parked. When I got out, I caught the reflection of my ridiculous astronaut suit in the side view mirror. Figuring that get-up made no sense while in a DQ, I slipped it off and tossed it in the back seat.

Once inside, I immediately recognized the girl behind the counter as the missing sister. Her features were identical to Kat's, but she had a short blunt haircut.

"Can I help you?" Her sweet, genuine smile was vastly different than her sister's.

I stood there uncomfortably, trying not to stare. Her name tag confirmed she was Jenn. I figured I should order something, and studied the menu board. I cleared my throat and said, "I'll have a small German Chocolate Blizzard, please." Normally, I'd ask for extra chocolate, but under the circumstances, I played it cool.

As she worked the register, I glanced in the back kitchen and wondered if one of the guys back there was Kat's Ex. "That will be $3.59."

I was momentarily distracted by her thick southern accent. It was even stronger than Kats. As I handed her a five-dollar bill, I tried to think of what to say next. The girl certainly appeared to be fine and she didn't look to be injured or mistreated. It was the oddest thing since I had fully expected to have to save a timid, frightened girl.

After Jenn gave me my change, I watched her make my Blizzard. She turned my cup upside-down as trained, to prove its thickness. When she handed it to me, I was delighted to see the ice cream was especially chocolaty.

I took my treat to a booth to observe her and hopefully come up with a strategy. The chocolate melted in my mouth leaving the crunchy coconut and pecans. I enjoyed the Blizzard so much I almost forgot my purpose for being there.

Once I had drained the last of the ice cream, I followed my usual modus operandi and winged it. I tossed my cup in the trash on my way to the counter and said, "You look a lot like a girl named Kat who I met on the movie set in Tulsa."

Her eyes flickered for a second then looked down. "Oh really? That's funny. I don't know anyone named Kat."

From my years of teaching, I had learned people who wouldn't look you in the eye were usually lying. And in this case, Jenn was lying. I was positive she knew Kat since they looked identical.

"Here, look at this." I lifted my phone and showed her the video I had taken of Kat describing aloud what she had done to someone. Jenn slapped her hand across her mouth and looked at me with eyes narrowed, "Who are you?"

In a cordial tone, I tried to explain, "My name is Kitty Kole. I'm a music teacher in Broken Arrow, but I got to know Kat on a movie set this week. Today, when I was googling an Alabama band, I accidentally found an article that reported you as missing." I took a breath and watched her grow more confused. "Did your sister kidnap you and bring you to Oklahoma?" I leaned in and whispered, "Do you need help?"

She cocked her head in genuine surprise at the notion, then said, "Kidnap?" Then she asked, "Wait. Who thinks I'm missing?"

Then, I became the one confused. How could someone not know they had been kidnapped? I quickly found the write-up on my phone and showed it to her.

As she read the article, her face flushed and her eyes flickered. I thought she might faint. "Why don't you come sit down?" I pointed to my booth.

She turned back and said in a wobbly voice, "David, I'm taking a break for a sec. Can you watch the counter?"

"Sure, Jenn." A gangly teen with a name tag marked, David, Assistant Manager, put a carton of milk in the refrigerator and stood at the register.

The tall replica of Kat walked around the counter and slid into the booth across from me. She put her head on her hands and spoke quietly, "I really don't understand any of this. Kat said she had gotten me a job here in Jenks and wanted me to come right away, so I did."

"Did you tell your parents?"

"No. I didn't, but Kat assured me she had told them." She picked at her fingernail and said, "It was the weekend of our 21st birthday. We had gone out to celebrate. She woke me up early the next morning and said, 'Time to start a new life." She said she had already packed my stuff and we were going on an adventure. Kat was so happy about going that I got excited too."

"So, you went with her willingly?" I was a little disappointed that maybe Kat wasn't the monster I had made her out to be.

"Sure. Things weren't going well at home. I had just broken up with my boyfriend, my parents were mad at me and I had just lost my job." She shrugged. "So, it was perfect timing for us to move here. I just don't understand why the police think I'm missing."

"Did you tell anyone you were leaving?"

"No. Like I said, Kat said she had worked it out."

I could see Jenn's wheels turning as she realized her sister had lied to her. She said, "My parents really don't know where we are? Kat said she told everyone. Maybe she had a reason."

A family of four walked in and stood at the counter. The little girl looked like one of my first-grade students, so I was distracted until I realized it wasn't her.

I turned to Jenn. "Well, I don't want to cause trouble, but I have something important to ask you."

She looked at me with sincere green eyes.

"Besides the unusual manner in which she brought you here, do you think Kat has any violent tendencies?"

"Kat?" She rolled her eyes. "Well, yeah. She has a terrible temper and has been in trouble pretty much all our lives. She was kicked out of two schools for fighting, has lost every job she's ever had and doesn't keep friends very long. As a matter of fact, she stormed out of our apartment last week and I haven't seen her since. I didn't even know she was going to be in a movie." Jenn lifted her hands in amazement.

I worried about asking the next question and took a deep breath. "Do you think she is capable of something more serious…like plotting to murder someone?"

I watched her reaction, expecting her to defend Kat, but instead, Jenn pushed her short hair behind her ears and said, "I hope not, but I just don't know." She leaned forward and whispered, "Sometimes she scares me." She bit her lip.

Not happy with the answer, I asked, "What did she do to make you scared?"

"She's threatened to kill me before. I know she never would, but normal people just don't say that stuff, do they?"

I gave a shrug. "Not usually. We should alert the Alabama State Police and tell them that you are okay and where you are. After all, they are trying really hard to find you and your sister."

"Right." She nodded. "And I need to let my parents know I'm OK." She cocked her head. "Now that I think about it, when I told Kat a couple of weeks ago that I wanted to call Mom, she threw a fit. She stormed around and threatened if I did call anyone, she'd make me move out of our apartment." She shook her head. "Then she ended up moving out anyway. My sister has issues."

I wondered what Kat's motive was for moving here and all the secrecy. It was so bizarre. I pulled up the online article and said, "Here's the number. Want to call the police or your mom first?"

She took her phone from her pocket and started to dial as the young family walked by with two giggly kids licking their cones. I was startled when something cold hit my ankle. I looked down to find the little boy had dropped his dipped cone on me! The frozen scoop slid from my ankle to my foot and was already dripping into my shoe soaking my sock. When the kid started wailing, Jenn stood up and moved away.

The horrified father apologized to me and ran to get napkins. He handed me a stack and started cleaning up the mess on the floor. Embarrassed, he shook his head and said, "I'm so sorry."

I assured him, "It's really fine. I teach elementary school and believe me, this is nothing."

It was however the first time I'd had ice cream oozing into my shoe. I picked up the blob of ice cream and put it in some napkins. Then I took off my shoe and tried my best to clean it out.

As the frazzled mom rushed to the counter to order a replacement cone, the kid stood there crying right by my ear. In full teacher mode, I patted the toddler on the head and said gently, "It's OK. Mommy's getting you a new one."

Then I made up a rhyme in order to get him to hush while I cleaned my shoe with a napkin. "Drip, drip drop, the ice cream went kerplop. Don't cry or say boohoo. No one's hurt, except my shoe. Drip, drip drop."

The little boy's sniffles lessened as he stared at the crazy lady singing about ice cream. By the time his mom appeared with the new cone he was totally fine.

After the family was seated, I tried to listen in on Jenn's side of her phone conversation, but my phone buzzed. It was a text from Kim. "Did you find her?"

I quickly typed, "Yes. At DQ. Busy now. Will call later."

I eavesdropped again and was surprised when Jenn said, "Oh my. I never saw it….she never said anything about that either."

I blinked in confusion at the disjointed conversation. What was she talking about now? Jenn continued, "I haven't seen him in a week. I thought they moved in together…. Yes, just a second…"

Jenn walked back to my booth and handed the phone to me. "The detective wants to know where he can find Kat. Can you talk to him?"

I said into the phone, "Hello? This is Kitty Kole."

"Ms. Kole, can you tell me where you last saw Katherine? And do you think she's still there?"

"Yes. She's in Tulsa at the fairgrounds working as a stand-in for the actress, Alison Baxter, in the movie they are filming there. My sister is keeping an eye on her now, but I can be there in 30 minutes."

"Good. I'll call Tulsa police and explain what is going on. We'll arrange for them to meet you at the fairgrounds."

"Okay here's my phone number." I told him, then added, "You might want to send plain-clothed officers. If Kat gets spooked, there's no telling what she will do. As a matter of fact, I'll probably wear a disguise."

The other end of the phone line grew so silent, I thought we had lost connection, but the detective finally said, "You really think a disguise is necessary?"

"Well, in my case, it is." I left it at that. Being banned from a movie set wasn't something I wanted to explain to anyone, especially the law.

The officer said, "Thank you for finding Jennifer. Her family has been very worried."

"Of course. Anything to help."

He cleared his throat. "Oh, and Mobile Police will be glad to find Kat too since they have a warrant out for her arrest."

I held Jenn's phone closer to my ear and asked, "Can you tell me what she is wanted for?" I closed my eyes and expected to hear him say murder.

"I'm not at liberty to tell, since it's a pending investigation."

After hanging up, I turned back to the girl, who sat with elbows on the table and head in her hands. With no inflection in her voice, she said, "I guess my sister was busier than I thought. She took my dad's gun."

"What?"

"When Dad found it missing, he called the police who dusted for fingerprints. They found Kat's all over the gun cabinet." Jenn closed her eyes.

I assumed Kat had been arrested before in order to have her fingerprints on file. Yikes.

"I'll bet Dad regrets giving us the combination to the gun safe."

I shook my head at the thought that Kat could be armed, then asked her, "Did your parents ever try to call you?"

Jenn opened her eyes. "Yes, according to the detective, they called repeatedly, but I never knew about it because I didn't have my phone." She laughed in disbelief. "Kat told me she lost it while packing. She made a big deal about getting me a new one with a new number once we got to Oklahoma." She sighed. "Poor Mom and Dad. They must be frantic with worry. I can't believe I was so gullible. I even followed her directions and didn't send my new number to my parents because supposedly she already had. Now I have to decide if I want to press charges against my twin sister."

"Don't be hard on yourself, Jenn. Your sister is very cunning and lying seems to come naturally to her. I believed her stories at first too. Do you have any idea why she did all of that?"

"It sounds like she's wanted for something serious in Mobile. That would explain her need to get out of town quickly."

I nodded. "The detective mentioned that. I wonder what she did?"

"No telling." She looked up at me. "But…there's one more thing. I'm afraid Kat's boyfriend, Rodney, is missing. He was working here last week, but I have no idea where he is now. What if…" Jenn's sentence trailed off and her lip quivered.

Movie Watching Tip #13
Pay attention to the details of each scene.

Oh wow. The new information about Kat was a little scary. I put my hand on Jenn's, and said, "I hate to say it, but Kat might have been involved in some suspicious activity on the movie set. I need to go now to meet Tulsa police so they can confront her. Will you be okay?"

"I'll be fine once I talk to my parents. Thanks for letting me know."

Jenn looked so sad that I felt bad for being bearer of bad news. I stood and nodded. "Call if you need anything."

On my way to the door, I threw away the wet napkins then walked to my car while texting Kim, "I'm on my way – with police. Don't tell anyone."

As soon as I plugged in my phone it dinged and I read a text from Ree, "I'm at Caitlyn's working on an art project. Can she spend the night at our house tonight?"

I replied, "Sure. I'm not at school. Should be home in time for dinner." At least I hoped I would be.

I drove back to 21st and Yale where my giant boyfriend stood a block from his new murderous clone. Why hadn't the police called me yet? I parked and sat for a few minutes, wishing I'd asked more about the bizarre semi-kidnapping. The phone rang and I pushed the car's green phone button. "Hello?"

A woman's voice asked, "Is this Kitty Kole?"

Too impatient for niceties, I said, "Yes. I'm in the east parking lot of Expo Square. Is someone on the way?"

"I'm calling from America's Best Bank. You've been pre-approved for a credit card."

Oh brother. "I'm waiting for another call and I'm not interested in another credit card at this time but thank you." I hung up without a reply and hoped I'd get the real call soon. It was almost four o'clock and I didn't want to stay in the car all day.

When the phone rang again, I jumped. "Hello?"

"Hi Kitty?" a male voice said.

I answered quickly. "Yes. I'm in the east parking lot of Expo Square. Are you on your way?"

"No, but I certainly can be." There was a slight giggle on the other end. "I just wanted to touch base about our date, but I can meet you in 15 minutes if you're that anxious to see me."

Seriously? It was Kenny. "Oh, Hi Kenny. I'm sorry, I thought you were the police."

"Police? Are you in trouble?" His voice squeaked.

"No. I'm fine, but I can't talk right now. I have to catch a call. Bye." I hung up again.

When the phone rang again, I answered with much less excitement. "Hello?"

"Hi, is this Kitty Kole?"

"Yes." Just in case it wasn't them, I figured I'd forgo giving out my location again.

"I'm Sergeant Matthews with the Tulsa Police. I'm approaching the fairgrounds now. Can you tell me your location?"

Finally. "Yes! I'm in the east parking lot of Expo Square in a dark gray VW bug."

"I'll be there momentarily."

I jumped out of the car and donned my disguise, minus the faceplate for the time being. A car, so nondescript it blended in with the gray sky, pulled in a few spots away. It just screamed 'unmarked police car'. A handsome 50-something man dressed more like a lawyer than a policeman exited. He straightened his tie and approached me, and squinted at my odd outfit. "Ms. Kole?"

"Yes." I started my explanation. "OK, so someone, possibly Kat, has been plotting murder on the movie set. Nobody believed me when I told them my suspicions. Then I was banned from the set yesterday. So now I use a disguise to enter."

He nodded slowly and said, "That's actually disturbing."

I nodded in agreement, "I know. So, what's the plan? Are you going to frisk her? Did you bring a gun in case she's packing? Or did you want to do something more subtle? You should probably have a fake name and story? I can introduce you once we're in."

He smirked. "No need for theatrics. I'll talk to Ms. Hobart. If I need assistance, there is backup down the road. She can't get far."

"But I know her. She could be dangerous. We must be careful."

"As far as I know, she hasn't done anything violent. The sister came here willingly."

"Well, What about her dad's gun? She took it!"

He shrugged. "She was given the combination." He gave me a 'so there's that' look. "Let's just see how this goes. I'll check-in and ask to speak with Kat in private."

"Wait! Did you know there is a warrant out for her arrest? It could be for something awful."

He shrugged. "Look, I'm just supposed to bring her in for questioning and we'll deal with the rest later."

I was disappointed by his lowkey approach but nodded okay. He probably did know best. With anticipation, I asked, "So, what about me? What's my job?"

He rubbed his chin. "You should just stay here. I'll fill you in when I get back. I can't condone you entering a place where you are forbidden." He turned and strode toward the building where Rita checks people in.

Well, that was a bad idea. He may not know it, but he needed me. I refused to just sit in the parking lot. Besides, he wouldn't be condoning my actions if he didn't know what I was doing. Once Sergeant Matthews disappeared in the building, I put my faceplate down, grabbed my welding gun, and walked through the other breezeway.

I spotted the production crew standing under the giant white hanging screen. Kat and Pat were standing at the back entrance of the I.P.E. building watching Team 1 film. I snuck through the crowd, tiptoeing between background actors until it dawned on me that a welder probably wouldn't tiptoe. So, in my manliest gait, I ambled to the middle of the throng and watched the action. A few people stared at me because my faceplate was down. Perhaps it wasn't the best disguise after all.

A hand grabbed my arm making me jump. I almost screamed but managed to squelch it. I turned and found Kim staring at me. "Tell me everything."

I lifted the clear faceplate and whispered, "OK. Kat's sister is safe in Jenks and a Tulsa police detective is getting ready to interview Kat. I don't know the whole backstory, but according to Jenn, Kat might be capable of orchestrating the problems here." I surveyed the area and said, "Who is directing today?"

She whispered, "Luckily, Mr. Mason flew to LA for the Academy Awards, so it's the blond guy. But why are you here?"

I was relieved to hear Joel Mason wasn't around. I figured he must have gone to support Aaron Winston. I turned back to Kim. "The detective told me to wait in the parking lot, but he'll probably need me, so here I am."

She smirked. "A case of FOMO?"

I shrugged. I always did have a fear of missing out. I watched Rita make her way through the crowd and whisper something to CowboyHatGirl who rolled her eyes. Then she sighed and walked to the blond director. Whatever she said didn't seem to faze him.

He called out, "Kat Hobart?"

Kat turned around. Pleased that the director knew her name, her face brightened. She glowed as she said happily, "Yes?"

"Can you go with Rita? Someone wants to talk to you."

In an instant, her brightness dimmed and her eyebrows turned from thrilled to suspicious. Then, remembering her large audience, she lifted her nose in the air. "Of course!" She followed Rita back to the building, swinging her hips as she walked.

I wanted to follow along and witness the confrontation, but for the life of me couldn't think of how to manage that. Shoot.

The blonde director shouted, "Team 1 in." I really needed to learn his name. He was too nice to just name him a hair color.

I leaned over to the frumpy old lady next to me, lifted the faceplate, and whispered, "What's the name of this director?"

There was a slight pause and the woman said in an annoying voice, "Pity?" I turned to the old woman and saw Shelly's eyes staring from under a gray wig. The rest of her face was unrecognizable with lines drawn in for wrinkles. Her eyes bugged out and she squawked, "You're not supposed to be here! You were banned from the set by Joel Mason himself! I can't believe you snuck in here with that stupid disguise!" One of her gray eyebrows flew off, but I didn't dare laugh.

"Shhh. Shelly. I'm here to solve a kidnapping case."

"Oh, sure you are!" Her face was twisted. "I'm telling on you!"

That didn't surprise me. Shelly was just like an uppity twelve-year-old who thrived on getting others in trouble.

She raised her hand above her head and waved wildly, shouting, "Mr. Hart! Mr. Hart! There's an imposter on the set. She was banned by Mr. Mason but snuck in here wearing a disguise." Then, with a smug expression, she yanked off my mask, took some of my hair with it, and pointed triumphantly at me.

The whole crowd turned and stared. I gave a big sigh and rubbed what I could only assume was a bald spot on my scalp. Mr. Hart (at least I found out his name) walked over to me, parting the crowd like the red sea. I remembered him being a nice guy so could only pray he wouldn't have me arrested. He had a twinkle in his eye when he said, "Hello? Do you have a good story to go along with your get-up?"

Kim stepped forward and said, "She really does."

My sister's confidence was contagious and I stood a little taller. Then I realized Mr. Hart's question wasn't rhetorical and he was waiting for my explanation. I cleared my throat. "I discovered that Kat, the girl who just left, is hiding something. I believe…" I stopped, remembering all the people in earshot. I couldn't make information public before Kat was formally charged. I leaned in and whispered to him, "Well, she's wanted by the police in Alabama for kidnapping and for something else, but I don't know what. TPD is interviewing her now. I'm convinced she had something to do with the incidents that happened here too."

I leaned back and watched Mr. Hart's surprised face. Realizing I hadn't answered his question about my outfit, I added, "Since I was banned from the set, I had to put on a disguise so I could come back and investigate."

A low familiar voice said, "So, she might have had something to do with the fire in my dressing room?" I turned, shocked to see Aaron standing with eyebrows raised. I was so hellbent on explaining myself that I didn't even notice that he and Alison had arrived and were listening in.

So, it was his dressing room that caught fire. I said, "Maybe?"

Aaron cocked his head, "You know, I tend to believe Pity. She's a friend of mine and if she believes this Kat girl is a bad apple, it's most likely true."

I smiled at Aaron, relieved to hear he still liked me. Then I had to back paddle a bit, "We don't know anything for sure yet. It's all speculation."

Alison joined in. "There is definitely something fishy about that Kat girl. She told me she tricked her sister into coming to Oklahoma and that she put something in her boyfriend's drink."

I noticed the old woman, aka Shelly, petting Alison's arm. I made a face at her to stop, but Shelly seemed to have gone into a trance from standing so close to her idol. It was rather hilarious.

Alison finally turned to Shelly and literally shook off the pest, saying, "Excuse me? Would you please leave me alone?"

Shelly snapped out of her stupor and stepped back. Then, I watched as she reached into her old-lady handbag and pulled out her phone. She turned around and took a selfie with Alison in the background. Alison rolled her eyes, and said, "Amateur," then walked away.

Did Alison actually say Kat had put something in her boyfriend's drink? Why would Kat admit that to anybody? I turned to the director, "Excuse me, I have to tell the policeman something. I'm so, so sorry I interrupted your scene. I'll let you get back to work and leave you alone, I promise."

As I turned to leave, Mr. Hart said, "Wait. Weren't you the stand-in for Ms. Baxter before this Kat girl?"

"Yes." I sighed. Of course, he remembered what I did. Reluctantly, I turned back and looked at the ground in shame.

He stepped toward me and said quietly, "If this girl ends up being extradited to Alabama or is suspected of anything here, we can't have her on set. We're about to wrap today, but would you be willing to stand in tomorrow? We're only working a half-day so that Aaron can leave for Los Angeles."

I was shocked and flattered at the request and bubbled, "Of course, I can. But I have to go back to teaching on Monday."

The kind director nodded. "That's okay. We'll have time to find a replacement. Looks like we owe you thanks for finding someone who could be dangerous. So, thank you very much."

I shrugged and said, "You're welcome." I nodded to him and Aaron then walked away beaming.

Kim caught up with me and gave me a soft shove. "Pity's a friend of mine…"

"I know! Can you believe Aaron hasn't given up on me, even after I yelled "cut" the second time? And, I get to come back tomorrow! See? I'm not so crazy after all."

She followed me and kidded, "Yeah, well that's debatable."

As we passed a tall guy and another man wearing a hat, I chuckled to myself. I had been so certain those two guys were up to something. Silly me. But my steps faltered when I realized Kat couldn't have operated alone if she was truly responsible for the murder attempts on set. She would have needed help. I turned back and stared at the two men. Sure enough, the tall one was the same man Kat had been talking to earlier in the week. I gulped and kept walking.

Kim kept up with me. "Where are you going in such a hurry? You are acting like CowboyHatGirl."

"Didn't you hear what Alison said? Kat put something in her boyfriend's drink and now he's missing! I need to tell Officer Matthews. And I may even have more information for him. I need to catch him before he leaves."

She nodded and turned back to the scene being filmed. "Look, I'd better get back in case they need me. Call me later."

"Will do." A moment later I was entering the building where Kat and Rita had gone. As I rushed down the hall, I peeked in doorways looking for the meeting area, but all rooms were empty.

Rita stood by the back door and I asked her, "Can you tell me where Sergeant Matthews and Kat are meeting?"

"They just left. You might catch them in the parking lot, but I'd be careful. That girl is not happy." As if she just realized who she was talking to she said, "Hey, what are you doing here? And what's with the get-up?"

As I stepped through the door, I said, "I'll explain tomorrow. Mr. Hart is letting me come back!"

I zipped out to the parking lot and started looking for my car. When I saw it, I started to run, but my jumpsuit was so baggy I couldn't move very fast. The gray detective car was backing up and I ran towards them, waving my arms. Sadly, Detective Matthews pulled away, leaving me in the dust, figuratively of course, since there was no dust on the pavement.

Looking at my phone's recent calls list, I pushed redial. I leaned on my car to catch my breath and waited for him to pick up. "Detective Matthews." Now I could put his face with that deep voice. I collected my thoughts. "Hi! This is Pity, I mean Kitty. Do you have Kat with you?" I couldn't help think that sounded weird.

"Yes."

"Well, I have more information I haven't told you. Alison Baxter said Kat told her she slipped something into her boyfriend's drink and now he's missing. Doesn't that sound illegal? Maybe you can get her for that. I thought you should know. I also think I know who might have helped her with the murder on set."

"Okay. If we need more information, we'll let you know."

"You have my number, right?"

"Yes."

"Are you trying not to say much because she's there?"

"Nope."

"Is it because it's a secret mission?"

"Nope. Just not a real talker. "

"Oh. Well, keep me informed, please."

He must have gone into a bad zone because the phone went dead before he could answer. I gave a big sigh, satisfied that I had caught the bad girl and had been invited to go back to the set tomorrow. All was right with the world. I drove home, singing along with the radio.

Movie Watching Tip #14
Keep track of your personal belongings.

Exhausted from my afternoon of playing hooky, I arrived home to find an empty house. Ree was still at Caitlyn's and Ren was probably working late on the school newspaper. I hollered "Hi!" to Edgar and opened the back door to get some lovin' from my sweet Harriet. She didn't immediately come to the door, so I figured she must have fallen asleep in the sun. I walked out to my quirky backyard for some fresh air.

While strolling around the row of glass shower doors planted upright like dominos, I looked to see if Harriet was visiting with the neighbor dogs. Nope. I passed the snow-ski-lined tool shed and continued on to the 20 pine trees that lined the back fence. I brushed my hand along the spoons I'd hung from a branch and listened to their lovely tinkling sound. Then breathing in the sweet pine fragrance, I relished in the knowledge that I had solved a kidnapping and possibly a murder.

After stepping around my four colorful bottle trees I made my way beyond the wall of mirrors but didn't see Harriet anywhere. When I reached my tall clump of bamboo, I was pleased to find the plant had survived our icy winter. I peered in the pond, but couldn't see either Dave or Buster in the water. The bright orange koi must have been hiding under a rock.

The last place Harriet might have been was in her dog house. I followed the glass brick path to her home I'd spray painted periwinkle blue and peeked inside. Still no pup. Where was she?

After edging my way along the side yard to the gate, I found it open! We rarely left our gate open but if we did, Harriet wouldn't leave her oasis for long. I ran around to the front yard calling her name, but she wasn't on the front porch or anywhere to be seen.

I gasped. Somebody must have stolen my baby, my sweet dog I rescued from the pound just after my divorce eight years ago. She has been my confidant all these years. I rushed inside, grabbed my phone, and called the police. While I waited for them to arrive, I checked the backyard one more time but didn't find a trace of her. Why would someone snatch her from our yard? She wasn't the type people steal for dog fights and definitely wasn't a show dog. In fact, once a man at the dog park said, "Now that's a face only a mother could love." I disagreed. For one thing, you couldn't even see her face with all the hair, and furthermore, everyone who knows Harriet thinks she's adorable.

I sucked in my breath. What if Kat stole her? But that was ridiculous, she didn't know where I lived and besides, she was with the police now.

I couldn't just sit idly by waiting, so I went to my computer and made a bunch of "Missing Dog" posters with a photo of Harriet and my phone number. My mind reeled as I fretted.

I went downstairs just as the door opened. Ree and Caitlyn entered and behind them was Caitlyn's Grandpa Brian, who had brought them home. He was holding a box of art supplies and his granddaughter's overnight bag, while the girls carried their backpacks.

I hugged Ree and choked out, "Harriet is missing. I think she may have been dognapped." How weird that I dealt with two possible "nappings" in one day.

I continued, "The police will be here soon. Would you girls go hang these signs up in the neighborhood?" I handed them the flyers and gave them a staple gun.

Ree's eyes started to fill with tears. Brian, said, "I'll be glad to drive the lasses around to post the flyers."

His adorable Irish accent always made me smile, but today I was too upset to enjoy it.

"Thank you, Brian. I'll stay here and wait for the police."

They walked to his luxurious BMW and he said, "We'll keep an eye out for your wee doggie."

Within minutes, a police car drove up. I ran to the officer and as soon as he opened his door, I said, "Somebody stole our dog. She's a 50-pound shaggy sheepdog." I handed him a few pictures. In most of them, her hair covered her eyes.

He stood to his full height which seemed to be 6'5". I was momentarily taken aback by his rugged good looks, but shook it off and squeaked, "She's my best friend."

He said with a smile, "She looks kind of like a mop," but he wrote a report on our missing dog. After I showed him the open gate, the handsome Officer Potter, (I read his name tag) said "We'll look for your special hairy pup."

He was about to leave when Ren drove up from school and walked over to us. She said warily, "Mom, what's wrong?"

A tear escaped my eye as I said with a shaky voice, "Honey, I'm so sorry to tell you this, but Harriet is missing. She may have been dognapped."

Ren closed her eyes and hung her head. I put my hand on her shoulder to comfort her. When she opened her eyes, tears stained her face, but instead of crying, she said with uncontrollable laughter, "Mom, don't you remember last week when you asked me to take her to the groomer today? Well, I took her a few hours ago."

My first reaction was Hallelujah, my loveable Harriet was just getting a bath and not being held for ransom by a madman. Then, I felt complete humiliation. I turned to see the policeman smirk and rip up the report.

He smiled and said, "It's okay, I'm glad you found your shaggy baby. He gave me a sweet nod and walked to his patrol car.

In my extreme embarrassment, I managed, "Thank you?" just before he shut his door.

Ren looked me in the eyes and said, "I should write a book about all of your crazy stunts."

It was true. I was a dope. "Let's go inside." I started up the driveway and stopped short with my mouth open wide. "Oh no! Ree!"

Ren asked, "What? Was she kidnapped too?" Her smirk was not welcome.

"No, she's posting lost dog flyers." I ran to the garage to get my car and try to flag down Brian, but I heard the trio come in the front door.

I didn't particularly want to be present when Ren told them how stupid her mom was, so I quickly maneuvered my bug around his new luxury car so I could take down the flyers myself.

As I pulled down the last sign, I got a call from Paw Magic saying Harriet was ready to be picked up, so I drove straight there to retrieve my baby. I smiled as I entered, despite the combined smell of perfume and wet dog. A new receptionist stood at the counter, wearing a pink, poodle-covered smock.

"I'm here to get my shaggy sheepdog, Harriet."

She gave a little laugh and handed me the bill. I added a tip and paid with my card. The girl turned around and said, "I'll get her."

A man entered and nodded as he stood behind me. He was probably picking up his dog too. When the woman returned, she led a large, short-haired gray dog. She held out the leash.

I moved out of the way so the man could take it. He shook his head and she held the leash up to me. I waved her off. "Oh, that's not my dog."

"Yes, it is."

Was she delirious? I said calmly, "No, mine has long white hair." Seriously, this dog's hair was no more than an inch long. It was cute and wagged its tail happily, but it sure wasn't mine.

She tapped her toe. "Ma'am. This is your dog. We used a size four blade."

I shook my head. "No. That's not Harriet."

Upon hearing the name, the strange dog pulled on the leash and tried to get to me. Suddenly I recognized those big brown eyes. Could it be Harriet? Confused, I leaned down and cocked my head. "Harriet?" She jumped into my arms and slobbered on my face. It was indeed my angel. She had just transformed into a completely different dog without hair.

I was in disbelief. "Why did you cut her hair?" My mind was reeling and I couldn't calm down. Then I added before the girl could answer, "All I wanted was a wash and dry and to have her toenails clipped."

She shrugged, "The girl who brought her in said to do the usual. We didn't have records for her. For us, the usual is a wash and haircut."

"Well, I don't know why you don't have records. We've been coming here for years."

She rolled her eyes as she walked around the counter. "What's the last name?"

Kole with a K.

She screwed up her mouth as she flipped farther back in the card file. "Oh. Here it is in the K's. I must have looked in the C's." She shrugged and said, "Well, I mean, she was in dire need of a haircut."

I glared at her. "No, she was not. She was perfect." Then I took a deep breath and told myself, her hair would grow back. Harriet seemed fine so I calmly said, "It's alright."

She smiled sheepishly, "I can give you a coupon for your next grooming if you aren't satisfied?"

I never turn down a coupon. "Okay, but can you please make a note on her chart to leave the hair long from now on?"

As I drove Harriet home, she looked out the window panting happily. It may have been the first time she could see clearly without hair in her eyes. When I walked her into the house, Ree did a double take. Ren said, "What the hell?" And Caitlyn stared.

Harriet was the only one who didn't seem to mind her haircut. After the shock wore off, we were all so happy to have her back again that we didn't care how she looked. I relaxed in the recliner and turned on the TV before fixing dinner. Every now and then, I caught a glimpse of my dog and thought there was a stranger in my house.

The doorbell rang and Ree and Caitlyn raced to the door. After they opened it, they were unusually quiet until Ree said, "Mom?"

I answered. "Ree?"

"Umm, you need to come here."

I trudged over to the door to find out what had silenced the normally noisy teens. As I approached, they stepped aside to reveal a massive black limousine that took up our entire driveway. What the? A stocky stoic man, wearing a cap and black suit, stood outside the driver's door. I turned my head to see the girl's faces agog. Could it be that Aaron sent a limousine for me? My heart started racing and I yelled to the driver, "I'll be ready in a minute."

I hurried to the bedroom, where I combed my hair and changed into my cutest little black dress. I threw on some earrings and applied make-up. As I put on the black shoes I wore for Saturday's blind date, my excitement withered. I looked at the clock and saw that it was six. I sighed. The person in the limo was probably not Aaron Winston, but Kenny. My heart sank. Duh...the flowers had been delivered yesterday, so "tomorrow night" was actually now.

My spurt of energy also dissipated as if I had been zapped. I'd lost all interest in going out, but here I was, dressed up and a limo awaited me. I walked to the teens, who whistled at my appearance. I frowned and admitted, "I thought it was Aaron Winston, but it's probably Kenny, the guy from my blind date Saturday."

Ren chuckled and said, "You're a nut, Mom. Why would it be Aaron Winston?"

She made a good point. Why would it be him? I shrugged and said, "Wishful thinking, I guess."

Ree said, "Who cares? You get to ride in a limo, Mom!"

Caitlyn agreed, "Yeah, that's cool, Mrs. Kole. You'll have to tell us about it when you get home."

I took a deep breath and said, "I'm sorry I won't be here for dinner again. Can you handle it on your own?"

Ree pushed me out the door. "Yes. Go see who's in the limo."

I shrugged and stepped down the driveway to the long black vehicle. When I reached the front door, I could only see my reflection in the dark shiny windows. I nodded to the driver as he opened the back door for me. I bent down to peek in. Sure enough, it was Kenny. He yelled, "Surprise!"

I gave a polite smile to the bland-looking man. He wore both a goofy smile and the same shirt he'd worn Saturday night, but this time it was buttoned up to his neck. Oh, fun.

"Hello, Kitty. I thought you deserved a special ride for our special date. And…this is for you." He pulled an enormous bundle of pink flowers from behind his back. Upon closer inspection, I realized it was a wrist corsage. I wondered how I could wear something so big on my arm and forced a smile as I took the huge pink grouping from him.

"Hi, Kenny. Thanks. I sure wasn't expecting a limousine."

"I wanted to treat you to an evening full of surprises. Sit wherever you would prefer." He motioned across the large space.

I'd either need to sit on the seat beside Kenny or ride facing backward which would make me carsick. I stepped into the vehicle and sat next to him. I was tired, but it was my first ride in a limo. I might as well enjoy the experience.

Kenny lifted a lever and two metal trays magically appeared; one with an assortment of crackers and cheese and the other with glasses half full of light-colored liquid. My eyes lit up. Although I don't particularly like champagne, I could sure use a drink to help me relax. I lifted a glass, feeling rather elegant, but the first sip told me it wasn't champagne.

"Is this… apple juice?"

"Yes. They have a choice of every kind of drink imaginable, but I thought we should enjoy some of nature's nectar as we go to our first location in Tulsa."

Nature's nectar? Great. I mean, it was cold and sweet, but alcohol would have been better today, especially while riding in a limo. I looked at the other silver tray, happy to find my favorite cheese, smoked gouda, as a choice. Maybe the evening wouldn't be so bad.

I was amazed at how smooth the ride was. I snacked and watched out the window as I entered Tulsa for the third time today. Through the tinted windows, the city seemed to glow. What made the drive seem surreal was the lack of street noise. It was like gliding through town in a bubble.

When I noticed other drivers staring at the car, a little jolt of excitement went through me. They probably thought we were celebrities.

"Our first stop will be brief. I'm excited to have you meet the author of the new book, 'How to Solve a Sudoku Puzzle in Under 10 Minutes.' She has a book signing at T-Town Books!"

"Hmm," I nodded, wondering why he thought a book like that would interest me? I have tried Sudoku puzzles twice before but gave up both times since I had no patience or aptitude for the puzzles. Now if it was an author like Stephen King or Sophie Kinsella, I'd claw my way to the front of the line. Oh well, I was up for a new experience.

The chauffeur pulled right in front of the entrance to the bookstore. Then he opened my door. With a polite smile, the tall man held his gloved hand out to me.

Before I took it, Kenny said, "Wait! Your corsage!" He fumbled as he slid the enormous bouquet onto my arm. Once my wrist was fully donned with the hideous pink corsage, I took the driver's hand and exited like a princess. I could get used to that!

Kenny followed me as I walked into the book store. He said, "Did you notice I wore the same shirt as Saturday night?"

"Oh, yes! I see that." I nodded my head as if it hadn't been my first thought.

"You said you liked it, so I thought I would wear it again just for you."

I managed to produce a smile at his strange logic.

Inside the store, two people were in line to have books signed by a lady with frizzy gray hair and a wrinkled jacket. I got in the short queue feeling over-dressed. I was also a bit embarrassed by the formal mode of transportation.

When I reached the table, the sudoku puzzle author said, "Which of my books would you like to buy?"

I looked at the display of the five books she offered and opened my mouth wondering how I could politely say, 'None thank you', but Kenny answered with, "We want two of each of your books."

I turned to him and said, "No, Kenny, I don't need any books. Just get some for yourself."

"Nonsense. This is your night. You get the royal treatment."

The woman brightened and asked sweetly, "And what is your name, you lucky, lucky girl?"

I quickly tried to think of anyone I knew who liked Sudoku that I could give the books to, but couldn't come up with anyone, so I suggested, "How about you just write, 'friend?'"

She opened 'The History of Sudoku' and carefully wrote a greeting that filled half of the first page, then she began to inscribe the other four books. While waiting, I wondered what the rest of the evening would hold. I kind of wished I had stayed home since I had to get up early for filming and I only had two days to prepare for my Oscar party.

Once the woman had signed all of my books, I thanked her. While she worked on Kenny's stack, I held mine, trying not to smush the enormous bunch of flowers on my wrist. I stepped over to the table stacked with newly released fiction novels and wished he had offered to buy me one of those instead of the puzzle books. Stop it, Pity. You are being ungrateful.

Kenny appeared, standing uncomfortably close to me with his new books in hand. "Ready for the second surprise of the night?"

"Sure." I smiled appreciatively. "And thank you so much for the books."

I usually love surprises, but if all of his "surprises" were as exciting as this, I wasn't sure I could take it. He motioned to the door where we met the chauffer he called "Roberto." As I stepped inside the luxurious vehicle, I took a closer look at its opulence. It must have been new because the scent of leather was very strong. I rubbed the smooth seat and was impressed that Aaron and Alison got to ride in this kind of luxury every day. I looked at Kenny sitting next to me. He wasn't bad looking. He had an average, albeit extremely pale, face with dark blond hair that was a bit long and looked like he might have cut it himself. His clothing choice was off-putting to me; dressed in pleated khakis and his repeat shirt buttoned up to his neck. It looked very uncomfortable. He reminded me of some characters from the show, 'Big Bang Theory'.

I tried to think of a way to start a polite conversation. "So, have you lived in Broken Arrow long, Kenny?"

"I've been here for 7¾ years. My brother and I are from Oklahoma City."

"Oh?" All I could think was how he added a fraction to count his years. Who counts years in fourths?

He continued, "We went to Oklahoma City Preparatory School, then I went on to Dartmouth where I studied Egyptology. A critical study of the ancient cultures from 3400 B.C.E. to 100 in the Common Era...."

As soon as I heard Egyptology, I zoned out. I remembered his long, one-sided discussion about the different thicknesses of menu paper at dinner last week and knew it was about to go on and on. My eyes would have glazed over, but luckily, there were beautiful city lights to focus on as we approached downtown.

I hoped against hope he would take me somewhere interesting this time. As he droned on, I tried to pay attention, but when I heard the phrase, "captain of my chess team", I tuned out again. I was mindful to nod every now and then. At one point, I heard him say his father had invented some oil field part.

"What have you been doing lately, my dear?"

It took me a while to realize Kenny had asked me a question. The only person I'd ever known to call me 'My Dear' was little Mrs. Garmin and she was 80. I turned to him. "I've actually been working as an extra on the set of the movie being filmed in town, 'Crude Town'."

"Well, I'd better keep a close eye on you or you'll get snatched up and made into a movie star." He chuckled as he patted my shoulder awkwardly.

I smiled at his compliment and imagined being discovered, then pictured my name on a marquee next to Aaron Winston. But then Kenny ruined everything by crooning, "You are the most beautiful woman I've ever seen." I opened my eyes to find him staring at me with obvious adoration.

I scrambled to think of how to politely point out I didn't feel the same way about him, but the car slowed and stopped, saving me for the moment. There, just outside my door was the convention center with an enormous banner reading "Repticon: A World of Reptiles." While I scrunched my face in horror, Kenny turned giddy.

A smile engulfed his face. "I thought we could look around here and grab a bite to eat, then go to our final destination."

I was aghast. We were not going to a reptile show, were we? Maybe something else was going on in the huge event complex.

I quickly said, "Kenny, I can't stay out late. I have to get up early tomorrow."

He patted my arm. "Oh, that's fine. I never stay up past ten. We can leave whenever you want. You're going to love seeing the world's largest albino alligator."

I had absolutely no interest in looking at alligators or any kind of reptiles, especially snakes. Although I like our iguana, the only reason we have Iggy is that a friend didn't have room for her huge aquarium anymore and Ree begged me to take her in.

I made a sorry attempt at a smile as we exited the limousine. The enormous lobby of the Tulsa Convention Center was plastered with banners advertising snake clubs, amphibian groups, and exotic pet stores. Kenny walked to a table and paid the entrance fee for both of us and we were off for what he called "the adventure of a lifetime".

I expected to see information booths and aquariums displaying reptiles for sale. What I didn't anticipate were shoppers casually walking around holding their creepy crawlies. I nearly bumped into a boa constrictor wrapped around a guy's neck. As I jumped back, I came face to face with a large lizard that stuck out its bright blue forked tongue at me. When I couldn't help but make a horrified face, the owner gave me a weird smile and caressed the creature to show me its tame nature.

As much as I didn't want to, I opted to stay close to Kenny at the nightmare of a convention. When he spent far too long watching the featured giant white gator, I wondered if it was too early to say I wanted to go home. As I rubbed my tired eyes, trying to erase the vision of reptiles from my mind, I felt something tugging at my wrist. I looked down to find a huge bearded dragon eating the flowers from my corsage. Resisting the urge to scream, I leapt over to Kenny and blurted, "I'm ready to leave now."

He grinned, "Not before I buy you a t-shirt." Kenny took my hand in his sweaty grip and pulled me over to a table that had hundreds of shirts with silly reptile puns. He motioned to the stacks and said, "Choose whatever you want!"

I didn't want a shirt but figured I'd better pick one or we would never get to leave. One read, 'I have a reptile dysfunction.' I sure hoped he didn't choose that one. After searching through many stupid sayings, I finally found a cute one; 'What's a reptile's favorite movie? The Lizard of Oz.' I pointed to one in my size. He snatched it up and paid for it along with another for himself.

In a flash, he threw his new bright orange t-shirt on over his button-up. I read the saying on his shirt. It read, 'You are one in a chameleon.' He pointed to me and winked.

I fake chuckled a "Hehe"

"Put on your shirt!" He lifted his eyebrows so high I thought he might knock his glasses off.

Seriously? I said, "Over my dress? Um. I'm sorry Kenny, but I'd really rather not. It's really cute, though. Thanks." I stowed the shirt in my purse.

My stomach growled and I said, "You know, I'm getting pretty hungry. Any chance we could go somewhere to eat?"

"Of course. I have friends who are saving us a place."

I wondered who his friends were and what restaurant we might end up at. There are so many cool pubs nearby. I started to walk toward the lobby door, but Kenny turned me around and led me back to an elevator. When we entered, he pushed the up button. Oh no. Don't tell me we were going to eat in the convention center.

While riding up the empty elevator, he gave me an oddly seductive stare. All I could think was, please don't make a move. Please don't make a move. But Kenny moved toward me. Before I could duck, he patted my head as if I were a child or a dog. He said with his voice quivering, "Your hair is so lovely."

Movie Watching Tip #15
Don't be disappointed if the plot isn't what you expect.

That did it. I could never ever go out with Kenny again. He was kind, seemed smart and obviously wealthy, but we had nothing at all in common. Plus, if my first reaction is to duck when a guy reaches out to me, there is a problem. I'd just have to make it through the rest of the evening and be done with him.

The elevator doors opened to a large room with a buffet set up on one side, a drink station on the other and about 25 people milling about. A man in a black apron walked up to Kenny and said, "Mr. Dicks, everything is ready. Would you like to inspect the line before we invite people to eat?"

OMG, I had forgotten Kenny's last name was Dicks. How unfortunate. Then I wondered why Kenny would have to inspect the food? I watched as my date walked along the table, nodding and giving a big thumbs up to the man I assumed to be the caterer.

Kenny said aloud, "You, my love, get to be first." The other guests stared at me. I couldn't exactly argue with him in front of his friends, so I smiled and got a plate. I was sure my face was red because I felt embarrassed with the attention.

The food was well presented and smelled amazing. Why, there was more salad, roast beef, potatoes, and asparagus here than these people could eat in a week. I stood, holding my filled plate, and waited for Kenny to direct me to his friends' table. Instead, he waved his hand across the room as if I should choose any seat. I walked to an empty table, put my plate down, then went to get a drink. I took a glass of iced tea and sat down, looking forward to the caffeine. Again, I was wrong. It was Kenny's favorite, good old 'nectar of the earth'.

When he joined me, I said, "So, how do you know these people?"

Kenny shrugged. "Well, I don't actually know them. I sponsor a reptile watching club, but I can't go to the outings because I'm allergic to pine and many of the watching areas have pine trees. So, I thought I'd treat them to dinner tonight."

This evening was getting more and more bizarre. Did he have any friends at all? I took a bite of the delicious beef and said, "Well, that was very nice of you to buy them dinner, but I think you ordered enough for my whole school to eat, Kenny. You are going to have mega leftovers."

He smiled as if I'd said something funny. "I love to hear you say my name."

That shut me up and we spent the rest of the meal in silence. It was hard to cut my meat while wearing a corsage on my wrist. I should thank the lizard for thinning them out so much. A plumeria fell in my potatoes at one point, but I managed to eat around the flower. The other guests were busy visiting and not one of them talked to us, which was totally fine with me.

When we finished eating, Kenny gave a check to the caterer and talked to him a while. I can't imagine how much this huge spread must have cost. He came back and said, "Time to go to your final destination."

As we rode in the limo to the last location, I wondered why in the world Kenny hadn't just driven a car? None of these places was limo-worthy. Sure, it was fun to see how the rich folk traveled, but all I could think of was how much more fun I'd have to ride in the limo with my girls, Lin, Kim, or for that matter, anyone besides Kenny. Be nice, Pity.

The drive was short. When we stopped, I peered out the window, excited to see a cool coffee shop. Maybe I could at least have something to drink other than apple juice tonight.

Roberto helped me out and I practically skipped to the door in anticipation of something more my style. Although a pub would have been even more exciting.

Kenny followed me in and the hostess nodded at him. She took us to a table right up front, near a stage. Cool! Live music? Wait. Not so fast. A woman with frizzy gray hair, resembling the Sudoku lady, stepped up to the microphone. "Welcome to Poetry Night, A time to share your favorite poem, whether an original, written by you, or a classic penned by one of the greats."

I tried to keep an open mind, since I have written over a hundred songs and lyrics are similar to poetry. Maybe there would be some clever wordplay. The woman cleared a frog in her throat and said, "Our first reader is Jerry Muldune, who will read one of my all-time favorites by Ann Bradstreet."

A man in an argyle sweater vest stepped to the stage and opened a book. He took a deep breath and began to read, "As Spring the Winter Doth Succeed." I listened carefully, trying to catch the meaning behind the poem, which was, I assumed, about the upcoming Spring, but some of the words were unfamiliar to me. What in the world did 'succored' mean? After he finished, there was a polite spattering of applause.

The emcee returned to the mic. "And now, Star Fannin will recite a poem she wrote about her cat."

A tall black woman with a purple scarf tied around her head swished her long colorful skirt as she moved by our table. She leapt onto the stage in a catlike manner, and by memory recited 'Ode to Marmalade', "With every flick of your sandpaper tongue, I felt your love. Your soul spoke to me with every purr. We were one and the same Cat/Woman/Cat/Woman. How can I wake without your whiskers tickling my lips?"

The more she described her love affair with Marmalade, the more disturbed I got. By the end of her monologue, she was weeping. Everyone but me clapped enthusiastically.

The emcee introduced the third reader who was to recite a free verse about a trash can lid. I tried to listen to the poem, if you can call it that. It didn't even rhyme. It went on forever, so I pulled out my phone and started looking at new outfits for my bitmoji. A text from Kim popped up. "R.A. is coming back tomorrow, cast as an old man extra." She added a laughing emoji and "See you tomorrow!"

I sent a thumbs up and wondered what you had to do to get a drink around here? Since Kenny seemed to be enthralled with the avant-garde trash can lid poem, I excused myself and wove through the small tables to the coffee bar where the barista yawned, probably as bored as I was. I whispered my order and paid her. I enjoyed watching her make the two cups of decaf caramel macchiato much more than listening to the boring poem. The man droned on with occasional bursts of banging noises.

I took the drinks to our table and handed one to Kenny. He put his hand to his mouth in disbelief and looked like he might cry. I wanted to say, "Let's go", but when I looked at my watch, it was only 8:45. That amazed me since it felt like midnight. So, I sat back down and focused on my hot, yummy drink. With my eyes closed, I imagined listening to jazz in a pub in New York City. When people clapped, I snapped out of it and heard the announcer say, "Our next reader is Kenny Dicks."

My jaw dropped as Kenny rose to his feet. He nodded at me and stepped up to the stage, facing the audience with a calm, self-assured air. He spoke softly, "My heart in her hands, the sun in her smile, she warms me with care, passion and style."

He read his poem with confidence and I was pleasantly surprised. I continued to drink my coffee and listen. "From the moment we met, I trusted my soul to the sweet, sweet love of Kitty Kole."

I sucked in my coffee, sputtered and coughed. A man behind me patted my back which helped with the choking, but it didn't change the horror I felt hearing the poem Kenny wrote about me!

Once recovered, I ducked down trying to make myself disappear. I knew my face was turning red with embarrassment, but Kenny continued with flowery statements about our love.

Love? It was only our second date, and most definitely our last! He had gone way too far this time. When he finished, he got a great reception from everyone except me.

Kenny beamed as he returned to our table. I grabbed his hand and led him out the door onto the sidewalk. I looked him straight in his eyes and said, "I can't believe you did that. You don't even know me, Kenny. And to be honest, I don't feel that way at all about you." There. I had said it.

He looked at me and said, "Don't worry. I understand. You may not feel the same as I do right now, but in time you might."

I shook my head but tried to force a smile, "I don't think so. You are a very nice person. I appreciate all you've done for me: the flowers, the corsage, the Limo ride, the books, and the t-shirt. But none of those things will change my mind. I'm just not interested at this time." Adding 'at this time' was the least I could say in order to keep from hurting his feelings too much.

He nodded, seemingly non-plussed by my declaration.

I said, "Look, I'm ready to go home. Tomorrow is going to be a long day and I have company coming on Sunday. I have to get the house ready and prepare a lot of food." I wasn't about to tell him I was hosting a party, or he might show up.

He said with a smile, "Well, let's go then." He flicked his hand for Roberto to come pick us up. As we walked to the limo, I heard a loud group of people walking into a pub next door. I was shocked to see Alison Baxter and Aaron Winston among them." When Aaron caught sight of me, I gave a little wave. He nodded back with an eyebrow raised as I got in the limousine. I would have given my right arm to stay with them rather than take another ride with my obsessive date.

I spent the ride home gathering my "goodies" and thinking back on the evening. Was it really that bad? I mean it was flattering, albeit creepy, that someone wrote a poem about me. Plus, dinner was really good even if it lacked the ambiance and company I like. Furthermore, I got a t-shirt and books to give away as gifts. And I saw Aaron. I'll chalk it up to experience.

Roberto pulled into my driveway and opened my door with a smile. "Here you go, Ma'am."

"Thank you, Roberto. You have been very sweet."

He nodded. "Take care of yourself."

Kenny stepped out and walked me to the door. He said, "Thank you so much for coming with me tonight."

I said, "You put a lot of money and planning into the evening. Thank you for the meal and presents."

"If you let me, I will shower you with gifts, Kitty."

I sighed and looked him right in the eye, feeling like I was getting ready to reprimand a 3rd grader who refused to follow directions, "Kenny. We talked about this. I don't need gifts, I need space."

He straightened his glasses and nodded, "Right. Got it. I have several business trips in the next few months and that will give you a chance to miss me." He nodded his head and said, "Have a nice evening, My Dear."

OMG. With a "Thanks again," I closed the door behind me.

"Ree and Caitlyn barreled around the corner. They pelted me with questions so fast, I wasn't sure who asked what. "How was it? Was the Limo cool? Did you go somewhere fancy for dinner? Did you feel like a movie star? What's in the bags?" They were so excited, I had to laugh. I sure wish they had gone instead of me.

Which question to answer first? I said, "Limousine was nice, but not too exciting. Didn't feel like a movie star. No fancy restaurant." That was an understatement. "I got you a t-shirt, Ree. Caitlyn, if you like sudoku, you can have one of the books I got."

Harriet, who still shocked me with her new look, was as excited to see me as the girls, but she was much less vocal. She pranced as she followed me to my recliner and licked my face. Funny how I didn't duck when her slobbery tongue came at my cheek, and yet just the thought of a kiss from Kenny caused me to repel.

I reclined as the girls ran off to Ree's bedroom with my bag, then I focused on an episode of Dateline that was just wrapping up. I know I shouldn't watch that show because it always pumped up my imagination.

Maybe there would soon be an episode called "The Missing Alabama Twins." I imagined Keith Morrison leaning against the wall with his distinctive voice, "What drove Kat to kidnap her sister? Was she protecting her twin or was it something much more sinister?"

Just before the ten o'clock news aired, I got a call from Rita. "Sorry it's so late, Kitty, but I wanted to tell you the start time for tomorrow. We'll need you from 7:00 until 2:00. Also, do you have any other friends that might want to work tomorrow? Maybe someone easier to work with than your friend, Shelly?" She gave a little laugh.

I was glad Rita couldn't see my face as I stammered, "I meant to tell you, she is not my friend, despite what she said. But I do have an actual friend named Lin, who might be free tomorrow. I gave her Lin's phone number, thinking how much fun it would be to have my best friend on set with me."

"Thanks! I'll see you at seven in your regular outfit…not the disguise."

I laughed briefly and hung up before going to my bedroom to watch the news. Harriet followed and in a moment of weakness, I let her join me on the bed. She curled up at my feet, leaving no room for my legs. At least she smelled good after her bath. I dealt with the lack of space by leaning against my headboard.

The lead news story on TV was about a robbery at a convenience store. Then, there was a feel-good story about a kid raising money to buy blankets for homeless people. I jotted the number down to make a donation as the anchor began to talk about "Crude Town."

He said, "The drama continued today on the movie 'Crude Town'. Not only has there been an accidental death and a dressing room fire, today the girl working as the stand-in for Alison Baxter was arrested." Good. I'm glad she was officially charged. Then I remembered I had told everyone I was the stand in for Alison.

Now my friends would think it was me who was arrested. But the next thing out of the anchor's mouth was, "One local extra, Kitty Kole, was instrumental in the arrest of Katherine Hobart." A trio of photos popped up, two taken from the internet story of Kat and Jenn and the third picture was of me. Unfortunately, it was the terrible photo taken at the audition. It looked like a mugshot from a DUI.

The announcer continued, "Katherine Hobart is wanted in Alabama for the disappearance of her twin sister, Jennifer Hobart. Ms. Kole was the one who found the missing sister in Jenks. Another warrant for additional crimes is out for the suspect, known as Kat. She will be extradited to Alabama tomorrow." I ran the news report back and recorded the report on my DVR.

"Oh My Gosh, Harriet, I was on TV!" I ruffled the dog's short hair, an act not nearly as satisfying as it was with her long hair. She looked at me briefly and then lay her head down, hoping I wouldn't make her get off the bed.

My phone buzzed with a text from Kim. "Wow! You're famous!" It was the first of many texts.

I chuckled as I read Lin's text. "Girl, you got some 'splainin' to do. See you tomorrow!"

Then I got one from Becca. "Worst picture ever. But congrats, sleuth!"

I got a few more messages and was amazed by my sudden fame. After the messages stopped, I fell asleep immediately.

In the morning I found my crumpled 60's outfit on the closet floor and put it on. It hadn't been washed, but it wasn't that wrinkled and it smelled okay. I sprayed it with a bit of perfume, just to make sure.

I arrived on time and walked up to Rita, holding my head a little higher than normal. I could be sort of a celebrity around these parts because of the news report, but nobody even mentioned it. Rita was happy to see me though and said, "Back in your usual get up, I see."

"Hi, Rita. Yes. I'm here legally this time."

She laughed and said, "After Hair and Makeup, go to the holding area and wait for directions."

I skipped over to Hair, where I found Lin with a new bouffant do. She squealed when she saw me and just like a sorority girl, I made the same annoying noise. She headed to Make-up, while my pink-haired stylist began on my hair.

When Kim appeared, I gave her an excited thumbs-up but couldn't move much while being teased and prodded.

After getting gussied up, I took on a more dignified presence and made my way to the pavilion for a day of serious acting. The great domed building was filled with people, some I'd seen before and some new. I hunted for Lin but didn't see her. There was no sign of Pat either. I vowed not to suspect anyone now that Kat was in captivity. I would just relax and enjoy the experience.

With a cup of coffee in hand, I stood and waited for someone familiar to arrive. CowboyHatGirl stormed in with her usual flair. I tapped her on the shoulder and she whipped around so fast that her hat nearly fell off. She lifted her eyebrows.

"Um. Should I have a script today? And is Pat here?"

"Yeah, he's got yours in the cafeteria." She turned back and started hollering directions at a group of extras.

I walked to the next building and snuck up behind Pat. "I'm back!"

He turned around and peered over his glasses at me. "Man, the first stand-in is killed and the second gets arrested...what's my fate going to be?"

"You just wait and see!" I gave him a maniacal laugh.

He smiled and handed me the script. "You won't believe it, but the first scene today is to be filmed on top of the I.P.E. building."

Did I hear him right? I said, "How do we even get up there?"

He shrugged. "Beats me. Here, read this." He leaned over pointing to the description of what we were supposed to do.

I had only read the first few words when CowboyHatGirl rushed in and said, "Team 2, this way!"

She led us inside the large building and started climbing up a super tall vertical ladder. It looked like the one in my parent's garage that I hate climbing, but way taller. I hesitated then followed. Since my upper body strength is pathetic, I had trouble pulling myself straight up. When I finally reached the top, I stepped out onto the slightly pitched roof and looked for something to hold onto. Luckily, there was no wind. With the slope and my fear of heights, I was afraid a slight breeze would put me over the edge, literally.

I moved away from the ledge and said to our leader, "A handrail would be nice."

Cowboyhatgirl scoffed, "Maybe when you're a star. For now, just don't fall." She pointed to a spot for us to stand. When Pat and I were put to work, we didn't do much but walk back and forth. I could only hope the actual scene would be more interesting than what we were doing. Again, I was glad I wore Mom's sensible flat shoes but still was careful not to lose my footing.

Surprisingly, Aaron and Alison climbed the same steep ladder just the way we had. I was impressed. Aaron gave me a wink and a smile. Alison even gave me a little wave, which surprised me. Maybe seeing me getting in a limo had impressed them.

Pat took my arm as we stepped behind the cameras to watch. It didn't take long to see why. We were only a few feet from the edge of the roof and a 30-foot drop-off.

I know they film movies out of order, but this must have been the final scene of the movie because Aaron said goodbye to Alison. He looked as though he would jump. I wished I had read the script beforehand because I was terrified the scene would take a tragic turn. With real tears streaming down her perfect cheeks, Alison begged him not to jump but in a shocking moment, he did!

I was dumbfounded. What in the world? Then, in a burst of noise and wind, a helicopter rose from where Aaron had jumped. There he was, standing in the doorway of the chopper, waving at

Alison. She wiped her eyes, laughed, and blew kisses as the copter flew away.

I watched, mesmerized, as they filmed the whole crazy scene a few times. What an exciting ending.

On the 3rd take, I saw movement out of the corner of my eye and turned, expecting to see a bird. What else would be up so high? About 10 feet above my head, two men were climbing the oil derrick. They were at the fake Golden Driller's waist. What were they doing? I squinted as I tried to see between the steel girders. Was that the tall guy and hat guy I'd suspected earlier? They both wore black and carried tools of some sort. Odd.

I nudged Pat and pointed to the guys. He looked, shrugged, and turned back to the actors.

I watched the two workers a bit more wondering how high there were in the air. The four-sided framework of the oil derrick had six sets of X-shaped steel crossbars. Each X was about 8 feet tall. Since the guys were in the 5th X, I calculated they were about 40 feet off the ground. Just looking at them up there made me dizzy. I sure hoped those guys were paid well to work so high up with no safety net. I guess I should feel lucky to stand safely on a fairly flat surface.

Movie Watching Tip #16
Give credit to stunt performers.

I turned back around from gawking at the workers and watched the stars. It wasn't much longer when the blond director announced, "Cut. Print! Take 30 minutes and on to Scene 8."

I followed Pat back down the steep ladder and was relieved to be on solid ground again. We walked to craft catering where I grabbed a muffin and bottle of water. I saw my brother-in-law sitting at a table dressed like an old man in a suit and fedora. Across from him sat a guy, who I hoped was his sound man friend. I rushed over to R.A and upon closer inspection, I saw heavy wrinkles had been drawn on his face. He truly looked old. I said, "Hey old man, at least they didn't have to color in your white beard this time." I asked, "Is this your friend?"

He nodded and said in a gravely old man's voice. "You bet your sweet bippy, little youngin'. This is Jesse. And this is my sister-in-law, Pity, and her cohort, Pat."

Jesse nodded at us and I sat next to him while Pat took the chair by R.A. Jesse appeared to be in his 40's with beautiful skin the color of chocolate milk. I said, "So, I heard you may have taken some video from the day of the accident?"

He pulled out his phone. "Yeah. Ray said you wanted to see them. Now, to clarify, I was just filming the equipment and the order of events for reference when I make my independent movie next month. I'm sure there's nothing you'll find very interesting." He knitted his brows. "But I could be fired for having this."

I made a face. "Understood. I won't tell anyone. I just need to see it. Wait. Did you just call him Ray?"

"Yeah. It takes too long to say R.A."

My brother-in-law smirked. "It's better than some other things he's called me."

I smiled at the two who obviously knew each other well. Jesse scrolled through the videos, cued one up, and handed his phone over to me. He said, "I didn't film the guy getting squashed."

I nodded. "Good. I don't ever want to see that again."

I opened my bottle, took a drink, and sat back, relaxing in the plastic chair as best I could. I turned the phone on its side so the picture filled the screen and watched the first video:

Close-up on the boom operator.

Pan to the director.

Pull back to wide-angle on the entire scene.

I scanned the video for anything suspicious. There was no sign of Kat. When Mason made his signature 'sneeze', I watched as I came into view and walked up to SmugGuy. Wow. That was really me on film. I looked pretty good except I should have sucked in my tummy.

The first video ended and I played the next one.

Close-up on camera operator.

Zoom in on Kat. I squinted to see if she was doing anything unusual, but she was only drinking from a bottle of water looking around. She didn't look nervous or suspicious at all. The camera then zoomed to an extreme close-up of her face.

I turned to Jesse who was looking over my shoulder. He shrugged. "What? She's pretty."

The video pulled back, showing Kat waving to a guy who walked by. Her eyes scanned him from head to toe. She only seemed interested in good-looking men.

The next shot was filmed straight up at the fake Golden Driller while suspended from cables. The camera zoomed in on the big Styrofoam man and it panned down his body to the oil derrick he would use as an armrest once in place. As the camera slowly scanned further down, I noticed movement between the crossbars of the metal structure. I willed the camera to stop and zoom in, but it kept going down and switched to a full-screen shot of Kat's big flirty smile.

I rewound the video back to the part I needed to see up close and pushed pause. "Hey, Jesse, can you zoom in on something?"

"Sure." He took the phone and clicked something in his editing app and zoomed in. At first, we only saw the top of the derrick, but he panned down on the still frame of the oil derrick until I said, "There! Stop! Look! Do you see someone standing on the roof of the building?"

"Yeah, I do. Let me get even closer."

The more he zoomed, the grainier the photo became, but it was clear enough to see a man standing on the roof holding what looked like a long stick. He wore a ball cap turned backward. I instantly recognized him as one of the two men I saw climbing the oil derrick moments ago. I squinted at the image and realized the stick was actually a gun!

Just as I noticed the weapon Jesse said, "He's got a long gun!"

Upon hearing that, R.A. and Pat ran around the table. The four of us stared at the tiny screen.

My voice quivered, "Can you go to the next frame without doing all that editing again?"

Jesse pushed a button on his phone and the man on the roof moved slightly, lifting the weapon a bit."

R.A. said, "It looks like an AR 500. I've never seen one in person since I think they're banned."

In slow motion, the scene unfolded frame by frame. We watched as the guy who I definitely recognized as the ball cap man I'd suspected all week, held the rifle-looking gun to his shoulder and looked through the site to aim.

Then, the frame switched to a close-up of Kat looking up. Still moving in super slow motion, her eyes widened. Her face revealed shock as she watched the oilman fall. Tears filled her eyes and her hand covered her mouth. I suddenly realized this girl, shown so upset in the extreme closeup, had nothing to do with the murder of Sean Marco. The video ended, frozen on the terrified face of Kat.

We were all stunned. I shook my head and broke the silence, "I guess my theory about Kat was wrong. She wouldn't have reacted like that if she had anything to do with Sean's death."

Pat touched my shoulder. "But now you have proof that the whole thing wasn't an accident."

Jesse rubbed his hand across his forehead and said, "I'll call the police and turn the video over to them right away,"

R.A. shrugged and said, "Good thing you noticed that, Pity. I never would have spotted him through the girders of the derrick, especially on the phone." He shook his head. "That guy must have used an armor-piercing round to go through the heavy steel cable."

Jesse nodded, "And he had to be an expert marksman to hit the cable in one shot."

I rubbed my eyes in disbelief. The shooter in the video had been standing atop the IPE building, just where I stood today. I shuddered at a new thought and said, "Hey guys, I'll be back."

I exited the room so fast I nearly ran into a woman carrying a tray of food. Once my path cleared, I raced around the building to the oil derrick. I counted up five X's and studied the place where the men had been earlier, but they were gone.

The fake Golden Driller, now planted in his correct spot, loomed over me. His hand rested atop the oil derrick, just as the real statue did a half-block away. I worried the men had tampered with the metal frame instead of repairing it. This was a terrifying thought since Aaron was scheduled to climb the structure after lunch. Was he the target all along?

My mind raced back to the first Golden Driller incident. What if Aaron was supposed to be under the boot and because someone had yelled Team 1 instead of Team 2, the stand-in was there in his place. And then, what about the tall guy who held up his silver burrito/gun. He may have aimed it at Aaron while he looked out the window of the car. We'll never know since I interfered and the guy disappeared.

My sinking feeling gnawed at the pit of my stomach. I should tell someone about my new suspicions, but I needed to prove there was a problem before making a fool of myself again. I only had a few hours, so there was only one thing to do. Climb the oil derrick and look for damage!

I ran to my car, which was parked relatively close to the building, and searched for anything I could use for my plan. The faceplate was of no use. I wished I had been trained in welding in case there was damage to the frame. I grabbed R.A.'s tool belt and tightened it around my waist, glad to find a pair of old leather gloves in its pocket. I searched my trunk for a rope but could only find a spool of gold ribbon for tying balloons together for the Oscar party. I put a carabiner in a pocket, knowing that mountain climbers use them. A screwdriver or wrench would have been nice, but of course, I didn't have either, so I put the gloves on and ran back to the base of the derrick.

I took a deep breath and pulled myself up to the flat crossbar by stepping up to the middle of the first black steel X. The beam, although thinner than an I-beam, was still awkward to hold onto. I was thankful for the leather gloves.

As I climbed straight up for the second time in a day, I found it more challenging than you would think. It felt as though I was leaning backward, but I kept going. When I was sure I had gone most of the way to the top, I looked down and realized I was only six feet off the ground.

I persevered, just like my cowboy song lyrics advised, and finally made it up to the second set of crossbars. That was when I made the near-fatal error of looking down. I'd say the room was spinning, but there was no room. I felt nauseous and my ears were ringing. Everything pointed to vertigo. I closed my eyes and breathed evenly until it passed. Then I took a deep breath and moved upward, avoiding looking down again

As I continued to pull myself up, I heard R.A.'s frantic voice, "Pity, what in the world are you doing?"

I didn't look down, but shouted, "I'm going to prove that someone has tampered with the oil derrick!"

Surprisingly, I heard my sister's voice next, "Pity, come down. First of all, you're scared of heights and secondly, if it is unstable, you could fall!"

Hmm. That was a good point but I was almost there and refused to be a quitter. "Well, I've gotta try. I'm wearing Mom's good shoes and I have the guitar-shaped carabiner you gave me!"

"That's a keychain, Pity! It won't hold your weight!" Kim added in exasperation, "Did you tell your girls goodbye?" Her voice changed direction. "I can't watch this R.A. Do something."

I climbed up to the middle of the third X and looked right and left for anything suspicious. I ran my gloved hand along the cold steel to see how everything was connected. The bolts seemed to be perfectly in place. Before pulling myself up to another rung, I yanked hard to make sure the bar was solidly attached.

Feeling more confident, I looked up to see how much further I had to go. Not a good idea. My stomach did a big flip and vertigo came back. I thought that only happened when looking down. Good to know. Once my head cleared and the dizziness stopped, I started repeating the phrase, "I think I can. I think I can," and kept climbing until I was at the 4th set of X crossbars.

I could faintly hear R.A. shouting. He wasn't that far away, but the pounding in my ears impaired my hearing. I listened carefully and heard other voices too. R.A. came through louder this time. "Pity, come down. Let me do it. I've climbed every kind of tower."

I replied, "I'm almost there!"

After pulling myself up to the next flat bar, I realized I had made it to my destination. I wrapped my arm around the metal framework, happy it wasn't as cold as earlier in the week, or I'd be stuck to it. I inched my way to the right, looking for anything unusual. All the bolts were nice and tight. I made my way slowly a bit farther and accidentally glimpsed the ground again. With my secure hold on the tower, my stomach didn't flip this time, but I did see a crowd of people forming to watch me. Dang! Why was I wearing a dress? Everyone could see right up my skirt.

Amid the crowd of people below, the tall guy and ball cap guy stood together pointing up at me. The shorter man started climbing the derrick, but the tall one turned to leave – moving quickly at that.

I carefully wrapped a leg around a pole and loosened a hand to wave and point. I yelled, "Kim! He's leaving! Do something!"

After a brief delay, I saw her shrug and say, "What? I can't hear you."

I shouted louder – "The tall guy is getting away!!!" I pointed to the parking lot. "Do something!"

Kim rushed in the opposite direction. At the same time, R.A. started climbing the derrick.

"Kim! The other way! He went the other way!"

In frustration, I must have unwrapped my leg for I lost my balance and reached for the next bar before having a chance to check it. Right when I touched it, the bolt that held it in place plummeted to the earth and the bar swung free. Just in the nick of time, I reached out and grabbed a secure bar with both hands. Feeling a little safer, but still terrified I would fall, I stepped on a beam. Then the unthinkable happened. It came loose. In a flash, I found myself hanging by my hands, 40 feet above the fairgrounds with both my feet dangling in the air.

Mr. Garner, my elementary school gym teacher was right; those chin-ups and pull-ups would be useful later in life. Why hadn't I worked harder to strengthen my arms? If my grip slipped, I was going to be a Pity Pancake. I didn't even have a chance to say goodbye to everyone. Had I actually bought that life insurance policy or just planned to do it? Who would take the girls? Todd and Shelly? No, No No! Kim and R.A. needed to take them in. These thoughts whirred senselessly in my head. I didn't have the stamina to hang on much longer. But, thoughts of my daughters and my parents kept my hands gripping tight, despite my lack of upper body strength.

I heard screams from down below and I realized the crowd was worried about me. I knew if I moved, I would only compound my problem, so I just hung there.

Suddenly keenly aware of all my senses, I felt the cold air, marveled at the bright blue sky, and heard a motorcycle engine, (a motorcycle?).

I heard R.A.'s shouting again. He was closer now. "Hang on, Pity! We're on our way." Then there was metal clanking as he and several workmen climbed up. I sure hoped they brought better tools than I had. I hung on, wishing I had locked my guitar carabiner to something, or better yet, hadn't climbed up at all.

I called to him, "Hurry! The screws are loose." I could only imagine everyone below thinking I was the one with screws loose for getting into the predicament.

A surprisingly close voice growled, "I'll get you, Bitch!" I couldn't resist craning my head down to see who had spoken. It was the ball cap guy, the one who had shot the cables. When a new chill ran through me, I realized I was actually more afraid of him than of falling.

The man had almost reached me when I yelled at the top of his head, "You can't get away with this. I know you were involved in the stand-in's death."

"You won't be talkin' to nobody, blabbermouth!" He grabbed my ankle and pulled. The extra weight made the bar much more difficult to hold onto, which I assume was his plan. With my free foot I tried to kick away his hand and missed, but miraculously found a piece of angled metal to rest that foot on and give my hands a break.

I squawked, "We gave the video of you on the roof with a gun to the police. They are on their way now." Even if the statement wasn't true yet, I hoped it would make him leave me alone.

He sounded even angrier, "I don't believe you. You've been a thorn in our side since this began. You should have minded your own business."

As strained as I was, I had to admit he wasn't the first person to tell me that. I tried kicking my foot to loosen his grip, but he held on tight, trying to pull me down.

Suddenly a huge wind and deafening noise surrounded me. Another tornado? Talk about bad timing! I hadn't heard a siren, but sometimes they pop up without warning. I could barely hold on to the bar now, much less during a tornado.

I heard a crack and suddenly my hands and my ankle bore an unbearable weight. The bar the man was standing on must have given way and now my leg was being pulled down by his full body weight. I had lost my footing and hung only by my hands again. My shoulders felt like they were going to come out of their sockets. I tried to kick my feet in an effort to release his grip but I was just being stretched as my hands grew weaker and weaker. I said a little silent prayer for a miracle and kicked with all my might.

Amid the whirlwind and din of the tornado, I was shocked to hear my brother-in-law's voice loud and clear below me. He yelled, "Let go of my Pity!" Then R.A. must have done something because the ball cap guy loosened his hand from my ankle and grabbed my foot. But because Mom's shoe was already loose, it slipped off taking him with it as it fell. Thankfully, once he let go, my body became substantially lighter. I didn't see the man plunge into the sea of people below, but the distant screams were telltale.

R.A. said, "Don't give up. We're almost there, Pity."

I closed my eyes and tried to feel for that place to rest my feet and give my hands some relief again. My legs flailed around, but I only found vertical bars. This was it. I was going to fall. Down I would go along with the murderer and Mom's shoe. I opened my eyes and yelled down to R.A. "I can't hold on anymore. Tell everyone I love them. And please take care of my girls."

Suddenly, a hand appeared in front of my face. I looked up and saw a wingtip shoe standing in the loop of a thick rope just to the side of my head. What the… Well, this was a no-brainer. No matter who the hand belonged to, it would be better than falling. I let go of the metal bar with one hand and grabbed the offered hand. It was warm and strong and felt much better than the one that had grabbed my ankle.

A familiar voice, shouted, "That's right. I got you. Now, give me your other hand."

As much as I wanted to, I didn't have the courage to let go of the bar. "I can't! I'll fall!"

"You have to. Just trust me!"

I thought of my sweet daughters and decided to trust whoever was hovered above me. I closed my eyes tight and in a sudden burst of courage, released my final grasp from the steel bar. I waited for my body to plummet to the ground with a splat. But, instead, I rose into the air swiftly and smoothly, both arms were above my head, and my feet still dangled. Was I being lifted into the eye of the tornado, like Dorothy in the "Wizard of Oz"? Now in a daze, I felt the wind encircle my body as thunderous noise grew even louder all around me.

My eyes were still squeezed tight as someone grabbed my waist and pulled me into an incredibly loud room. I had a strange sensation of sitting still but also moving. Maybe I had fallen and was actually dead. My arms hung by my side. With effort, I lifted my hands and touched my legs, torso, and head. All seemed normal. If I was dead, at least there was no pain.

I began to feel a bit more secure and opened my eyes. The first thing I saw was the face of Aaron Winston staring at me. Could this be heaven? My eyes flicked to an open doorway, revealing blue sky. I heard the pulsating sound of blades slapping the air and I finally realized I was in a helicopter.

The movie star gave me a grin and said, "You okay, Pity?"

I slowly started to piece the event together and asked incredulously, "Was that you on the rope?"

He shrugged and said with a twinkle, "See how great it is to do your own stunts? Why let someone else have all the fun?"

Still processing the whole ordeal, I said, "You saved me?" I realized the depth of that question and repeated it as a statement with tears in my eyes. "You saved me!"

"Hey, I'd been practicing standing on the rope most of the morning...and I couldn't see another way out for you." He winked.

Although relieved, I was still so shaken and confused that I couldn't think of an appropriate response.

While Aaron talked to the pilot, I took off R.A.'s gloves and rubbed my raw, bruised hands, thankful that they had held on so long. I had nearly plunged to my death! I shuddered when I thought of the other guy. Had he died?

My stomach lurched when the helicopter dipped abruptly. Panicking, I found a seatbelt and put it on, tightening it so I wouldn't fall out and join the man on the ground below.

The helicopter leveled out and I felt much safer. Being strapped in next to a movie star didn't hurt either. I took a deep cleansing breath, but when I caught sight of Tulsa from the amazing vantage point, my breath was taken right away again. It was gorgeous!

As we hovered right over the Golden Driller. I frantically hunted for my phone and found it in R.A.'s toolbelt which was still strapped to my body. I snapped some awesome photos of my tall golden boyfriend from above. Then glancing at Aaron, I figured I should document the incredible moment. I shouted to be heard above the din, "Mind if I take a picture of my lifesaver?"

Instead of the flirty pose, I expected from the gregarious star, he seized my phone and frowned. "Yes, I mind!" I was shocked by his denial and frankly was afraid he would throw it out the open window. But then he gave me a cheesy smile and put his head so close to mine I could feel his beard stubble on my cheek. He smirked, "How about a selfie of the two of us?"

I beamed as he snapped a couple of photos of us with the Tulsa skyline in the background. Then, he backed up and took one of me pointing down to the golden driller just as we started to descend.

From the birds' eye view of the neighborhood. A police car followed a motorcycle with lights flashing. Was that the other bad guy, the tall one? I watched as the cycle darted in an alley and just like in a movie's high-speed chase, the cruiser drove right past him. I felt helpless as the cycle took off in the opposite direction, escaping capture. Dang.

Moments later, I watched the crowd part as we descended to a spot near an ambulance. EMT workers lifted a stretcher through the back doors of the vehicle. That must be the guy who fell. A clear oxygen mask covered his nose and mouth and an IV bag was attached to the gurney. Although he had tried to kill me, I was glad to know he was alive.

When we were only about ten feet off the ground, I turned to Aaron and shouted through the noise, "Thank you so much for being my hero, Aaron!"

"Well, I'm pretty sure you saved my life too. I was supposed to climb the derrick today. That would have been me hanging on."

Movie Watching Tip #17
Sometimes the movie is even better than the book.

I looked at my handsome hero and hollered above the helicopter noise, "Any idea why someone would want to hurt you? We discovered those two guys were the ones who shot the cable holding the Golden Driller. Maybe they were aiming for you!"

Aaron screwed up his face at the thought of someone wanting to hurt him. "Seriously? I thought they were just crew members."

My body jolted as the chopper touched down. I was so happy to be back on solid ground, I felt like kissing the earth, and quickly unbuckled my belt. When the blades wound down completely, the ungodly noise and wind finally stopped.

I cringed and said to Aaron, "What can I say? My sister loves me."

I jumped down to the ground and gave Kim a big bear hug, thankful to be alive. I sobbed, "You were right, I'm way too impulsive and it was a stupid thing to do. I was so close to falling."

She sniffled. "And R.A. tried to be a hero and go up after you."

With my head still resting on Kim's shoulder I looked at my sweet brother-in-law and said to him, "Thank you so much for climbing up to save me." I pulled away from our embrace and wiped my nose with one of R.A.'s life-saving gloves.

He said, "Well, I tried to get to you, but that jerk got there first." He shook his head in disgust.

Aaron whined, "Hey, I'm not that much of a jerk."

Horrified, R.A. blushed and stammered, "No! Not you, Mr. Winston. That was really cool how you did that. I was talking about the guy who climbed up and grabbed Pity's foot."

Aaron winked, "I know. Just wanted to watch you squirm."

R.A. blew out a big sigh of relief and we all laughed. Guess he didn't mind being kidded by a movie star.

A boisterous voice burst through the small crowd of people who stood gawking at us. "Oh My Gosh! You'll do anything for attention, won't you, Pity?" I turned and smiled when I saw Lin, all dolled up in a pink mini skirt and Go-Go boots. She said with a snort, "I just about died when I saw you climbing up there in your dress. I thought you were scared of heights, but you just kept going up, up…" Lin stopped short. Apparently, she had finally noticed Aaron Winston standing behind me.

I turned and watched my movie star friend smirk at my three-person fan club. "Aaron, this is my sister Kim, her husband, R.A., and my best friend, Lin."

He nodded, "Nice to meet you all."

With tears in her eyes, Kim said, "Thank you so much for saving my crazy sister."

He puffed out his chest and said, "All in a day's work, my dear. All in a day's work."

I asked the trio. "Do you know if the guy who fell is OK?"

R.A. said, "He's in pretty bad shape…broken ribs, leg, and arm, but they think he'll live."

"That could have been me, huh?" I winced.

My sister, brother-in-law, and friend all nodded at me.

I unbuckled R.A.'s toolbelt and handed it and the gloves to him. "Those leather gloves saved my life."

As a kind gesture, or maybe because he saw me wipe my nose on them, R.A. said, "You can keep the gloves as a souvenir."

Then in a stage whisper, I said, "Maybe we shouldn't tell the girls or Mom and Dad about this."

Kim nodded, "Good idea."

Aaron climbed down from the helicopter, thanked the pilot and we all walked over to the blond director, who was talking to two police officers.

The director, (Oh yeah, his name is Mr. Hart), patted Aaron on the shoulder and said, "That was some fine work you did there, Winston. Wish we had it on film."

Aaron pointed to me, "You know, Pity should be the one commended. She not only found a fugitive on the set yesterday, but she saved my life today. She believes the same guys who caused this were responsible for the stand-in's death."

Mr. Hart nodded. "I've already spoken to the police. Evidently, Jackson got away. I don't know why they wanted to hurt anyone." The handsome director's face was drawn. "But, once Simon wakes up, we should find out what there were up to."

I felt bad and shrugged. "I'm sorry, Mr. Hart if I made a mess of today."

He patted my shoulder and brightened. "Are you kidding? I'm grateful for your detective work even if it was rather risky. He shook his head. "I still wish we had recorded your stunt – you were amazing. It might have been a good addition to the film."

I shrank a little from the recognition. Then I rubbed my sore hands, trying to get the feeling back in my fingers.

Aaron cleared his throat and said, "Look. I'd like to stay and chat, but I should get going. I have to at least pretend like I have a chance at winning an Oscar." He faced Mr. Hart and said, "I guess we'll film the oil derrick scene next week since we had a slight delay today."

The director nodded. "After we make repairs, we'll get back to it. Your Limo is waiting over there to take you to the airport."

Aaron gave a friendly wave to us all, turned, and walked toward the sleek black limo parked by the next building. I started to tear up as I realized I'd never see this cool man in person again. Just then, he turned and said, "Hey, Pity, walk me to my ride?"

"Um. Yes?" Despite my achy body, I skipped over to catch up with him. I glanced back at my entourage and gave a shrug just before joining him.

He nudged me. "So, I saw you with a guy last night. Is that your boyfriend?"

My face dropped and I gave an emphatic "No. He'd like to be, but I'm not interested at all."

He stopped and smiled at me. "I hope you find someone that can keep up with you and bring you the excitement you crave."

How did he know that's the type of guy I liked?

We stopped when we reached his limousine and he shifted on his feet. "I thought you might like to know that Sandra Ellington and I have been talking and we're giving it another go." His lips crinkled up on the edges. "I'm really excited about it." Aaron was adorable and looked truly happy.

Oh, I'm thrilled for you. She's so beautiful and talented! You are perfect together. Will she be your date for the Oscars?"

"Uh-huh." He looked into my eyes and took my hands. "Just want you to know that anyone who can keep me calm in a tornado, has the gall to shout "Cut" in front of Joel Mason, and would climb a tall tower just to prove a point, is A-O-K with me."

I blushed at the compliment and stammered, "Thanks, Falcon."

He cocked his head in my very favorite way and asked, "What did you call me?"

"Falcon. I finally thought of a nickname for you. I mean you swooped down from the sky and picked me up just like a hawk grabbing its prey."

"Oooh. I love it. Maybe Sandra can use it sometimes too." He waggled his eyebrows. "Look, I'd better get going. But first, can I have a goodbye hug?"

"Um, yeah!" Like I would turn down that request.

I wrapped my arms around his waist and he hugged my neck. We stayed like that for a few seconds until I said, "Thanks again for saving my life, Aaron. I'll never forget you." I blushed. What a stupid thing to say. Nobody could forget him.

"And I'll never forget you."

I looked up at his blue eyes and thought, "maybe, maybe not," but, it was sure a nice thing to hear. After our hug, he slid through the door, waved to me, and shut it. Since I'd actually been in one, I could now picture the inside of the elongated luxury vehicle. The front window rolled down and I was surprised to see Roberto in the driver's seat. He winked at me as he slowly drove away.

Wow! I was so happy my life could have ended then. With a grin plastered on my face, I suddenly remembered, my life had actually almost ended today and the grin faltered.

When I was five feet away from my cronies, Lin shouted, "Oh My Gosh! Aaron Winston hugged you! And he knows your name! And he saved your life!"

I shrugged as if it was no big deal. "Yeah, so what?" Then I started to giggle hysterically.

A heavy-set policeman with a ruddy complexion walked up to me and said politely, "Miss Kole, may we ask you some questions? The medical team wants to check you out as well."

"Of course." I turned to Kim and Lin and said, "I'll call you later. Go on home."

I was led to a table and chairs set up by the main building. Medics came over and checked me out. A dark-haired EMT said, "Well, you are sound of body, but I'm not sure you are sound of mind to do what you did." I chuckled at her.

I spent an hour trying to explain the whole situation, describing the men in detail and answering a million questions. Finally, the policeman allowed me to leave. It was only 3 p.m., but it seemed much later with all that had happened since morning.

When checking out with Rita I said, "It was so nice to get to know you, Rita. If you're ever filming here again, please call me." I gave her a card with my contact info.

"It's been a real treat, Kitty. Take care of yourself now."

As I drove home, I thought back on my ridiculous day and was relieved the cameras hadn't been rolling during my crazy stunt. The last thing I needed was to see myself hanging from a bar in a dress. Although, it would have been a stellar scene to add to my Oscar video. I mean that would have been a true show stopper.

When I pulled up in my driveway, I checked myself over to make sure I looked normal, then composed myself and walked into the kitchen with as much confidence as I could muster. I sure didn't want the girls to find out what happened.

As I entered, Ren was getting a glass of water. She turned to me with a look of horror, "Mom, you have to see this!" She led me to the dining room. Had she already seen something about my stupid stunt on TV?

She held her hand out ala Vanna White. "Look!"

The dining table was overloaded with aluminum pans and Styrofoam containers. There were so many I could barely see the tablecloth. I lifted the foil lid from a pan and saw what looked like the very same asparagus stalks I'd had eaten the night before. Another container held rolls and yet another was filled with the delicious roast beef. I said in disbelief, "Did Kenny bring this?"

"No. It was delivered by two guys wearing black aprons."

I looked in awe at the spread. "Wow! That is a lot of food." I put my hand on my head, and said, "I guess Kenny decided to share the leftovers from our exciting date."

Ren squinted, not knowing what I was talking about. I'd forgotten she had spent the night with Jennifer and hadn't heard about the date. Glad to have another story to tell besides the one where I nearly fell to my death, I said, "Let's try to find a place for all this in the fridge while I describe my bizarre evening."

Minutes later, the food was put away and the story was told. Ren said, "Why in the world did that Kenny guy think you would like those places? If he knew you at all, he would have taken you to a flea market, a movie, or to a pub."

I shrugged. "Yep. We are sooo not a match made in heaven."

She said, "At least we don't have to make food for the Oscar Party." Then, she said, "Oh, Grandma and Grandpa are stopping by in a bit. He has some book he wants to show you."

It would be nice to see them. I showered, trying to wash away my mistakes of the day. The warm water pulsated over my sore shoulders and soothed my mood. I couldn't decide whether to laugh or cry about the day's events. I opted not to wallow in the memory, dried off, and got dressed."

I took Edgar from his cage and sat on the recliner with the big gray bird. He bent his head down so I would pet him.

I stroked his soft feathers then leaned my head back.

"Pity? Are you okay?"

I opened my eyes to find my parents and both girls standing over me with worried expressions. Edgar was back in his cage. I must have fallen asleep.

Ren said, "Mom, you scared us. We couldn't wake you up."

I said in a froggy voice, "Oh, I was just really tired."

Their faces relaxed as I sat up straighter and said, "Hi, Mom and Dad."

Dad said, "I brought something that might interest you."

I nodded as he pulled a nondescript book out of a bag and handed it to me. He explained further, "It's on the oil industry in Tulsa and is a first edition."

I opened the old book, focused my sleepy eyes, and flipped through, careful not to damage a page. The first thing I saw was the brand-new Golden Driller statue. I shuddered, remembering my pathetic high wire act. Was that just today? It must have been since my shoulders screamed at me with each page turn.

I found black and white photos of the first International Petroleum Exposition and looked at my father. "Dad, you won't believe it, but the movie set inside the IPE building looks just like this, except the fake version is in color."

Dad said, "You know the real version was too." He winked.

I chuckled. "Yes. I assume it was in color."

He said, "Well, that sounds like a movie I'd like to see."

I flipped through a few more pages and saw a big piece of equipment with a young man standing beside it. The caption read, 'Seymour Dicks, inventor of the Industrial Compression Gasket. His discovery will forever change the future of oil drilling.' I shuddered again, this time because of his awful name that reminded me of a Simpson's episode. I cocked my head thinking of the name, Dicks. That must be Kenny's father. Maybe he gets residuals from his dad's invention and that's why he is so rich.

I pondered this as I handed the book back to Dad "Very cool. Thanks for showing me."

Mom's voice came from the kitchen, "We were in Broken Arrow today because we wanted to check out the grand opening at the new book store on Main Street."

Mom entered with glasses full of lemonade. "I found several Agatha Christies that I don't have." Her face turned solemn. "Pity, we saw on the news that you found that girl from Alabama. Why are you getting involved with out-of-state investigations?"

I shrugged; just happy she didn't know what I'd done today. In order not to spill the beans, I changed the subject. "Mom, look in the refrigerator." I took her back into the kitchen and explained the story again. "I'll send some home with you."

When we returned to the living room with a bag full of food for Mom and Dad to take home, my father said, "Pity, do you mind if we turn on the evening news? I ran out of blank videotapes and couldn't record it."

"Sure." I smiled at my dad who refused to enter the 21st Century and still used videotapes. "I also have your copy of the latest "Not Quite the Oscars" video for you, but you'll have to put it in the DVD player. I picked up the remote and turned to channel 2 then ran upstairs and retrieved a copy of my recording.

When I returned to the living room, Shelly was on TV, standing atop the roof of a red Cadillac holding an umbrella. She must have had a wind machine aimed at her because her skirt and hair were blowing sideways. She yelled above the wind noise,

"Our March prices will blow you away!" Just then, her umbrella turned inside out and she spouted her standard line with her signature wink, "You'll get the max from Big Jack's Cadillacs."

We all gave a collective eye roll and Mom said, "Oh, we saw her today. She and Todd were at the bookstore." Mom continued as she nodded to the TV, "Miss Priss looked so out of place. Has she ever even read a book?"

Dad shook his head. "She sure didn't have anything good to say about you, Pity. Did you really make her dress up like a nun?"

I laughed. "No. I had nothing to do with that." I figured she would blame me for her unfortunate role.

The doorbell chimed and Edgar imitated it perfectly. Ree ran to the door and came back with a somber face. In a loud stage whisper, she said, "Speaking of the devil."

I stood reluctantly. "Why is Shelly here?" I didn't really want to know the answer.

Ren sighed with a pained expression, "Oh, yeah. I forgot we said we would spend tonight at Dad's. He wants to take us to some special rodeo."

I nodded, "That's ok. Maybe it will be fun." The girls left to pack and I went to the door. Shelly stood there with a scowl. Todd's hands gripped her shoulders, possibly to keep her from throttling me.

Ignoring Shelly, I spoke over her head to Todd, "Rodeo?"

He nodded.

"That's fine. As long as I have them back by four tomorrow. I'll need them to help with the Oscar Party."

Shelly's demeanor switched and I realized my fatal error. Her eyes lit and her lip curled unnaturally. . She squealed, "Oscar Party? Is Alison coming? I know Aaron can't come because he's in Los Angeles. What time does it start and what should I wear?"

My eyes grew huge. "No, Shelly. Alison isn't coming. I didn't invite any of the people from the film. Just my school friends are coming." Why did I even answer her?

She raised a skeptical eyebrow like I was lying and all of Hollywood would be rolling up in limos.

Todd shook his head. "Believe me, sweet cheeks, it's a lame party. No movie star would go to one of her Pity Parties."

Shelly pursed her lips and released her breath reluctantly. Keeping her eyes on me, she sang, "Girls, let's go!"

Ren and Ree gave us hugs and started to the door with their overnight bags.

Shelly said, "I brought you each a cowboy hat to wear tonight. They're from our Cadillac Stampede Sale."

The girls, who had just crossed the threshold, both did a 180 at the thought of wearing pink or purple rhinestone-studded hats. In order to keep the peace, I gave them a sympathetic shrug, twisted them back around, and gently pushed them out the door.

As Shelly turned to leave, she cooed, "Hot Toddy, let's go eat at the Golden Corral to get us in the mood for the rodeo."

Hot Toddy? In all the years I've known Todd, it never once occurred to me to call him that. Gross.

I shut the door and joined my parents, who were watching the five o'clock news. I hoped there hadn't been a report about my antics on the set. But since neither Mom nor Dad mentioned anything, I assumed I was in the clear.

I sat beside Mom and leaned my head on her shoulder.

She said, "You okay, sweetie?"

I almost cracked and told her the whole story of what happened today, but I stopped myself and shrugged. "I'm just tired. Maybe I need something to eat. Want to go to Goldies?"

Before she could answer, Dad, stood and said, "Sounds good."

It wasn't until I had a pile of Goldies bread and butter pickles in front of me and my glass of iced tea that I felt better. When the burgers arrived, their smell made my mouth water. The flavor of the first bite almost made me melt.

We chatted about anything and everything, except my secret on-set drama.

Movie Watching Tip #18
Give sports movies a chance.

Back at home with a full belly, I watched the week's TV shows I'd missed while I prepared for my party. First, I got my big box marked 'Oscars' from the garage. I pulled out my red carpet, star-shaped bowls, gold plates and movie-themed wall decorations. I smiled with each item I unpacked. Online I found ballots and bingo sheets designed for this year's awards show. Once I had printed them, I attached them to clipboards for each guest. Tomorrow, I would buy the prizes and have the girls blow up the balloons. I was way ahead of where I was last year, mainly because the food was already prepared.

After my quiet evening, I kissed Harriet goodnight and went to bed. The next thing I remember was the doorbell ringing. Why was someone here in the middle of the night?

I blinked at the clock. Was it already 9 a.m.? Darned blackout curtains. I jumped from my bed and pulled on my pants, groaning aloud as my sore muscles resisted.

I yelled, "Just a minute!" as I tried to remember what day it was. Oh yeah…Sunday. I was very glad I hadn't agreed to direct the children's choir at church this morning, or I may not have made it. Who would come over on Sunday morning? Mrs. Garmin probably needed something.

The face behind the door took my breath away. It was Kat! Wait. No, it wasn't. I relaxed and said, "Jenn? Come on in." I started to apologize for my appearance, but the next question trumped it. "How did you find out where I live?"

As I led her in and to the couch, she said with a twinkle, "You're not the only one who knows how to use Google."

I nodded, still trying to wake up, and said, "So? Why aren't you back in Alabama?"

"I stayed here to pack. I'll drive home tomorrow but wanted to tell you the outcome of the investigation."

I sat next to her and said, "Before you begin, would you like some coffee? And maybe a Pop-Tart or bowl of Life?" I had a reason for my overt hospitality. My stomach was growling and also, I couldn't focus without my morning java.

She shook her head. "No, but maybe some water?"

I started the coffee, got her a glass of ice water, and threw a Pop-Tart in the toaster for myself. From the living room, I heard her say, "I saw you on TV the other night."

I couldn't see her around the kitchen wall but hoped she wasn't making fun of me. I hollered, "Yes. Sorry I managed to get your name and photo all over the news."

"It's OK. I appreciate your research and can't wait to grill my sister in person. Hey, did you ever find out if she was involved in the problems on the movie set?"

I came back around the corner with her water and said, "You'll be pleased to know that we no longer consider her a suspect in the incidents on the movie set." I realized that sounded very official and said, "Well, they have one guy in custody and another is on the loose, but I really don't think Kat was involved."

She nodded. "Oh, that's good." I heard true relief in her voice.

The toaster popped and I went back to retrieve my preservative laced pastry and coffee. I sat down across from Jenn. "OK. Tell me everything." I took a big drink and could feel the caffeine pulsate through my veins.

She started, "As you know, Kat has been extradited to my hometown."

"Yes?" I bit into my warm Pop-Tart and the cherry filling melted in my mouth. I tried not to groan as I savored the flavor.

She said, "My parents met Kat and the detective at the airport yesterday. According to Mom, there was a big scene. They had gone to welcome her home, but Kat wouldn't speak to Mom or Dad and was very rude."

I nodded, thinking it was awful, but wasn't that surprised. "Did you find out what else she's wanted for and what happened to the boyfriend?"

Jenn pushed her short hair behind her ears. "Not yet. But listen to this; For some reason, Kat wasn't restrained and she ran off. TSA had to chase her through the airport, causing quite a ruckus. They finally apprehended her. She was cuffed and taken to the police station."

"Seriously? What was she thinking?" That Kat was crazier than I thought.

"I told you she's impetuous. In addition to everything else, she's considered a flight risk. The detective even called and told me Kat's not cooperating and won't answer questions. In the meantime, I've decided to take matters in my own hands and have been looking for clues about Rodney."

"That's Kat's missing boyfriend?"

She nodded. "I found out a few things, but I need your help to get more information."

"I'm sorry, Jenn." I shook my head and laughed. "But I'm out of the detective business. Besides, I'm hosting a big party tonight and have to get ready for school tomorrow."

"I think my plan will only take a few hours. Please?"

Jenn's eyes begged so sweetly I couldn't help but consider helping her. I constructed a mental list of reasons I should:

1. I had started the whole Kat investigation - why not finish it?

2. I was nearly ready for the party and could probably spare a few hours, especially since the food was already done.

3. I was getting pretty good at this sleuthing thing.

4. I have trouble turning people down.

Even though I figured it was a bad idea and two hours can often turn into six, I said, "OK". You would think I would at least ask about the plan first, but nope, I didn't.

Her face beamed. "Great! Do you happen to have a tape recorder, a crowbar or a bowling ball? The tape recorder made sense to me, the crowbar scared me a bit and I couldn't help but wonder why she wanted a bowling ball.

Embarrassed to admit it, I said, "As a matter of fact, I have all three. I mean, you never know when you might need them."

I gathered the three items, including my favorite, my gold bowling ball engraved with the name Marybell that I'd gotten at a garage sale. It was just my size. "Do I need bowling shoes too?"

"If you have them."

I grabbed some socks and my college bowling shoes. We took off in her car to points unknown to me.

I listened to her slow thick accent as she told me the plan. And to think, some people think Okies have accents.

She said, "I called Rodney's roommate and he said he hasn't seen him for a week. He said he might be stayin' with his brother."

"Did you get the brother's name and address?"

"Only his name, Michael. And he works at the Dust Bowl in Tulsa."

Now I knew where we were going and the reason for a bowling ball. I asked, "Is it open on Sundays?"

She nodded. "I called. They have a Sunday morning league and a few open lanes."

"So, Jenn, do you know why it's called The Dust Bowl?"

She shook her head and I couldn't resist giving her a little bit of Oklahoma history. I described the horrible dust storms of the 1930s. "As if the depression wasn't bad enough, people were displaced by an eight-year drought where dust covered everything and most crops couldn't survive."

She frowned. "Wow. I'd heard the term 'dust bowl' but didn't know it was that bad."

"Yeah, and some clever entrepreneur built a bowling alley and named it that."

After driving past the Art Deco churches and buildings in downtown Tulsa, we arrived at the Dust Bowl and parked out front. I said, "So, do we have a plan?"

Jenn gave an apologetic shrug. "That's why I brought you."

I took a deep breath and said, "OK. We'll just wing it. Let's go." I stopped. "Wait." I turned back to her. "Has this Michael guy met Kat?"

She shrugged again and said, "I don't know."

"Hmm. Maybe you should stay out here since we don't know how he would react to seeing you. I'm not sure if anyone has told you this, but you are the spitting image of your sister."

Jenn chuckled and gave a nod. "I've heard. Text me if you want me to come in."

I turned and opened the door to the sounds of clattering pins, laughing, and talking. I loved the way the owners gave the bowling alley a vintage look; perfect for the eclectic clientele of the upscale area. It was like stepping into the early '70s with clean lines, cool lights, and bright-colored couches. A bar in the corner looked more like a retro nightclub than a snack bar. I half expected to see The Dude from Big Lebowski hanging out there.

A banner hanging from the ceiling read "Sunday Morning Bowling – Pray for a strike." Well, that was just plain silly. My attention was drawn to the counter where a tall guy handed a pair of shoes to a cute college-aged girl. He said, "You are on lane six. Good luck Miranda."

When she walked away, I stepped up and said to the guy who may or may not have been Michael, "Do you have a lane available? It's just me getting a little exercise today. I have shoes."

He nodded. "You get the last one. It's $20 an hour." Wow. That was a bit pricey, especially since I hoped to only be there for a few minutes. But since I had no plan yet, I pulled my card out and paid. He gave me a small pencil and a scorecard. I stared at them. I wasn't playing miniature golf. I made a quick glance at the lanes and saw no electronic scoring monitors. Wow, they took retro to a new level. I had forgotten how to keep score manually and started to panic, but remembered I wasn't really there to bowl, so I shook it off. I hauled my bowling bag to lane five and watched the group next to me throw the ball while I got my shoes.

When the girl, Miranda, walked by me, I asked, "Excuse me, but do you know if the guy working over there is named Michael?"

She said, "Oh. Yeah. Mike's a doll." She bounced off and promptly threw a gutter ball.

Since I still had no plan, I figured, I might as well throw the ball a few times. Even though I hadn't bowled in five years, I slipped on my shoes, casually chalked the soles and walked to the lane. My lucky Marybell weighs only 10 lb. but she felt incredibly heavy today, probably because my muscles were still weak from yesterday's nonsense. I dried my stiff fingers at the little fan and placed them in the holes. Then I took my standard two steps, slid on the third one, and released the ball. I watched as it raced down the lane and knocked all the pins down! A strike! Cool!

Once the ball returned, I shook out my arms and fingers and picked it up. I made my approach to the foul line and let go with a little less force. OMG, another strike.

"Way to go!"

I turned to see my bowling neighbor, Miranda, clapping for me. I couldn't help but smile. Of course, I would get two strikes when my girls or R.A. weren't around to see it. In my excitement, I tried again and by golly, I knocked them all down again. What a crazy fluke. I had never bowled more than three strikes in a whole game. I didn't want the euphoria to stop so once my ball was returned, I repeated and got yet another strike. By now, the guys bowling with Miranda were watching my incredible lucky streak.

"Come on! Do another!" one guy yelled.

I chuckled. I had just gotten 4 strikes in a row. What were the odds? I shrugged and said, "I'll try."

I walked up to the line feeling my sore wrist this time. I took my usual steps and watched the ball go a bit to the left. This would stop my run of good luck for sure. The ball tapped the side of the headpin, knocking down all but one. I turned around and gave an 'oh well' shrug. But the guys started to whoop and holler.

I turned and saw the last pin had fallen. What in the world? I wish someone had recorded that. Heck, I hadn't even been keeping score. Nobody would believe this.

One of the guys next to me said, "That's a turkey, right?"

A voice behind me said, "Three is a turkey. She's got a five-bagger."

I turned to see Michael lining up balls on a rack. He didn't seem particularly impressed. I suddenly remembered the reason I was there. I was supposed to be investigating Rodney's disappearance and poor Jenn was outside waiting for me. I swallowed. I should stop, but I had an actual audience watching me."

"Are you a professional?" Miranda asked in awe.

"Oh, heaven's no. I haven't bowled in years. I don't know what's going on."

"Well, keep it up. I want to see you get a perfect score."

My fans waited to see what I would do next. My heart raced. I looked down at my bruised palms and wondered if I could pull off number six. I took a deep breath, walked to the front and followed my usual protocol. This time, probably because my arm was completely worn out, I didn't throw with much force. As it slowly made its way down the center, I was sort of relieved that my streak was over. It inched its way to the front pin and one at a time they all toppled over as if in super slow motion. Was I being pranked?

I started laughing uncontrollably. The small crowd around me cheered and Miranda yelled. "Sweet! Mike, what do you call six strikes in a row?"

He said with a little more interest, "A six-pack or a wild turkey. If she gets seven, it's a seven bagger."

I took my phone from my pocket and offered it to Miranda. "Would you mind recording my next shot, just in case I get it?"

She took the phone and held it in position to record my next turn. If I got another strike, I wanted proof.

All eyes were on me. I shook out my hands and walked to the ball return, picked up my ball, and focused on my approach. I gave a big smile to the camera then did my backswing and released the ball. To my horror, I threw it right in the gutter.

I heard a collective groan from my audience. I should never have hammed it up for the video. The spell was broken.

Miranda handed the phone back with a sympathetic face. "Six is better than I've ever seen."

"Thanks."

Once everyone had gone went back to their own lanes, I felt a bit dejected but snapped out of it. I needed to tackle the task at hand. Michael didn't look busy, so I walked up to him and said, "I don't even know how to score that. Can you help me?" I handed him my scorecard and he wrote a 140 and explained I needed to keep bowling to a final score. I nodded and said, "I wish I had recorded the first 6 strikes."

He nodded. "It was pretty cool."

"My sister won't believe this. Have you ever tried to impress your siblings?

He laughed. "My brother is only impressed by money or pretty girls." He smirked.

I nodded. "Do you see your brother often? My sister and I are inseparable."

He tied the laces of some shoes together and said, "Yeah. He's been pretty busy with a new girlfriend lately, so I haven't seen him in a week or so."

Gee. What else could I ask him without seeming nosey? "Well, I'd better go throw a few more gutter balls before my hour is up so you can finish the scoring for me."

As I went back to my lane, I texted Jenn. 'Sorry for the delay – come in and meet me at lane five.' When Michael sees Jenn, we'll be able to tell if he has met Kat. But I wanted to talk to Jenn first.

When she walked in, I kept my eyes on the counter. I told Jenn about my crazy luck bowling and about my brief conversation with Michael. I whispered, "We need to broach the subject with him. After I finish my game, will you go over with me so we can talk to him?"

"Sure, but did you really make six strikes?"

If she didn't believe me, how would anyone else? I called Miranda over. "Would you tell her I did make all those strikes?"

I held up my phone and recorded Miranda bubbling away, "This girl was amazing. She threw a strike, then another, then another and ended up with a six-pack – six strikes in a row."

I turned the phone around to show me in the frame, or people wouldn't know who "this girl" was.

I thanked her and told Jenn, "My spell was broken when I got cocky and tried to record a seventh strike. Guess I'd better finish up." I picked up my ball. By now, my wrist felt like spaghetti. I did my usual thing and only knocked down one pin.

I finished with mixed luck and said, "I'll ask Michael to tally my score. Ready?"

She said, "Let's go."

I changed into my street shoes and packed up my stuff before we walked to the counter. When he saw Jenn, his eyes narrowed in confusion. "Kat?"

She shook her head. "No. I'm her sister, Jenn." She spoke before he could react. "Have you seen Rodney lately? I am a little worried about him."

He looked at me and back to her, probably wondering what I had to do with her. "Um. No. Rod said he was going to be out of town for a few days with you, I mean her. Are you twins?"

She raised her eyebrow at me before nodding to him.

I asked, "Have you tried calling him?"

"No. What's this all about?"

Jenn took a deep breath and said, "I worked with your brother at DQ. He stopped coming in and I've been worried about him. Just humor us and call him, please."

Michael scoffed, "As if keeping a job at Dairy Queen is a concern for him." He gave a quick eye roll while calling his brother. When there was no answer, he shrugged and said, "Just because he didn't answer doesn't mean he's in trouble."

Jenn said, "Well...I don't want to alarm you, but my sister, Kat, sort of kidnapped me and brought me to Oklahoma. She was arrested yesterday and taken back to Alabama for that and other crimes. I want to make sure he's safe before I go home to Mobile."

Michael looked skeptical but small lines formed in his forehead. He punched in another number and said, "Mom, have you talked to Rod this week?"

We watched as he listened to his mother's response. There was no relief on his face. He put the phone down and said, "I'll call his roommate."

Jenn frowned. "I already asked Jacob. He hasn't seen him."

I perked up. "Michael, do you happen to have the "Find My Friends" app on your phone?"

His eyebrows went up. "Believe it or not, I do. My mom made us both download it so she could keep track of us." He pulled up the app and looked at it. Then he picked up the landline phone on the counter and made a call. "Mac, can you come watch the desk? I've gotta go somewhere."

After he hung up, he said, "Wanna come with me?"

We looked at each other and said in unison, "Sure."

I laid my bag behind the counter and followed the handsome young man and adorable girl, thinking they would make a great couple. We climbed into his open-air jeep and he took off. As I tried to buckle my seat belt, we lurched through the streets at breakneck speed. When we got on I-244, we headed West. I imagined possible destinations; Sand Springs? Sapulpa? I hoped it wasn't Oklahoma City since I had a party starting in five hours.

I finally yelled through the wind, "Where do you think he is?"

He didn't hear so I repeated my question louder. He responded, "Turkey Mountain!"

Turkey Mountain? Well, at least that wasn't far away. On one hand, I was glad Rodney wasn't tied up in a house somewhere, but I wasn't too thrilled to hunt for him in the wilderness. Turkey Mountain is by no means an actual mountain, but a very large hill with 300 acres of wilderness. Unless his app took us directly to him, we might not find him for hours. It had been years since I'd hiked there, but recalled the red trail is easiest, blue is difficult, and yellow is expert. I sure hoped we would use the red trail.

Michael pulled into the main parking area and the three of us jumped from the Jeep, easier said than done for this sore gal. Phone in hand, Michael followed its signal to the yellow trailhead with us close behind. I took a deep breath and released it as we hurried up the dirt path. And up and up.

After what felt like miles of rushing and nobody talking, I wanted to slow down, but Michael and Jenn plowed through. Without warning, Michael took a turn and walked into the brush. I stalled and finally broke the silence, "Um, where are you going?"

He yelled back, "I'm following his signal. He must be this way – just a quarter of a mile."

Jenn had already taken off after him but I stood catching my breath. I wondered what to do. I would feel silly staying behind and so trudged through the thicket after them.

I pushed aside dead branches and tried to keep up with the two. Since I lagged so far behind, I followed the sounds. When I heard excited yelling, I picked up my speed, hoping for the best, and ducked underneath a group of branches. My heart was racing as I came into a clearing, but I stopped short when I saw a body lying on the ground!

Movie Watching Tip # 19
Invite like-minded people to watch with you.

I slapped my hand across my mouth in horror to see the prone body. Michael's back heaved as he kneeled beside the man whom I could only assume was his brother. To the side, a pretty girl in her twenties stood uncomfortably while talking to Jenn.

I took slow steps towards the group, feeling just terrible that we were too late. Then I froze when the body slowly pushed up to a sitting position, yawned and rubbed its eyes. He was alive! Relief flooded through me and I realized Michael hadn't been crying over his brother, but laughing at him.

My heartrate started to slow and my shoulders relaxed. I rushed over and stood by the men with a smile. "Rodney, I presume?"

He blinked and squinted at me then nodded.

I knelt down and asked, "Are you hurt?"

"No. I was taking a nap."

Jenn gave a slight shrug, "It seems like he's fine. He was just on a hike with his new girlfriend and decided to rest."

I said, "So, you weren't kidnapped by Kat?"

He chuckled. "No, but I could see her doing that. She's possessive with a capital P."

I sat down on the bed of pine needles and said, "Oh?"

"Yeah, I ditched her as soon as she told me how she'd threatened to kill a girl who was dating her ex-boyfriend."

Jenn stared. "In Alabama?"

He nodded. "Sorry Jenn, but apparently Kat even held a gun on the girl. Yeah. No. I don't want to be around anyone like that."

Now I knew the reason for Kat's arrest warrant in Mobile, but my stomach tightened with the news of her extreme jealousy. With how much she wanted my stand-in job, I realized she truly could have gone after me.

I watched the new girl who must have been thinking the same thing for she said cautiously, "Is this Kat girl close by? Should I be worried?"

Jenn took the girl's hand. "No. You have nothing to worry about. She's been sent back to Alabama."

Michael jiggled his head back and forth. "Wow! You sure know how to pick 'em, Rod." He turned to the girl, "Present company excluded." To Rodney, he said, "But, you might try answering your phone so we don't have to bring a search party."

Rodney scoffed. "Like you haven't gone AWOL for a few days." He turned to me. "And exactly who are you?"

I filled him in on my involvement, then said, "Rodney, Kat bragged that she put something in your drink. Did she do that?"

He looked confused then nodded slowly. "Ahhh. So, that's why I fell asleep last week. It was just after I told her to move out. I slept for hours and when I woke up, she was gone, along with some of my money. Man, I had a hell of a hangover."

Michael patted his brother on the shoulder. "Unbelievable. I'm glad you're alright Bro, but I've gotta go back to work. Please call Mom."

As we turned away to leave, I shrugged. "Sorry to interrupt your hike."

Rodney yelled after us, "It's nice to know someone cares!"

After walking the easy two miles downhill to the jeep, we rode to the Dust Bowl. Then Jenn drove me to Broken Arrow. On the slower ride with her, I relaxed, knowing Rodney was okay and I still had time to prepare for my party. I texted the bowling video to R.A. then asked Jenn, "Why the crowbar and tape recorder?"

She shrugged. "I just wanted to be ready for anything."

I realized Jenn might be just as spontaneous as me and before she left, I said, "Let's keep in touch, girl. And watch out for that sister of yours."

I arrived home at 2:00 and got to work immediately. I vacuumed the living room, set up the red fabric runner on the floor, and placed the life-sized cardboard cut-out of Oscar in the front entryway for red carpet photos. I pinned large gold stars to the wall, which added to the Hollywood-themed backdrop.

Then I ran to the dollar store to buy candy and other prizes. In addition to those, I give my guests a photo of them on the red carpet. I hoped to find gold or movie-themed picture frames but found little gold ceramic stars attached to cute paper clips that would be perfect to hold the Oscar photos this year.

Back home, I sat on the stairs and checked my camera to make sure there was enough room on my SD card for the new photos. Ren and Ree walked in and I brightened. "Hi girls! How was the rodeo?"

They rolled their eyes, which told me all I needed to know. "Well, you're just in time to blow up some balloons and make prize baskets. Then, you'll need to get ready."

Strangely, my girls just stood in the entryway and said nothing.

When cold air blew in through the open door, strong perfume wafted in with it.

No. Not Shelly. I stood and put my camera down to open the door further. Shelly peeked around the corner, probably scanning the room for movie stars. I sighed, "Hi Shelly, can I help you?"

"I just wanted to see if your party had started yet." Dressed in a super short red dress, she brushed past me into the living room, scratching me with a huge bow on her sleeve. I rubbed my arm wondering if the bow was made of steel wool?

I sighed. "Nope, it hasn't started yet. I haven't even showered, but I really need to do that before my 'guests' arrive." Hint hint.

"It is alright that I come, right? I mean we're practically family. I really want to meet Alison. Baxter."

"I'm so sorry, Shelly. I only have seating and food for the number invited." I winced as I said the next sentence. "Maybe next year? And as I told you, Alison is not coming, nor will anyone famous. It will only be school teacher friends and my sister. Todd was right, we just sit and watch the show. I honestly think you would be bored to death." This was the absolute truth. I also had no interest in hearing her whine all evening.

"Oh, well. I guess the girls can tell us all about it on Tuesday." She took Ree's face between her acrylic-nailed fingers and squeezed. "Little Marie, would you like to have me do your make-up for tonight?"

Ree's face started to sag at the thought, but she held it together enough to say, "No, thank you, Shelly. I'll be fine. Ren usually helps me." Ree rubbed her chin where she'd been squeezed. Somehow, Ren had escaped to her room.

"Thanks for bringing them home," I said as I opened the door to usher her out.

Reluctantly, Shelly left. I imagined her staking out the house all night waiting to see if any stars would arrive.

Once the door shut, Ree said, "Mom. I was so scared she'd stay. That would have ruined the evening."

I nodded. "It totally would."

Within minutes, Ren's bestie, Jennifer arrived.

I got serving plates and bowls and asked the big girls to start heating the meat while Ree set up the prize baskets. Harriet scratched at the door and I let her in and fed her. After a quick shower, I dried my hair, made up my face and put on my new, used dress. I donned my special earrings and necklace, both with dangly gold stars. I looked like a million bucks. Okay, maybe 20.

The doorbell rang. It was only 5:40. Oh, it was probably Caitlyn. When I walked into the hallway from my bedroom, there stood sweet Caitlyn with her wicked mother. Trish wore a gold sequined gown, glittery shoes and a huge matching fascinator clipped to her hair. She looked as if she was going to the Kentucky

Derby. My heart started to thump. Trish was the last person I wanted attending my party, other than Shelly, of course.

Caitlyn ran into Ree's bedroom and they immediately squealed about something.

Trish remained planted by the door, with her nose in the air. She was striking in her get-up, but that didn't change the fact that I've never met anyone as controlling, conceited, or confrontational as Trish. At least Shelly is fake at all of that. This woman has always been downright scary. Although the thin woman is only 5' 5", she seemed to tower over me as she gave me her condescending look.

Her nose wrinkled. Perhaps she smelled Shelly's leftover cologne, but her attention was on Harriet, who sidled over to say "Hi". I watched, anticipating a scuffle between woman and dog but Harriet took one look at her and kept walking. Maybe even the not-so-shaggy pup could sense Trish's Cruella Deville vibes.

With a curled lip, Trish said, "Caitlyn tells me you bought her a used garment. You wasted your dollar. No daughter of mine will wear a filthy article of clothing. Here." She shoved a plastic-wrapped dress on a hanger, into my arms. "This is more appropriate, even for this…" her eyes scanned the room, "party."

I sighed and said, "Come on in."

"Why? You don't actually think I would be a part of this?" Her eyebrows lifted as she pointed to my living room accusingly.

Relieved she wasn't staying, but sick of her rudeness, I said in a hick accent, "Well, then thank you for bringing Caitlyn. I'm sure she'll look just dandy in this dress from…" I looked at the bag with Nordstrom's marked clearly on the side and said with a quizzical expression, "Nord Storms?" as if I was so backwards that I'd never heard of the store.

She turned to me, tilted her head back and laughed, proving to herself once and for all, that I was a bumpkin. She chuckled. "Of course, you wouldn't know." With her hand to her throat she said, "Well, I'll be attending a real Oscar gala tonight. It's being held at the Petroleum Club in downtown Tulsa. I hear several of the stars from the new movie, "Crude Town", will attend." Normally, this would have impressed me but not this year.

She smoothed her dark hair back, which was already swept up so tight that not a hair could escape. "I should go now. The Judge has to be punctual. He must think of his career, you know." She studied me sincerely and said, "I pity you being just a teacher and never getting to experience a real gala."

I kept my mouth shut but honestly, I would take my kind of party over a stuffy event any day. "The Judge" Trish referred to is Caitlynn's father, the most influential judge in Tulsa County. I can't imagine poor Caitlynn, their only child, living with such strict, protective parents. I pictured the atmosphere at breakfast in a silent room; The judge at one end of a long table, Trish at the other, and poor Caitlyn sitting in the middle with a folded cloth napkin on her lap waiting for the help to bring her a perfectly cooked scrambled egg. No wonder she practically lives at our house.

I wanted to push Trish out the door, but instead, I said in my hick accent, "Well, have fun with all them there stars Trish. I need to get ma-own self ready. We have people comin' soon and I have to find my box of macaroni and cheese to cook up."

Funny thing is, I don't think she even knew I was being silly. Ha! As if I would serve boxed macaroni and cheese at my Oscar party. We may have it tomorrow for dinner, but I'd never serve it for my party guests.

Trish turned and shook her head. "It's always a kick to see how the other half lives." What a snob. Only Trish would say something like that aloud. I've always wondered how Trish turn out like that when she has sweet Grandpa Brian as her father? I watched her sashayed down the driveway to her new black Mercedes.

As soon as the door shut, Ree and Caitlyn crept around the corner. Caitlyn whispered, "Is she gone?"

"Yes." Finally, the two most annoying females I knew were both gone.

Caitlyn pointed to the garment bag and said, "I really don't want to wear that ugly dress, but my mother will be mad if I don't. I want to wear the long dress."

I said, "I know what! Put on the Nordstroms dress. I'll take your picture in front of the backdrop so she'll see you in it. Then, wear the other one to the party." I don't normally go against parents' wishes, but Trish's rules were ridiculous.

The girls grabbed the bag, obviously happy with my idea. I sat on the couch and made sure my camera was ready for the evening. Within moments, Caitlyn came out wearing a short, frilly dress that made her look like a 6-year-old beauty pageant contestant, rather than a 13-year-old. I stifled a giggle and positioned her in her ruffled pink dress in front of the gold stars. After snapping a few photos, I showed them to her. "OK?"

"Perfect." She smiled. "Now I'll go get my grown-up dress."

After a while, the girls paraded out, walking like awkward models in their long glamourous dresses. Ree's dark blue dress accented her eyes and I was dumbfounded by how beautiful she was. Caitlyn's modest dark green gown accentuated her beautiful red hair. The girls wanted their pictures taken so I snapped the giggly girls in several poses.

Next, Ren and Jennifer posed for their pictures, wearing glittery gowns, which showed off their figures. These girls were knock-outs. In one shot, they stood on either side of "Oscar" and kissed him on his cheeks, leaving lipstick marks. It was fun to see them so happy and excited, but I did make them wipe off Oscar's cheeks.

Lin arrived next dressed in her polka dot gown.

I said, "That turned out really cute!"

"Well, you look amazing in that!" She shook her head.

"Thanks, but you should have seen Trish turn her nose up at me a few minutes ago. After she left, I felt downright repulsive, so my dear, your compliment has lifted my mood considerably."

"Trish? Why was she here?"

"She brought Caitlyn." Lin had only met Trish once but had heard enough stories to believe anything I said about her.

I wanted to take Lin aside to discuss my close encounters with death and Aaron yesterday but was afraid my girls would hear.

The smell of roast beef drifted in from the kitchen, making my stomach growl. It also masked Shelly's lingering cologne. When Lin saw the spread, she said, "How did you afford to cater?"

"I didn't," I explained my unusual date on Friday as we set up the rest of the food along with wine, beer, tea, and water. It was almost time for the red-carpet events - one on TV and the other live in my living room, but I decided I should thank Kenny. I wrote a text saying how much I appreciated the food. Within seconds he wrote back, "Anything for my Pretty Kitty."

Ick. Before the other guests arrived, I had Ren take photos of Lin with me and then of us separately.

The other guests started arriving; Jules and her husband, Andrew, were dressed to the nines. Jana was more business casual. After placing their coats on my bed, I took photos of them on my fake red carpet. Although I don't care what people wear to my gathering, I'm careful to inspect each outfit to determine who should win the "best dressed" prize. The dress that got the most attention was not surprisingly worn by Becca. She waltzed in, literally, and twirled around the room in a glittery turquoise dress.

When Kim and R.A. arrived, I grabbed Lin and leaned into the three of them. "OK, you guys, remember not to tell my girls about yesterday's oil derrick stunt."

Lin zipped her lips.

R. A. said, "You can count on us too. But am I supposed to believe you bowled six strikes in a row?"

I nodded with a huge grin. "I'll explain later." After getting drinks and filling our plates, we started watching the red-carpet event on TV. I hadn't lied to Shelly about all the seats being taken. Tables were such a scarcity, people balanced plates on their laps.

I announced, "Remember to complete your ballots before the award show begins. Just put a checkmark by who you think will win in each category and keep score during the show. Then at the end of the evening, the best guesser will win a special prize."

While looking at the ballots, they all joked that I was the only one there who had seen all 8 nominated best picture movies. Once the ballots were completed, we focused on eating and the pretty people arriving on TV. Occasionally someone pointed out clothing or hairstyles.

Jana said, "This roast beef is delicious. Did you make it?"

"No. Remember my boring blind date, Kenny, from last week? You can thank him. It's a long story."

"It sure goes well with beer," said R.A. who took a drink from his bottle.

I felt giddy watching the stars exit limos and expected to see Aaron and Sandra Ellington anytime. I was sure she would be in the most spectacular gown. Then, I wondered if she was any relation to Duke Ellington. I should ask Aaron. What was I thinking? I would never get to talk to him again. I frowned. Then I remembered our bittersweet goodbye. Our friendship was probably just a fleeting memory for him but a dream come true for me. I sighed.

We watched another limo pull up. A tall driver in a chauffer's cap made his way around to the passenger side to open the door. Out stepped Joel Mason. I watched the director in disdain. He wasn't my favorite person, but in his defense, any director would probably oust me from the movie set after what I had done. The sullen director's face matched the red carpet. Why was he angry at this event? The two men talked for a moment and the driver handed something silver to Joel which he put in his tuxedo pocket.

When the driver walked back around to his side of the vehicle, he lifted his head and I saw his face. My jaw dropped. It was the tall guy from the set who had escaped on the motorcycle. The same one who tampered with the oil derrick and who had the burrito/gun! A gun! Did he just hand a gun to Joel Mason?

Should I call the Tulsa Police and tell them their fugitive is at the Oscars? But, what could they do? He was five states away.

I froze, trying to think of what I should do. The L.A. police wouldn't believe someone from Oklahoma who called in. My sister, Kay lives there, but she is miles away from the Dolby Theater and I couldn't see her stopping a possible shooter.

My heart beat wildly. I needed to call Aaron. OMG! What if Joel Mason wants to hurt him! But that's ridiculous. Why would he? I knew I was jumping to conclusions but I didn't care. I needed to warn Aaron, just in case.

I jumped up so fast my plate fell on the floor. I grabbed it and ran to the kitchen, leaving stalks of asparagus and a roll under my chair. Someone said, "Pity? What in the world?" and Ree said, "Mom, you made a mess." There was no time to worry about that.

I grabbed my phone and found Aaron's number. I dialed, hoping I could reach him in time. I certainly hoped this was a live broadcast, since warning someone about something that happened an hour earlier wouldn't do much good.

I stared at the red-carpet event on my tiny kitchen TV. Joel Mason stood to the side smiling a crooked smile. It looked strange to me, but then realized I'd never seen him smile before. I silently begged Aaron to answer his phone but figured it was on silent as he rode to the Academy Awards Show. Why even at my little party, I ask everyone to silence their phones. But there was at least a chance he would answer. The call went to voicemail and I accidentally hung up without leaving a message. I pushed redial and prepared my message in my head. Come on, pick up, Aaron!

While listening to the phone ring again, I kept my attention on the director who was talking to reporters and signing autographs. It was odd that he kept his eyes on the people arriving.

Before I had the chance to leave my message, the sultry voice of Sandra Ellington answered, "Hello?" Her voice is so familiar, I recognize it immediately in commercials and when she does voiceovers for animated films.

I was a bit star-struck but knew I had to spit out my message. "I need to speak to Aaron. It's an emergency."

I heard rustling and the familiar twang of Aaron. "Is there another tornado?" I could hear his light laughter through the line.

With a burst, I said, "No. Listen, please. Remember the tall guy who tampered with the oil derrick and got away on a motorcycle?"

"Uh-huh?" He giggled a little as if Sandra was tickling him.

I spoke even faster. "Aaron! I just saw him driving Joel Mason's limousine. I recognized him while watching the red-carpet event at my party. He handed something to Mr. Mason and… I think it's a gun!"

"Slow down, Pity. Slow down. Let me get this straight… You're at home watching the red-carpet event? And you saw the tall guy hand Joel something and you think it's a gun?"

"Yes. I think he's going to shoot you."

"Why would he do that?" He asked calmly

"I don't know, but please be careful! Are you already inside?"

"No, we're a few blocks away, but I'm not exactly prepared for a shootout. Forgot to bring my gun belt."

He didn't sound nervous or like he took me seriously. I gave up and said more calmly. "I don't know, Aaron. I just want you to be aware and protect yourself. I can't lose my newest friend." Then I began to sob.

"Hey, hey. Settle down. I'll think of something. It will be OK. You'll see. Look, I've gotta go."

The phone went dead and my mind whirred with thoughts of him being shot on the red carpet. I envisioned Aaron's blood seeping into the carpet as he lay gasping for breath. No!

With my phone still in hand, I asked Siri to dial the Los Angeles Police Department. I explained my story to the dispatcher who was very methodical and didn't seem very concerned. "And you're sure you saw a gun while watching TV?"

I stammered, "Well, no. Not really. But the tall chauffer handed Joel Mason something heavy and he put it in his pocket."

This time, her voice was more skeptical. "Joel Mason, the director?"

"Yes, but you have to realize there were several attempts on Aaron Winston's life in Oklahoma this week, and I think someone may try again tonight."

The woman said, "Ms. Kole, I'm not sure there is anything we can do, but I'll put in a report and have someone check it out."

I sighed, "Thank you!"

I went back to the living room where all eyes were on me. Kim, R.A., and Lin kept asking me what was up, but I tuned them out to focus on the TV. When it went to commercial, I gave all the guests a brief explanation of what I'd seen and suspected.

Kim's eyes were huge. "Was it really the same tall guy?"

"Yes!"

Her eyes narrowed and she bit her lip.

When the commercial break ended, my little crowd was riveted to the TV. John Jansen, who was emceeing the event was busy interviewing people. His big head was in the way so I couldn't see what Joel Mason was doing. A new limo drove up and I held my breath while waiting to see who would step out. It was just a female rapper who would be presenting an award tonight. Her gold dress was so similar to mine that I wondered if she had gotten hers at Goodwill too. Stop it, Pity. Focus.

I caught a glimpse of Joel Mason and thought it was peculiar that he hadn't gone inside the theater. All the other guests disappeared inside after a few minutes of schmoozing for the cameras. I sure hoped I imagined the threat, sure didn't think so.

Another limo drove up and the driver opened the door. Out stepped the glamorous Sandra Ellington, followed by Aaron. Her mocha-colored skin contrasted with his fair complexion. I couldn't help but think how beautiful their children would be. She wore the most heavenly, cream-colored gown with a sequined shawl that wrapped around loosely.

I watched carefully as Aaron stood and waved to the crowd held back by velvet ropes. What was he thinking? Why didn't he stay in the car? Clearly, he didn't believe my warning. The cheering was deafening as he played to his fans. I tried to find Joel Mason, but the camera was pointed directly at the beautiful couple and nothing else. So far so good. No problems yet. Maybe I was wrong. I prayed I was wrong this time.

The camera panned the scene as Aaron and Sandra made their way onto the carpet. I took a deep breath and let it out, relieved nothing had happened. Then, a loud pop pop rang out. No!

There was a big scuffle and the camera swayed as the cameraman tried to focus on the action. Major stars and reporters scrambled. The camera showed Sandra covering her mouth with her hand as she looked at the ground, but I couldn't see Aaron. Then we saw Joel Mason standing across the carpet, waving a real gun, not a burrito, in the air wildly. Several actors and bodyguards rushed to apprehend the crazed director and knocked him down. We could hear what Joel Mason was shouting as clearly as if he had a microphone pinned to him. "Somebody had to stop you, Winston. You sabotaged Swerve by undermining my directing every chance you got. I should have been nominated, not you! You're nothing but a B-rated actor and you'll never be more than that."

In a daze, the emcee sputtered nonsense words. My throat closed up so much I could barely breathe and everyone at my party was shocked silent. The broadcast abruptly went to a commercial break where of all things, Shelly lay on top of a Silver Cadillac SUV. She shouted, "It's March Madness here at Big Jack's Cadillac." I wanted to mute her annoying voice, but I didn't want to miss anything. I closed my eyes and tuned her out.

Did Joel Mason really shoot my Aaron! He must have. Otherwise, why would Sandra have stood there crying? Why didn't I figure it out earlier? But, who could imagine a respected director shooting someone because he was jealous?

Ren came over to me and said, "Mom, you were right about the murder plot. You were right all along." She gave me a hug.

I whispered through tears streaming down my face, "It didn't do any good to warn him. He didn't believe me."

I sobbed. "I'm just like that little shepherd boy. Nobody believes me because I cried wolf too often. Just look what happened: Joel Mason shot Aaron Winston!"

Ree hugged me and said, "We believe you."

That made me feel a bit better. After a few more commercials and me sitting on pins and needles, the broadcast finally returned. John Jansen said, "We are currently in an unprecedented delay in our coverage as officials decide whether to proceed with the ceremony or cancel after shots were fired on the red carpet just moments ago. An update will be given as soon as possible."

Just as another commercial aired, our doorbell rang. Ree's eyes flew to me and she lifted her shoulders wondering if she would get it. I wasn't expecting anyone but nodded for her to go ahead. I was so sick to my stomach I couldn't even stand if I wanted to. It was probably flowers from Kenny, or worse yet, Kenny himself. Or maybe it was Shelly looking for Alison Baxter. I put my head in my hands as Ree opened the door.

There was a muffled conversation and then the door shut. Ree came to me. "It's a delivery for you."

I opened my eyes and saw a small wrapped package. "You can open it. I don't want to look at anything from Kenny right now."

Ree joined Caitlyn where they sat on the hearth. They ripped the package open and Ree said, "Mom, it's not from Kenny. It's from someone named Falcon?"

"What?" I sat up quickly and wiped my eyes. She handed me a small velvet box with a note. I unfolded it and read, "To my lifesaver. From your friend, Falcon." I sniffed as I carefully lifted the lid. Inside, wrapped in a cottony fabric was a delicate silver charm in the shape of a tornado. I smiled, then burst into tears.

My whole group crowded around me, wondering what had caused such a reaction. I blubbered, "It's from Aaron Winston."

Everyone took turns looking at the charm. They were probably curious as to the significance of the tornado and why a movie star would send it to me, but nobody dared to say much in my fragile state. When the emcee returned, our attention swung back to the TV. He announced, "I'm sure you have been waiting for an update on the unusual activity here. It turns out Joel Mason has indeed shot Aaron Winston."

I cried out in pain and almost missed his next sentence.

"But due to a warning call Mr. Winston received only moments before he arrived, he was able to protect himself. He is heavily bruised and has some flesh wounds, but will be fine. Mr. Mason and his chauffer have been removed from the area and are in the custody of the Los Angeles Police."

Everyone at the party clapped and jumped for joy. Relief flooded me as I clenched the tiny box. Tears of joy replaced my terrified sobs. The group quieted to hear the announcer say, "We will move inside for the awards ceremony momentarily." My face brightened and I let out a sigh of relief.

Ree said, "Mom, you saved his life!"

I smiled. I had done it. I had saved my friend after all.

Ren said, "What did the note say?"

"It's a long story. I'll tell you after the show." I didn't even try to wipe the smile from my face as I attempted to resume party mode. After all, I was the hostess.

I stood in front of the group while more commercials played. I began my spiel with my still shaky voice. "Thank you for bearing with me during all of that. But, it's time to pay attention to your ballots and mark all the winners you chose correctly."

I was giddy with relief when the actual awards show finally began only twenty minutes late.

"Mom, you forgot to show your video!" Ree looked aghast.

I leaned my head back and said, "I guess I'll show you my Oscar video at a commercial break if that's okay?"

The presentations began with technical awards, foreign language awards, and supporting actors. Every now and then a guest shouted, "Got that one."

During a commercial break, I paused the DVR and showed my eight-minute Oscar video. Everyone laughed at the skits but especially when I carried Harriet on the stage. Iggy was a hit too. They always say, never act with children or animals or they'll steal the scenes, but I love to include at least one of our pets.

Becca shook her head. "Pity, you're such a dork, but a creative one."

I couldn't help notice that Ren had shaded her eyes in embarrassment during most of the film. Oh well, so only one out of the nine guests, wasn't a fan. That's not so bad.

While the group continued to watch the awards being announced, I popped popcorn, then ran upstairs to print their red-carpet photos. I watched the little upstairs TV so I wouldn't miss anything as I clipped their pictures onto their cute holders. I smiled when I heard occasional outbursts from downstairs. The doorbell rang again. Although I didn't figure it was another gift from Aaron, I ran downstairs as if it was.

I flung the door open and was horrified to see the real, actual LAST person I'd want to come to my party: Dr. Barry Love! What the hell was he doing here?

"Um. Hi, Dr. Love. What can I do for you?"

"I received an invitation to your party and I felt it my due diligence to stop by and see just what was going on?" He gave me a satisfied smirk as he held out a printed copy of my evite.

First of all, I hadn't sent him an invitation. Had I? I thought back frantically. Maybe when I was sending them to the girls, I somehow added his e-mail address?

"Uh." I stammered as I tried to decide if I should let him into my house or not.

He smiled and said, "Also, I'm here to tell you that you just may not have a job when you return to work tomorrow."

I was baffled. Why wouldn't I have a job? I said, "What?"

"You are not to have school functions past 10:30 at night."

"This isn't a school function. It's my own private party." I noticed my group of friends and family had gathered close behind me, which gave me confidence.

He straightened his thick glasses. "Maybe it is, but I've told you numerous times that your number one commitment must be to your students. You should always get plenty of sleep on a school night. We have a no moonlighting rule at Arrowstar."

I was shocked. How did he keep inventing new rules?

Becca piped up, "There is no rule like that in the Broken Arrow public school district."

Jules poked her head beside mine. "And even if there was, you couldn't possibly enforce something like that."

He stood his ground as he glared up at me. "Perhaps not. But, how do you explain being out of school three days last week? And on Friday, you went home sick. Clearly, you were not sick since television footage proves you were on a movie set. That is fraudulent, Ms. Kole. You have been caught playing hooky."

Oops. He got me there. I nodded. "You are right, Dr. Love. I was on the movie set Friday. But, in my defense, I actually did feel sick since I thought the situation was a matter of life and death. I already e-mailed H.R. and plan to call tomorrow morning to confirm having Friday's substitute pay docked from my check."

His eyes flickered as he scrambled for a good comeback. "We'll see about that, Ms. Kole. Be in my office at 7:00 a.m."

He took stock of the other guests who hovered behind me as if he was making a mental list, then he turned and left.

I shut the door behind him and let out a big sigh. "What next?"

Ree called, "Mom, they are announcing Best Actress now. Next up will be Aaron Winston's category."

We all returned to our seats to watch. The Best Actress went to Jolie Masterson, who played 'Eve' in 'The Best Temptation'. Ren stood up and said, "Yes!" Ree, Lin, and I shrugged with indifference. Jolie wore a pretty dress and did give a nice acceptance speech.

Then, last year's Best Actress winner, Gloria Ewing, came to the microphone. She gave a smirk and said, "This year's nominees for Best Actor include men with a variety of hair types; brown, black, blonde, red, and even a baldy." She paused so people could laugh at Enrico Romero who had shaved his head for his role in "The Forbidden Place."

As the actress read the names of the nominees, the camera panned to each actor who smiled and nodded to the camera. "The nominees are Enrico Romero for his role in "The Forbidden Place", Jon Crews from "The Best Temptation", Jimmy Banks for "Lost Again", Mike Nichols for "Wild Hearts of Mystic Canyon", and Aaron Winston for 'Swerve.'"

When she read Aaron's name, the audience clapped. I was afraid he was in some hospital room nursing his injury and they would just show a photo of him on the large screen. But there he was, big as day, sitting in the second row, smiling his crooked smile. His tuxedo jacket was left open, revealing a big bandage wrapped around his chest instead of a cummerbund. Sandra sat on his right. She held his hand and smiled beautifully at him. The little boy actor from the movie, "Swerve" was on Aaron's left. He looked older. Of course, it had probably been at least a year since they filmed his catchphrase, "fwuck". The lead actress sat on the other side of the boy. I was so relieved to see Aaron, I almost cried. He really was alive and smiling!

I held my breath as Ms. Ewing said, "And the winner is…. Aaron Winston!"

Everyone went wild - both at my house and in the Dolby theater. Oh My Gosh! He did it! I jumped up and down and laughed when I saw him jump too. Then he stopped and held his chest, wincing in pain, but then gave a smile.

Sandra kissed him, then he bounded to the stage, a little less hyper than normal. I beamed with pride as if he was my brother. And he thought he didn't deserve to be there. Silly guy.

Aaron caught his breath and leaned into the microphone and said, "Wow. Didn't expect this. I have nothing written, well I actually did, but…" He pulled out a piece of paper from inside his jacket pocket, "as you can see, I can't read it now." When he lifted the paper up, it had a big hole clean through it. The crowd reacted with oohs and aahs.

"Not sure I deserve this award when the other actors in the category are so much more talented, but I sure do appreciate the honor. Swerve is a special movie. The cast was amazing." He pointed to his co-stars. When the camera cut to the little boy, he was giggling.

Aaron looked down at the statue in his hands and said seriously, "And as for what happened earlier, I really hope Joel gets the help he needs."

Then he looked up at the audience and said, "I'd like to dedicate this Oscar…" He held the gold statue up in the air, "to my new friend in Oklahoma, Pity Kole." My heart stopped. I wouldn't have believed my ears, except that everyone at the party gasped and stared at me.

He continued, "She held my hand through a tornado and literally saved my life twice in one week." He looked right into the camera and said, "Pity, I am forever indebted to you. I hope your Oscar party is as much fun as this party!" He looked out at the audience and yelled, "Thanks again, Academy of Motion Picture Arts and Sciences!" He jumped for joy as he ran off the stage, whooping and hollering in his playful manner that helped make him a star.

I was speechless, dumbfounded and ok, thrilled. Now I knew what it was like to be on cloud nine. My friends pumped me for details as the wall phone rang off the hook. Then my cell phone buzzed with texts. The rest of the evening was a blur.

After the Best Picture, Oscar went to 'The Last Temptation", the party-goers tallied their correct answers. I was happy that Jana won and gave her the gift bag containing a Hollywood mug, movie candy, and a couple of movie tickets. She giggled as she looked at her haul.

It was time for my final award. "And for Best Dressed, the award goes to …Becca Marshall!" I handed her a bag holding clapper earrings, a glittery Hollywood t-shirt, and a deck of Hollywood playing cards. She hugged the bag and said, "I swear I'll wear them all tomorrow!"

Ree said, "Except for the playing cards." She laughed.

Becca pointed a finger at her. "Don't you be so sure I won't?"

I chuckled and said, "Anyone who didn't get a prize tonight, go get something from the prize basket."

Ree and Caitlyn jumped up and grabbed boxes of gobstoppers, and Jules got a coffee mug.

While the others chose something, I started up the steps to get the photo gifts, but Lin said, "Um Pity…look."

I followed her gaze to the TV screen. There, hanging from a bar on the oil derrick, wearing my blue 1960's dress was a clip of me! I watched as my legs flailed in the air. The reporter from the channel two late news said, "Up next. The local teacher who was mentioned by Aaron Winston during the Academy Awards show for saving his life, was actually rescued by him on Saturday. Exclusive footage up next on Action 2 news."

I closed my eyes and winced. Crap, the secret was out.

R.A. said, "I thought I saw Jesse recording with his phone, but I wasn't sure." He shrugged.

After deflecting a lot of comments and questions from my little crowd, we sat back down. My girls continued to give me what might be scowls or maybe just looks of amazement.

The anchor came back and said, "There was more excitement on the set of 'Crude Town' Saturday morning as Hollywood star, Aaron Winston, saved a Broken Arrow music teacher from falling to her death. Warning. Some parts may be hard to watch." There again was my body dangling from the oil derrick.

"Ms. Kole believed the crossbars of the oil derrick had been tampered with and decided to climb up to repair it."

My group stared at me in disbelief. I shook my head. "I wasn't going to fix it. I was going to confirm my suspicions." I shook my head. As if I knew how to repair something like that, and if I did, why on earth would I wear a dress to do that? Seriously.

The video captured the whole scene. It was just like an action movie, but without the music and proper editing. I looked like a damsel in distress hanging on for dear life when the villain grabs her foot. Just in the nick of time, a helicopter appears, dropping the handsome hero down to rescue the poor girl. And everyone lived happily ever after. It was absolutely unreal.

Becca said, "While you were up there, did I hear you yell, 'the screws are loose'? I think I know whose screws were loose - the one who climbed up there in the first place."

I smiled and nodded. I knew those words would come back to bite me.

None of us could take our eyes off the screen. I watched R.A. shove the ball cap guy which caused his hand to slip from my ankle to my shoe. When he fell to the ground, there was a loud gasp among those in our group who weren't expecting it.

The reporter said, "The man who attempted to hurt Ms. Kole was injured in his fall but is expected to recover. The other man suspected of helping him tamper with the derrick escaped on a rented motorcycle used in the filming of 'Crude Town.' However, due to a call to police, he was apprehended at the Academy Awards show tonight when he assisted famed director, Joel Mason in shooting Aaron Winston."

He continued, "Because of a warning from Ms. Kole, Mr. Winston was able to take precautions to save his own life."

I wondered exactly what precautions he took. Nobody ever said what actually happened.

"Filming may resume in as early as a week, once repairs to the oil derrick have been made and Aaron is cleared to work. Crude Town's assistant director, Jack Hart, will take the helm."

Once the report ended, everyone was wide-eyed except for Kim, R.A., and Lin. Ren said, "Mom…were you going to tell us about this?"

I bit my lip. "I hoped you wouldn't find out."

She shook her head and said to Ree, "Our Mother is crazy. Just think, if she had fallen, we may have had to live with Dad and Shelly."

Ree made a terrible face. "Mom. Don't do any more death-defying acts, please."

"I'll try not to."

Jules said, "You sure know how to make a party exciting."

I smiled and looked at the clock. "Wow. It's late. You all should go home. Let me get your gifts."

Jana hugged her bundle of prizes and said, "Gifts? You already gave us prizes and dinner."

"It's just something little." I ran upstairs, got their photos, and came back down carrying them in a box.

I asked Ren and Jennifer to hand them out.

When Becca got hers, Ren said, "Mrs. Marshall, you look like you belong on Dancing with the Stars!"

She took it and smiled. "I'm putting this on my desk at school so Dr. Love can eat his heart out."

Jules looked over Becca's shoulder and said, sarcastically, "He'll love it. Especially since your hand is holding Oscar's jewels."

We studied the picture and sure enough, Becca's hand was placed directly on the crotch of the tall cardboard statue. Only Becca! She shrugged and said, "He was the only available man here."

I was still shaking my head at that crazy girl when Jana leaned into me and said, "Don't worry about Dr. Love. There is no rule that teachers can't be out late on a school night. You're fine. Thanks for the lovely evening."

When my teacher friends were out the door, Lin said, "Well, you got your wish! Only you could accidentally fall in the arms of Aaron Winston and become his friend, then save his life twice and be saved by him. What's next?"

I winked. "You'll just have to wait and see."

She nodded and said, "Jennifer come on. You'll see Ren at school tomorrow, don't ya know." She winked at me. It was so cool that our daughters were best friends too.

R.A. said, "We'll drop Caitlyn off at her house on our way out. You have got to be exhausted."

"I am. Thanks." I put my hand to my mouth and turned to the cute redhead. "I almost forgot. Caitlyn, go change into your mom's dress, quick."

Both 13-year-olds said, "Oh yeah!" and ran to Ree's bedroom.

Kim gave me a long hug. "Pity, please take a break from all your sleuthing. You are wearing me out."

I nodded. "I will. I'm going to go do my lesson plans before bed and have a completely normal week."

R.A. said, "Normal? Your life is never normal." His twinkly blue eyes were filled with the love I adore.

I said, "I think I'll take the rest of the food over to Mom and Dad's tomorrow night – Wanna join us?"

Kim said, "Sure. We'll even make Eli and Alex come."

"Good. I was beginning to think I didn't have nephews anymore! They are so busy."

Caitlyn rounded the corner wearing both her frilly dress and a frown. Kim chuckled and said, "Come on, Little Bo Peep!"

I could hear their laughter as the door shut, leaving me alone with my girls.

"Well, that was a rollercoaster ride." I stepped to my girls and motioned them in for a hug. "I love you so much and I promise I'll be much more cautious in the future." I continued, "As I was hanging there, all I could think was what would happen to my babies."

Ree said, "I'm glad you have such strong hands, Mom."

Ren added, "And that you happened to know a guy with a helicopter who could save you. I hate to admit it, but you have to put that video in your Oscar movie next year."

That just about blew me away. Maybe she would come around and start liking my Oscar videos after all. I gave them each a squeeze. "Now let's get ready for bed."

The phone rang and I saw it was Mom so I answered. "Pity, are you trying to give us heart attacks?"

I cringed. "No. I didn't tell you what happened because I didn't want you to worry. I'll make it up to you by bringing a nice dinner tomorrow night. And I'll try to explain it all too."

"Alright, Dear. I am proud of you for saving that young man's life. But I still don't understand what people see in him."

I hung up, feeling exhausted but happy. I started putting food away and loading the dishwasher. My phone rang again. I picked up without looking at the number. My heart skipped a beat when I recognized Aaron's voice. "How was your party?" You have to be kidding. The man just won an Oscar and he called to see how my party was? This was unreal.

"Well, it was unbelievable - because of you!!! Congratulations, Aaron! I told you that you deserved to win."

"I still think it was a mistake. We're on the way to an after-party and I just wanted to thank you so much for the heads up."

"I'm just glad you are OK. But, please tell me how you survived being shot?" Suddenly, the line was staticky. I was afraid I'd lose him and said, "Aaron, are you still there?"

"Yeah, just went under a bridge. Um, well at first, I thought you were just being paranoid, but then I thought, 'Pity has pretty good intuition. What if she's right?' So, I looked around the limo for something to protect us. I didn't see any guns or bulletproof vests, but I found these small metal trays, kind of like heavy cookie sheets? I slipped two under my shirt and made Sandra wear one underneath her scarf."

"And it worked?" I could visualize the trays from my evening in the limo, but it was hard to believe silver could stop a bullet.

"Yeah. I wasn't sure if it would help, but I figured it would be better than nothing in case you were right. The police said even though it was only a small 9mm handgun, the bullet should have gone straight through the trays. But upon closer inspection, they discovered the trays were made of nickel and since he hit at an angle, they worked great."

"That's Amazing."

"You were a pretty smart cookie to recognize the driver."

"I think you were a smart cookie sheet to think of using the trays." Gee my jokes were bad.

He laughed and said, "Do you want me to send you your Oscar statue?"

I figured he was kidding, but said, "Of course not! You earned it. Besides, I already got my award: The silver tornado is adorable. I'll wear it always. It was the sweetest thing ever." I took a breath and added, "And thank you for mentioning my name in your acceptance speech! I was certainly the hit of the party."

"I'm glad you like the charm. Well, I do have just the right place for my Oscar statue. Maybe you can come see him sometime?"

"I'd like that. Now, you'd better get to your party and have some fun."

Simultaneously, we said, "Thanks for saving my life." Then again in unison, we said, "Jinks!"

We laughed, and he said, "Take care, Pity."

"Goodbye."

I hung up and held the phone to my chest. I knew I would never see Aaron again or go to his house. But, wow what a wonderful wild ride!

About the Author

Martha Kemm Landes is a former music teacher who wrote numerous musicals and hundreds of songs for her students while teaching music in Oklahoma. She is most known for writing the state children's song of Oklahoma.

After retiring early, Martha lives with her screenwriter husband and three adopted dogs just outside of Albuquerque, New Mexico. Besides writing mystery novels, she travels, makes quilts, and enjoys their log cabin in the nearby Jemez Mountains.

Martha loves to be outdoors and finds the weather perfect in New Mexico for hiking, gardening, and hosting weekly movies at their large backyard movie theater.

Like Pity, Martha and her husband love movies so much they hold an annual Oscar Party, complete with their own "Not Quite the Oscars" spoofs of the nominated films.

What's Next?

Pity the Garage Sale Addict

This time she gets more than she bargains for

Pity (Kitty Kole) is a self-proclaimed garage sale addict who finds excitement by bargain hunting. The busy divorced mom of teenage girls holds down two jobs, but still manages to get involved in plenty of extra-curricular mishaps, some even while shopping.

When Pity discovers notes in a small desk she bought at a yard sale, she is convinced they are clues to a long-ago murder. After she decides to solve the crime, her life and those of her daughters, go from unconventional to dangerously complicated.

In addition to her sleuthing, Pity gets in ridiculous predicaments while attending her daughter's swim meets, enduring a horrendous blind date, feuding with her strange principal and by continuing to try and ditch her persistent admirer, Kenny.

Despite the help of a crazy bunch of friends, family members and a very handsome policeman, Pity plunges head first into murderous situations - yet again.

9 781956 912005